KT-199-798

I WILL MARRY GEORGE CLOONEY
(...BY CHRISTMAS)

In 2007 Tracy Bloom was kidnapped by her husband to go and live in America for three years. Living with a brand-new baby but without friends and family close-by, she decided her only option was to set about making her dream come true (the one where she writes a book and gets it published, not the one where she marries George Clooney). Her debut romantic comedy novel, *No-one Ever Has Sex on a Tuesday*, went on to become a bestseller as well as being translated into over a dozen languages. Back in England, the dream continues as she carries on writing books whilst herding two children and a husband around the Derbyshire countryside.

I WILL MARRY GEORGE CLOONEY
(...BY CHRISTMAS)

TRACY BLOOM

arrow books

For Tom and Sally.
Get out of your own way and go for it.

Published by Arrow Books 2014

4 6 8 10 9 7 5

Copyright © Tracy Bloom 2014

Tracy Bloom has asserted her right under the Copyright, Designs
and Patents Act 1988 to be identified as the author of this work

This book is a work of fiction. Any resemblance between these fictional
characters and actual persons, living or dead, is purely coincidental.

This book is sold subject to the condition that it shall not, by way of trade or
otherwise, be lent, resold, hired out, or otherwise circulated without the publisher's
prior consent in any form of binding or cover other than that in which it is
published and without a similar condition, including this condition,
being imposed on the subsequent purchaser

First published in Great Britain in 2014

Arrow Books
Random House, 20 Vauxhall Bridge Road,
London SW1V 2SA

A Penguin Random House Company

Penguin
Random House
UK

www.randomhouse.co.uk

Addresses for companies within The Random House Group Limited can
be found at: www.randomhouse.co.uk/officcs.htm

The Random House Group Limited Reg. No. 954009

A CIP catalogue record for this book is available from the British Library

ISBN 9780099594734

The Random House Group Limited supports the Forest Stewardship Council®
(FSC®), the leading international forest-certification organisation. Our books
carrying the FSC label are printed on FSC®-certified paper. FSC is the only forest-
certification scheme supported by the leading environmental organisations,
including Greenpeace. Our paper procurement policy can be found at:
www.randomhouse.co.uk/environment

MIX
Paper from
responsible sources
FSC® C016897

Typeset by SX Composing DTP Ltd, Rayleigh, Essex
Printed and bound by CPI Group (UK) Ltd, Croydon, CR0 4YY

Prologue

George Clooney was a man you could always rely on to be out there and available, keeping alive the dreams of millions of women that one day, by some amazing miracle, they might be the one that he chose to spend the rest of his life with. That was until April 2014 when reports emerged he had become engaged.

I'm sure of course you will all join me in wishing George and this lucky lady the very best and a lifetime of future happiness. However, I hope they will forgive us for still holding on, in times of extreme adversity, to the impossible dream that George Clooney will rescue us.

Chapter One

Midlander Hotel, Saturday 7 September 2013

Michelle didn't like weddings.

She didn't like weddings because she hated the blatant and continuous lying that they required.

The weather was perfect despite the gale force winds and horizontal rain. The bride looked beautiful and had picked a gorgeous dress, despite the fact that no-one else would be seen dead in it. The service was extremely moving, although the vicar droned on for way too long and the groom sounded like a mouse on helium when he said his vows. The venue was so special, despite the fact that everyone had been to at least a dozen weddings there before, and eating the slimy, bland chicken main course yet again had made them want to throw up.

Yes, Michelle hated lying. Well, about most things.

Still, at least she knew there wouldn't be any chicken to squander false praise on at this wedding. Her best friend Gina was prone to many a brain malfunction, but that would be a step too far even for her. The fact that Michelle and Gina both worked in a chicken factory, and spent every day up to their elbows in giblets waiting to escape to the chicken-free utopia that is Netflix, was surely a guarantee that chicken would play no role in this wedding.

And yet, come 5.30 p.m. on Saturday 7 September, there Michelle sat at Gina's wedding eating slimy, damp chicken on a table full of co-chicken murderers, trying to ignore the massive menu faux pas. Not that the rest of the table looked concerned. A good majority appeared to be having a whale of a time. She couldn't really tell, though, as they were jabbering away in Polish and could quite possibly be in hysterics over the weird English wedding rituals designed to minimise enjoyment for all in attendance.

'Why don't you finish mine?' she said, sliding the

contents of her plate onto Big Slaw's – so called because no-one at the chicken factory could pronounce his name, though they knew it ended in *-slaw*, and he was bigger than the other Polish guy whose name also ended in *-slaw* (and he wasn't the Asian lad who everyone thought it funny to call Cole Slaw, despite the fact he wasn't from Poland and he wasn't black).

'Not hungry?' asked Big Slaw.

'No. I tell you, Big Slaw, if I'd served up this tasteless rubbish when I was training to be a chef I'd have been kicked off the course faster than you can say deep fat fryer.'

'You used to be a chef?' he asked.

'Well, I trained a long time ago,' she admitted. 'I was even offered a job in a top restaurant in London.'

'What happened? Why you end up in chicken factory?'

'Life, Big Slaw,' sighed Michelle. 'That's what happened.'

For the rest of the meal and throughout the speeches Michelle let herself sink into the background. She had no partner with her to take on the conversation pinging around their table so she'd fallen silent, not having the energy to be chatty enough for two in order to contribute properly. The happy babble swirled around her as she spotted, worryingly, that the print on her dress was almost identical to the pattern on the flock wallpaper lining the overused function room. She was actually becoming wallpaper, she realised, as she pulled down the hem of the quality outfit she'd purchased to show a willingness to have a good time. She'd thought buying a dress from Topshop would be enough to mask the tired-of-life slouch of a 36-year-old single mum who'd had her hand up too many chickens' backsides. Apparently not. Topshop was determined moreover to put her in her place, sending her into depression by making her wear a dress that was clearly two sizes smaller than the label stated. She hoped the scratchy gold and cream fabric would later prove as effective as Harry Potter's invisibility cloak, should she pause too long near a badly decorated wall. Just the look she was after.

She was grateful when the tinkle of fork on glass heralded the start of the speeches. The wedding was progressing. She could look forward to at least half an hour where she wasn't required to make small talk or eat any more of the hotel's bland offerings. But the words of love and good wishes for the future left her wishing she was still stuck in the overcooked-vegetable-phase of the wedding. She couldn't be happier for Gina, really she couldn't. Dumped in a playpen with Michelle at a very young age, Gina had apparently offered her the hand of friendship by stuffing rusks down her nappy. They'd been inseparable ever since. When Gina had met Mike, Michelle had been the first to tell her that they would be married within the year and she'd been right. But as sure as she'd been that Mike was the perfect man for Gina, she was just as sure that such a man didn't exist for her. As she watched Gina fighting back tears whilst listening to the one she loved declare his feelings to the whole world, Michelle felt depressed to the bone, knowing she would never hear a groom's speech crafted for her.

She was on the verge of wedding defeat, her happiness for Gina's future conflicting with sadness for her own prospects, when Big Slaw came to her rescue. 'Let's go Polish,' he announced, waving a bottle of vodka over his head. Perfect, thought Michelle. Anaesthetic. She offered her glass along with the rest of her table and tried to concentrate on the all-important art of toasting the happy couple in Polish.

*

'Who will you marry you?' Little Slaw asked Michelle some time later. The wedding had improved at her table. The apple pie, covered in congealing custard, had been abandoned in favour of learning 'cheers' in Polish, until Big Slaw had to pop out to the off-licence to purchase more vodka. Clothing was fast being discarded. Ties snaked over the backs of chairs, hats crumpled under furniture legs and shoes congregated in a heap under the table. Seating arrangements had also slackened as the weak sloped off for crafty fags, allowing comrades to shuffle up together and reorganise the plan more to their liking. Little Slaw had dived into Big Slaw's seat the minute he'd left in search of more vodka. He was one of Michelle's older Eastern European friends, many having joined the factory over the past few years. A wise man in his sixties, he'd come to be with his daughter and grand-children who had settled in the area. In Michelle's head he was actually Yoda, given his broken English, tiny frame, wrinkled face and his liking for asking deep, searching questions. Sometimes she imagined that she was Princess Leia whilst they chatted over lunch at the factory. Anything to escape the knowledge that she was spending yet another day of her life chewing on dry Ryvita in a chicken factory.

'Who will I marry me?' she replied, vodka chasers vastly improving the quality of her Yoda impression.

'Is that no good question, my young friend?' Little Slaw asked, looking confused.

'No, it's a stupid question.' She looked away, all good humour draining from her.

'Your daughter's father, where is he?' he asked.

'I've no idea.' She stared back, daring him to pursue this particular line of questioning. He understood. He was Yoda.

'So who will you marry then?' he repeated.

Reluctantly, under Little Slaw's intense gaze, Michelle considered the question. She mentally reviewed the years she'd dedicated to stopping anyone from wanting to marry her. Pregnant at twenty-one to a man who was best forgotten, she had successfully blighted her prime marrying years with the phrase, 'Would you like to come home and meet my daughter?' Matters had not been improved by her need for help with childcare, which had forced her into buying a house in the same street as her parents, in the small Derbyshire market town where she had been born and bred. Malton held few opportunities for meeting single men aside from its tiny nightclub, known locally as 'Vegas' due to its dazzling array of a dozen flashing light bulbs. Even there it was virtually impossible to meet anyone who you weren't either related to or who you hadn't had a scrap with when you were at primary school.

But she also had a further ace up her sleeve, quite literally a killer fact that was guaranteed to make any man run a mile: An older sister. A dead one, victim of a hit-and-run when Michelle was in her early twenties. Apparently this branded her damaged, incapable of forming attachments and psychologically disturbed. Who could possibly live through a trauma like that without significant baggage? The introduction of a dead sister seemed to overcrowd any relationship and force the man to back off rapidly as if she'd grown two heads overnight. Jane's death had not only left her bereft of any siblings; it had also dramatically cut down her options in the marriage department.

'I,' she finally declared wearily to Little Slaw, 'will marry George Clooney.'

Little Slaw laughed too loudly.

'Always the joker, you,' he said, slapping her on the back.

Well, that had actually been the plan, once, a long time ago. She could vividly remember her seven-year-old daughter's face as she pleaded with her whilst they were snuggled up together on the sofa after watching George Clooney play the perfect single dad in the movie, *One Fine Day*.

'I wish he was my daddy,' Josie had said, sniffing into her teddy. Michelle could almost feel her heart breaking.

'I wish he was too,' she'd said wistfully.

'Really?' said Josie, her eyes lighting up.

'Really,' Michelle replied, nodding vigorously.

Josie leapt off the sofa and started jumping up and down.

'Oh please, Mummy, please, please marry him!' she chanted over and over again.

'Okay, okay,' she'd said, laughing. 'I'll see what I can do.'

Suddenly aware that Little Slaw was still laughing at her, Michelle gave him a punch on the arm. She knew of course that it was ridiculous to say that you were going to marry Mr Clooney; however, that didn't mean that others were allowed to think it that hilarious.

'What's so funny?' she asked.

'Hey, listen,' said Little Slaw, shouting over the table to his daughter. 'Michelle say she will marry George Clooney!'

You'd have thought it was the funniest thing that Baby Slaw had ever heard.

'You all seem to be having a good time,' announced Gina, swooping by in her Pippa Middleton knock-off. Sadly she lacked the required arse, having been on an intense pre-wedding diet, so with her tall, skinny frame and flame-red hair she resembled a matchstick rather than a sexy bride.

'You look like a swan, Gina,' Brian shouted from across the table.

'Aw, thanks Bri,' replied Gina, blushing.

'A Swan Vesta,' he added, creasing up with laughter as the rest of the table sniggered.

'Ignore him,' cut in Michelle, leaping to defend her friend. 'You look amazing, really. They're actually all laughing at me because I said I was going to marry George Clooney.'

Gina stared at her, appearing to consider her statement carefully.

'Perhaps George Clooney is someone different in Poland. You know, like the Prime Minister or something?' she said eventually.

'Are you serious?' asked Michelle.

'Yeah, like, you know, maybe the Polish Prime

Minister happens to be called George Clooney. It would be pretty funny to someone from Poland if you said you were going to marry the Polish Prime Minister.' Gina turned to Little Slaw to clarify the matter. 'Is George Clooney your Prime Minister?'

Little Slaw gave his best confused Yoda look for the second time that day.

'No. He Danny Ocean.'

'Danny Ocean is your Prime Minister?'

'No, George Clooney is Danny Ocean.'

Gina turned to Michelle. 'He has no idea who George Clooney is. I don't know why they're laughing at you.'

'They're laughing because they know exactly who George Clooney is and they think it's hilarious that I could think he would ever marry me.'

'Well, they'd be right there, wouldn't they, Michelle?'

'Gina, you're supposed to be my mate.'

'I am, but do you seriously think short, dark-haired, curvy women whose boobs are just a bit too big for their bodies are his type?'

'What point are you trying to make, Gina?'

'Michelle, you know I love you, and I know you sometimes think I'm stupid, but even I know that

11

George Clooney would never go out with someone who looked as bog-standard as you.'

It was a good job that Michelle had always lived with the fact that Gina had never grown out of the blindingly honest phase that most kids go through when they are around five or six. Gina just never understood the point of holding back, and Michelle actually admired her ability to come out with the truth, even if it wasn't what you wanted to hear. Well, most of the time.

'I'm not talking about arm candy,' Michelle pointed out. 'I'm not talking about being a coat hanger with false tits. I'm talking about being his wife. George clearly doesn't fall for the supermodel type. They're just for show. What he really wants is someone like me. Someone real. Someone with something he can grab hold of, someone who'll stand up for herself.'

'So he could have his gorgeous show wife for when he's out and about, and he could have you at home,' said Gina.

'Oh, just forget it,' sighed Michelle.

'So my Cousin Jack is dying to meet you,' continued Gina.

'Cousin Jack?' questioned Michelle. 'Recently divorced Cousin Jack with the drug addiction?'

'Not drugs. Prescription painkillers.'

'He's a drug addict, Gina. And you want me to get off with him.'

'No, he's not,' said Gina. 'Doctors aren't allowed to give you anything that you could be addicted to. And he can't help it if he's depressed because he's impotent. You're funny. You could really cheer him up.'

'Fuckin' hell, Gina,' said Michelle. 'I'm not care in the community. I'm a lonely woman who wants a man with a good sense of humour, who fancies curvy women and who would like the odd shag every now and then. A depressed, impotent drug addict hardly fits the bill, does it?'

'He's got a really flash car,' Gina countered.

'What, like a penis extension-type car?'

'Exactly. A big red one.'

'I'm going to walk away now, Gina, because you are really starting to annoy me, and that's not allowed on your wedding day.'

Michelle stalked off, feeling a bit overwhelmed. This was proving to be a really difficult wedding. Vodka, George Clooney, Little Slaw laughing in her face, Gina being Gina, and Cousin Jack were all whirling around in her headspace. She needed a calming influence.

'Mum, this is a really shit wedding. I can't believe you've made me come, *and* forced me into sodding *lilac*,' said Josie sulkily, sliding up to Michelle as she leant against the bar debating whether more vodka or Diet Coke would have the necessary calming effect. Michelle had nearly cried when she'd first seen Josie in her knee-length, pastel silk bridesmaid's dress. It took her back to Josie's toddler years, when she'd constantly pestered to be dressed like a princess, in contrast to the dark, gloomy, vaguely Goth-like uniform she preferred now. Unfortunately the black nail polish and dark eyeliner had somewhat detracted from the otherwise angelic effect.

'Please don't talk like that, Josie,' she pleaded. 'Gina is my best friend and your godmother. No matter how bad this wedding is, you are not allowed to have that opinion.'

'Yet another opinion I'm not allowed to have, then?' said Josie. 'I'll add it to the list of thousands, shall I?'

Michelle breathed in and out slowly. She'd promised herself to try not to rise to the tide of teenage angst flowing out of her fifteen-year-old daughter. Their relationship was currently about as warm and cosy as one of the chicken chillers at work.

'What I meant was that this is Gina's day, and as far as she's concerned it's the best wedding we've ever been to.'

'You agree it's a shit wedding, though, don't you?'

'No. I think it's lovely. I'm having a great time.'

'You are such a liar. You hate weddings, I know you do.'

'I do not.'

'You do. Sean reckons it's because there's no chance you'll ever have one of your own.'

How could Sean be so stupid and yet so wise all at the same time? Michelle thought to herself.

'Oh, I wondered when Guru Sean would make an appearance,' she said, losing patience as she struggled to disguise her dislike for the seventeen-year-old waste of space her daughter had attached herself to. 'I was beginning to panic that you hadn't mentioned him within the last twenty seconds. Thought you must have had surgery to remove him from your hip. Oh, speak of the devil, here he comes. Sean, love. I was just hearing from my daughter how you think that I'm too ugly to get married.'

Sean stared at Michelle and emitted a barely perceptible grunt.

'Mum, you're embarrassing him.'

'*Embarrassing him?*' squeaked Michelle. She just managed to stop herself informing her daughter that her boyfriend was more than capable of embarrassing himself without her help.

Sean grunted again before reaching round to pull his shabby jeans out of the crack in his backside.

'You don't like him because he's honest,' said Josie. 'Because he's not scared to say to your face that you're never going to get married.'

Sean's grunt this time was accompanied by a barely perceptible nod.

'Actually, I'm going to marry George Clooney,' Michelle declared.

'Oh God, Mum, not that again! You're the one that's embarrassing.' Josie took Sean's hand and turned to move away.

'You think that's embarrassing?' flared Michelle. 'Let me remind you, young lady, that once upon a time you begged me to marry George Clooney. You recognised a smart, attractive, intelligent man when you saw one. What on earth happened?' She nodded in Sean's direction, who blinked back wide-eyed before dismissing Michelle's comment with yet another unintelligible grunt.

'You're just jealous because I've got someone, and all you've got is some stupid pipe dream.'

Michelle stood and closed her eyes. Yet another encounter with her daughter not to be proud of. Why could she never say the right things? She swallowed and lowered her tone, just like Supernanny on the TV said you should.

'But you're fifteen, Josie. Your job is to have pipe dreams. My job, apparently, is to settle for Cousin Jack.'

'Bye, Mum. Enjoy cloud cuckoo land or wherever the hell you think you are.' Josie stomped off, Sean's hand gripped firmly in hers.

Michelle decided she needed to be where other people were not, so she sidled off to the ladies, hoping for a quiet few minutes alone to gather herself before the next stage of hell presented itself, in the form of Daz's Double Decks Diamond Disco. Daz had been in her year at school and she'd gone out with him for nearly a year, but only because he was Gina's boyfriend's best friend at the time. It hadn't ended well.

'Hiya, love.'

This wedding was spiralling out of control. A few moments of peace were going to be shattered by a close quarters encounter with her mother, the formidable Kathleen.

'Hiya,' she replied before diving into the nearest cubicle.

'Doesn't our Josie look a picture?' shouted Kathleen through the thin plywood door.

'She does,' replied Michelle.

'So nice of Gina to invite Sean. Pity he couldn't have worn a suit, though, eh?'

'Yes, Mum.'

'I don't give it long, though, do you? She'll be off to uni before you know it and you won't see him for dust, you mark my words.'

'Well, I hope so. I haven't worked all hours in that factory for her not to go to university and make something of her life.'

'She takes after our Jane, that one. She's smart. She'll go far.'

Michelle emerged from the cubicle and brushed past her mother, not trusting herself to speak.

'You know, I can't help thinking of your sister on days like this. I keep wondering what her wedding would have been like, if she'd married Rob.'

Michelle switched the hand dryer on in an effort

to drown out Kathleen's maudlin reflections.

'Do you think she would have married Rob? He was a lovely lad, wasn't he? I wonder if he's married now.'

'I don't know, Mum.'

The dryer cut out and they stared at each other, not knowing what to say. Michelle thought Kathleen's blush-pink suit with matching hat and shoes had edged too far into mother-of-the-bride territory. She wondered if her mother had decided that attending her daughter's best friend's wedding was the closest she was ever going to get to such a role.

'If you save that suit then you never know, you might be able to wear it to my wedding one day,' she said, desperate not to get stuck talking about the past.

Kathleen laughed before frowning.

'Oh yeah. You can't even bring yourself to tell us the name of the father of your own daughter, never mind marry him, so it's clear to me that you're not the marrying kind.'

Great, thought Michelle.

'Actually, I'm going to marry George Clooney.'

'Oh, don't talk such nonsense, Michelle.'

'Why is it nonsense?'

'Well, just look at you for a start.'

'Look at what?'

'Well, you're not exactly film star material, are you?'

'And what do you mean by that?'

'You know what I mean.'

'No, I don't. You tell me what you mean.'

'You're too fat to marry George Clooney.'

'*Mother!*'

'You asked me.'

'But you're my mother! You're not allowed to say things like that.'

'It's *because* I'm your mother that I'm allowed to say things like that. You need to lose a few pounds and make a bit more of an effort to give yourself a cat in hell's chance of finding anyone who'll marry you, never mind George Clooney.'

'I suppose you think that you've got more chance of seeing Jane come back from the dead and getting married than me walking up the aisle, don't you?'

'Don't say things like that, Michelle, it's cruel.'

'You just called me fat.'

'That wasn't cruel, it was honest.'

'Honest. I'll give you honest. I bet you wish it was me that died and not Jane, don't you?'

Michelle stopped and stared at her mum. Her mum stared back. In over sixteen years, Michelle had never said that out loud. She turned and ran out the door.

Chapter Two

'Even when I offered to go to the doctor's to ask to be put on Viagra she wouldn't stay. Can you believe that? She started packing her bags and an hour later he picked her up in a Ford Mondeo. A Ford Mondeo, I ask you. With an 05 plate. So humiliating.'

Michelle stared numbly at Cousin Jack. He'd now taken her through his entire relationship history.

'My shrink tells me that I should be honest about my past relationships when I meet a prospective partner. Have you got a shrink? Gina said your sister died. They recommend shrinks for grief, you know. If you haven't got one I'd recommend mine. He's really helped me to open up about my problems. I can talk to anyone about them now.'

Michelle caught sight of her mum gliding over to Gina's mum at the opposite side of the room. All the tables were being cleared away and the hub of the wedding had moved towards the bar at the back of the room as everyone waited for Daz to set up his disco kit so the dancing could commence. Michelle's mum appeared to be making her excuses to leave. Gina's mum wiped a tear from Michelle's mum's face. Michelle knew exactly the kind of conversation they were having. Michelle's mother would have donned her persona of grieving mother as she always did at any major occasion and Gina's mum would be dutifully consoling her. She could understand it for the first few years after Jane had died, but she was convinced that it was now, at best, her mother's desperation to keep the memory of Jane alive, and at worst a form of attention seeking.

Michelle hadn't spoken to her mother since their confrontation in the ladies. She'd gone into minor shock after her outburst and had headed straight for Big Slaw to demand a vodka shot or two. Sinking into a chair in a daze, she'd hoped somewhere in the back of her mind that her mother would come and find her and declare a suitable response to Michelle's revelation. But she never came. More shots were consumed before Cousin Jack took up residence in the chair next to her and spent forty-five minutes sharing his life history whilst Michelle said nothing. Still her mother didn't arrive to rescue her.

As she gazed over to her now, she willed Kathleen to look towards her, to seek her out. Eventually she did.

She glanced up just as she put her coat on and caught Michelle staring at her. Their eyes locked. Kathleen raised her hand in a cheery wave, turned and left. Just like that.

Of course she'd left. Why had Michelle been stupid enough to think her mother would do anything else? She knew her well enough by now, surely. Michelle's deep, dark confession, spilt out following fifteen years of angst, would barely cause a ripple with her mother. Kathleen had chosen many years ago to deal with her youngest daughter at arm's length. Jane was the saint. Well behaved and clever. A college graduate with a good job in a large accountancy firm. Michelle was bright too, but driven to rebel against her parents' obsession with her sister's saintliness by not applying herself academically, preferring to pursue her desire to spend her life being creative with food. She didn't want to be Jane so she chose to be the opposite of whatever Jane was, especially when confronted with the constant nagging of 'Why can't you be more like your sister?'

Michelle's mum had simply passed off Michelle's desire for herself to be the one that was dead, rather than her sister, as yet another foolish thing that Michelle had said or done. She was sure that, in her mother's eyes, there were so many that this episode barely rated for any special consideration.

'So you can see why I held back on starting Viagra, what with all my problems with diazepam. I mean, I ask you – you'd have to be an idiot to start taking another drug when you're already addicted to one, wouldn't you? I'm depressed, not stupid.'

Michelle got up and walked away from Cousin Jack without a backward glance, and went to find Josie.

She found her in a dark corner sitting on Sean's knee, snogging, with his hand halfway up her lilac slub silk skirt.

'Josie,' she said, trying to ignore the absence of Sean's hand.

Josie and Sean looked up sharply. Sean's hand shot back into sight. He grunted.

'Oh, just leave us alone, Mum,' said Josie.

'No, hang on,' said Michelle. 'I've just got to say something to you. Sean, can we have a minute, please?'

'Whatever it is you have to say, you can say it in front of Sean.'

'Please, Josie. It won't take a minute, then I promise I'll ignore you for the rest of the night, if that's what you want.'

Sean grunted and shuffled Josie off his knee. He adjusted his belt then pushed past Michelle.

'That's so unbelievably rude of you,' cried Josie.

'I'm sorry. Just hear me out, okay?' said Michelle, trying to get her head straight despite the dangerous mix of high emotion and vodka swirling around inside her. 'I just wanted to tell you that I love you and . . .'

'Jesus Christ, Mum! Just 'cause you're pissed doesn't mean we have to have a love-in.'

'Just listen, Josie, please. I want you to know that you're the most important thing in my life and I care so much about you, and if you ever . . . ever think that I don't then you're wrong.' Michelle swayed a bit and had to steady herself. 'I know I don't say things right most of the time and I annoy you, but it's just because I want you to have a better life than me, that's all.'

'Is this about Sean?'

'I don't care about Sean. I just want you to know that I care about you, that's all.'

'So just leave me alone, then, and let me do what I want to do.'

'I can't do that.'

'*Mum!*' cried Josie. 'I don't want you interfering.'

Michelle's mum had left her alone. Ignored her, in fact, preferring to lavish her attention on Jane, even after she'd died. That was the last thing she was going to do with Josie.

'I will interfere if it means you don't end up like me.'

'You mean saddled with a daughter you don't want.'

'I *do* want you. You're the best thing that has ever happened to me and I wouldn't change you for the world, but I gave up on things when you were born, and now you're growing up I want you to have all the opportunities I didn't have.'

'But that's what you mean, though, isn't it? When you say you don't want me to end up like you. You don't want me to get pregnant and ruin my life like I ruined yours.'

'You didn't ruin my life.'

'Well, then, I don't know what we're arguing about. If getting pregnant didn't ruin your life then I might as well have sex with Sean.'

Michelle gasped and took a moment to work out the correct response.

'*Don't you dare!*'

'But you just said I didn't ruin your life. At least I care about Sean, and at least I'll remember his name after we've done it.'

Michelle gasped again, then bit her lip to stop the tears.

Josie pushed the knife in.

'At least if I do get pregnant I'll be able to tell my baby the name of its father,' she spat.

The biting couldn't stop the tears. They oozed out, taking half her mascara with them.

Josie took a step forward and pushed her chin into Michelle's sodden face.

'So you see, Mum, don't ever interfere in my personal life. Haven't you read the parenting guides? Lead by example, they all say. Well, luckily for you, I won't be following yours. I won't be getting drunk, shagging a stranger and having a daughter who will never know her father. I'll be shagging Sean.'

Michelle staggered backwards, recoiling from Josie's grim determination.

'But you can't, you're underage,' she said desperately.

'I won't be. Not on Christmas Eve, on my birthday,' declared Josie before going slightly pink and looking down. 'It's my Christmas present to him,' she mumbled at the floor. 'It's a surprise.'

Michelle thought she might throw up. She wanted to take Josie in her arms and tell her it would never be worth it, but before she could, Josie's head reared up, the defiance back in her face.

'Because I'll be sixteen then,' she declared. 'You won't be able to stop me doing anything. I'm going to have sex with Sean, and by the way, you may as well know, when I finish school I'm not going to uni. Me and Sean have discussed it and I'm going to get a job so we can get a flat together.'

'Are you *insane?*' Michelle exploded. 'You've got your whole life ahead of you. You can do anything. Don't throw it away on Sean. I won't let you. I *can't* let you.'

'What, like you did? Yeah, you really went for it, didn't you? Bet it's what you always dreamed of, working in a chicken factory. Well done you, Mum.'

'But I did it for *you*. I did it to save money for your

education, so you could go and do whatever *you* wanted.'

'But I never asked you to do that. Okay, so I asked you to marry George Clooney, but I was just a stupid kid then. I never asked you to go and work in a chicken factory. You can't blame me for your shit job and your shit life.'

Michelle stood stunned. How could she be hearing this? The sacrifices she'd made were all for nothing. She'd spent years in that factory, and her daughter was going to waste her life. This was her worst nightmare. She had to do something.

Josie turned away and bent down to get her bag from under the chair. Clearly she'd decided the conversation was over.

'So if I do what you asked, will you go to university?' Michelle said to Josie's backside.

'What the hell are you talking about now?' she replied, standing up and scrabbling around in her bag.

'If I marry George Clooney, will you go to university?'

'What are you on?' cried Josie, jerking her head up.

'No, come on. If I marry George Clooney, will you go to university?'

'This is ridiculous. *You're* ridiculous.'

'Answer the question, Josie.'

Josie snapped her bag shut and glanced past Michelle's shoulder, looking for Sean, no doubt. She shrugged.

'Yeah, whatever. If you say so. You marry George Clooney and I'll go to university.'

'Really?' cried Michelle.

'Well, it's never going to happen, is it? I mean, look at you. You're a middle-aged woman who works in a chicken factory. You're not capable of making anything happen.'

'I could, if I tried.'

'No way.'

'Watch me.'

'You're being ridiculous. Look, Mum, if you want to believe you can do it, fine. You marry George Clooney and I'll do anything you want, okay?'

'Anything?'

'Sure. No sweat.' Josie shrugged. 'I'll even give you away at the wedding,' she continued sarcastically.

'Okay, okay,' said Michelle, thinking fast. She was on a roll, she was sure of it.

'So you won't sleep with Sean either?'

Josie threw her arms in the air in amazement.

'This is so stupid. Okay, if you marry George Clooney,

31

Mother, I won't sleep with Sean either. How drunk *are* you?'

'Deal.' Michelle thrust her hand forward, keen to seal the unlikely agreement.

'Deal,' muttered Josie, allowing her mother to take her limp hand and shake it vigorously. Michelle grinned back at Josie, feeling momentarily relieved.

'You okay?' asked Gina, slumping down in the seat next to Michelle on the edge of the dance floor. She'd sat there alone for the entire Take That medley. 'Not like you to turn down a bit of "Relight my Fire".'

'Josie says she's going to have sex.'

'How do you know?'

'She told me.'

'Oh, Michelle, that's fantastic. Well done you!'

'Eh?'

'No, really. It shows what a great bond you have if she's prepared to share with you this key moment in her life. You see, you are a good mother. Haven't I kept telling you?'

'Gina, I can assure you it was not a tender mother–daughter moment. She's doing it to get at me. She thinks she's being really clever having sex with a boy she thinks

32

she loves rather than "shagging a stranger" like I did, as she puts it, and denying her a father.'

'Oh I see,' said Gina. 'Well, I guess she does have a point there.'

'I didn't shag a stranger, *okay*?'

'Alright, keep your hair on.'

'I'm not now and I never was a slapper,' Michelle insisted. 'It's complicated, that's all.'

'Believe me, I know you're no slapper. Quite frankly, you make Judi Dench look like a slut. But for the record, perhaps if you opened up a bit more to Josie about who her father is, she wouldn't think you're a slapper.'

'*For the record*, you've said that a thousand times and I still don't agree.' Michelle slumped forward until her head touched her knees and her hands grazed the sticky brown carpet. 'And she says she's not going to uni so she can get a job and move in with Sean,' she mumbled. She thrust herself back up quickly to avoid being sick and jumped as Little Slaw appeared in front of her, as if by magic.

'Sorry,' he said, pulling up a seat alongside her and Gina. 'Carry on,' he added with a wave of his hand as he took out his handkerchief to wipe his brow. 'The Spice

Girls, they make me sweaty. Don't mind me. Just a little rest I need.'

Michelle turned back to Gina.

'All I know is that I have a daughter who is heading down entirely the wrong track.'

'Not a lot you can do to stop her wanting to shag Sean, I'm afraid.'

'Can we not use shag and Sean in the same sentence; it makes me feel nauseous.'

'What is shag?' asked Little Slaw.

'Sex,' replied Michelle.

'Your daughter and sex?' questioned Little Slaw. 'Not good.'

'Exactly,' said Michelle.

'You should stop her,' said Little Slaw.

'I know,' cried Michelle.

'You lead by example,' said Little Slaw.

Gina started to laugh.

'I don't see what's so funny,' said Michelle.

Gina creased up even further.

'Enough already,' said Michelle.

'Sorry, mate,' Gina finally managed to splutter. 'But when it comes to not having sex, you're the finest example there is. When did you last have sex, exactly?

Have you managed to have any in the twenty-first century yet?'

'My sex life is not up for discussion here, thank you very much.'

'Last sex for me, 2005,' announced Little Slaw.

There was a polite pause for Little Slaw's revelation, followed by an open-mouth moment between Gina and Michelle. They all sat in silence for a while, thinking, staring at the sticky brown carpet and ignoring the Birdie Song, which Daz deemed a necessary part of any classy wedding.

'So I've told her that I will marry George Clooney,' Michelle declared eventually. 'And if I do, she promises she'll go to university and she won't sleep with Sean.'

No laughter this time, just a moment's silence.

'What the hell did you do that for?' exclaimed Gina.

'Because I had to do something,' said Michelle. 'She's throwing her life away when she should be following her dreams.'

Gina and Little Slaw stared back at her, incredulous.

'I don't know,' she said, throwing her hands in the air. 'It just came out. When I said I'd worked in the factory just to save money for her education she threw it back in my face, said she never asked me to. She only ever asked me to marry George Clooney, so I thought that if I did that, then she might drop Sean and do something with her life.'

'You're pissed,' Gina declared.

'Pissed and desperate,' said Michelle, shaking her head. 'How has my life got to this? Stuck here, trying to convince my daughter that under no circumstances should she get stuck here.' Michelle lashed out and kicked her discarded stiletto across the dance floor.

'You lead by example,' said Little Slaw, slowly nodding.

'You've already said that, Little Slaw,' huffed Michelle. 'And as you've heard from my great friend Gina, the not having sex bit is not a problem, but unfortunately my lack of sex life is not having the required influence on Josie.'

'You lead by example,' he repeated, turning to clasp her hands and stare deeply into her eyes. 'You do something with your life then your daughter do something with her life.' With a dramatic sweep of his left arm he continued. 'You show her possibility, opportunity, potential, the pursuit of dreams.'

Confused, Michelle stared into his mesmerising, pale grey eyes.

'You feel worthy, your daughter feel worthy,' he continued.

'Mmmm,' she murmured, his words somehow starting to pour some sense over her desperation.

'You get yourself out of this terrible rut you in.'

Something struck a chord.

'That's it!' cried Michelle, her eyes suddenly lighting up as she seized Little Slaw's shoulders. 'I've got to get out of this rut.'

'That's right,' agreed Little Slaw. 'You are worthy of so much more.'

'Of course,' she said. 'Lead by example. Show Josie that anything is possible if you try.'

'Even marrying George Clooney?' Gina chipped in.

'Yes,' Michelle shrieked manically.

'How, exactly?'

'Not a bloody clue,' cried Michelle. She slumped back down in her chair and gazed up at the ceiling, hoping she might find the answer somewhere in the stained, cracked plaster.

Chapter Three

Dear Mr Clooney,

I'm writing to ask if you would consider marrying me. Now before you toss this letter in the 'trash', as you call it, I beg that you read on and consider my proposal.

You see, I can't help but notice that, despite the fact that you can have any woman you desire, you have failed to meet a 'keeper'. I think this is because you are looking in entirely the wrong place. You see, as any woman could tell you, the pretty ones aren't always the nicest. Their good looks tend to instil in them a certain arrogance, which I'm certain, given your good nature, is the thing that is turning you off. If you would care to extend your horizons in the gene pool and look beyond the perfect bodies, I am sure you would find much to satisfy you. There's an army of women out there, including myself, who lack any pretentions and self-importance, and who are just waiting for the right man to come along. I think for me that could be you, and I think I could have qualities that you have never experienced before in the bland, tight-skinned women you have previously courted.

I should also mention, before we take this any further, that I have a wonderful daughter who could really do with a father just like you to guide her into adulthood, a role I'm sure you would find extremely satisfying.

So I'll leave it with you, then. I have attached numerous ways in which you can contact me and I look forward to speaking with you soon.

Kind regards,

Michelle Hidderley

Chapter Four

'And he never replied?' shouted Gina over the din of the conveyer whizzing past them, delivering a freshly dead chicken every few seconds, ready to be de-gibletted.

'No,' Michelle shouted back.

'Did you give him your mobile number?'

'Of course I did. I even called it a cellphone number because that's what they call it in America.'

'Really? That's just weird. Why can't they call it a mobile?'

'I don't know, do I? They just don't.'

'And when did you send him the letter?'

'Over two weeks ago now. The day you went on your

honeymoon. I sent copies to his agent and to all the major Hollywood film studios, and I even addressed one to George Clooney, Italy because he has a house there somewhere, apparently. I thought there was half a chance the Italian post office would know where he lived.'

'Well, I think that's really rude that you've heard nothing back,' shrieked Gina in Michelle's ear just as the conveyer came to a halt and a near silent hum descended on their section.

'Haven't they fixed that lung vacuumer yet?' Gina wiped her brow with the back of her blue-gloved hand. 'Still, at least it gives us a break. So are you going to write to him again, then?'

'Nah.' Michelle wrapped her arms around her chest to protect her from the chill blasters suspended above their heads. 'He must get a hundred letters like mine every day. I thought it might be worth a shot, but I suspect that something on a much more dramatic scale will be needed.'

'So what you thinking?' asked Gina as the conveyor spluttered into life again.

'Well, that's where I need your help,' Michelle shouted. 'I need your weird brain to come up with a truly cunning route to get to George.'

'What are you saying?'

'I'm saying that you don't think like normal people. Your special talent, Gina, is to take a situation and see it in a way no-one has ever seen it before. You don't apply any reason or previous knowledge, which occasionally makes you a genius. And that is what I'm relying on, for you to get me to George.'

'You're asking me to tell you how to marry George Clooney?'

'You got it.'

'I'd like to tell you, that is the biggest compliment you've ever paid me in the thirty-six years we've known each other.'

'Well, stop getting all emotional and crack on with it.'

'No problem, Michelle. You just leave it with me.' Gina nodded. 'I tell you, I still don't really get why you're doing this, but it sure beats the hell out of our usual Monday morning chat.'

'You mean, what type of crisps we've brought for this week's pack-up?'

'Exactly.'

It wasn't until lunchtime that Gina could reveal her thoughts regarding Michelle's quest. They raced to the toilets as they usually did, to avoid getting stuck in the queue and wasting valuable moments of their break.

Gina was just getting her lunch out of its Tupperware box as Michelle slumped down beside her on one of the long communal tables in the staff canteen.

'Monster Munch,' Michelle observed. 'So you've gone retro with your crisps selection this week.'

'Pickled onion flavour,' replied Gina. 'Mike's addicted to them. I'm not that keen, if I'm honest. Remind me too much of bloody school. But it's all part of being married, isn't it? Till death do us part, we shall take it in turns to choose which six pack of crisps we buy each week.'

'Classic plain Walkers for me today,' said Michelle, happy for once that she wasn't married and having to take on someone else's snack preferences. 'The crisp that is yet to be beaten.'

'Even by Pringles?'

'Even by Pringles.'

They fell into silence. Crisps debate over for the week.

'So I think I've sussed it,' Gina said finally.

'Sussed what?'

'You know, the whole George Clooney thing.'

'Great, hit me with it.'

'Well, I think going direct to George is too hard. He's,

43

like, such a megastar. So why don't you track down someone who knows George and see if you can get to him through them.'

'Good, good. I like your thinking. Continue.'

'So what about Brad Pitt?'

'Not really much less of a megastar than George, is he?'

'I know, but with Brad there's a way that's guaranteed to get you close to him.'

'I'm listening, Gina. You're getting me excited now.'

'Well, you know how Brad and Angelina have got like a million kids and some are adopted?'

'Yep. Carry on.'

'Well, there's your answer.'

'What?'

'Adoption.'

'What, I put myself up for adoption in the hope that Brad will take me? I really don't think you've thought that one through, have you?'

'Don't be stupid. You put Josie up for adoption.'

Michelle stared at Gina, speechless.

'I know what you're thinking,' said Gina.

'Really?'

'Yes. You're thinking it's a stupid idea, because there's

no way Brad and Angelina would adopt her because she's English. Well, I think you're wrong. They wouldn't allow themselves to be accused of discriminating. All you need to do is to explain that Josie is very deprived and in need of their help. They couldn't say no to that, surely?'

'Josie is not deprived,' Michelle retorted. 'The only reason why I work in this dump is to make sure she's not deprived.'

'I know, I know,' said Gina. 'But think what Brad and Angelina could give her. A family. And think what they could give you. George Clooney.'

Michelle looked at Gina. She'd been hoping for some ridiculous plan from Gina that might contain a shred of something that might just work. Not just a ridiculous plan, full stop. She sighed and started to gather together empty crisp packets and aluminium cans.

'I'm not feeling it, Gina. Besides, I don't want Angelina Jolie being mum to my Josie. She'll turn out all trout pout and get her backside branded by some freaked out religious sect.'

'Ooh, you're right. You don't want Josie getting mixed up in religion. That would be bad.'

'Yeah, those ten commandments are no way to live your life, are they, Gina?'

'Well dodgy if you ask me,' she replied. 'Love thy neighbour? God clearly never had to live next door to Asbo Alan or else he'd never have put that one in.'

There was no time for chat that afternoon as they were stationed on a conveyor belt, weighing and packing chicken breasts into their polystyrene nests. The mood was subdued as it usually was on a Monday, the day furthest from the weekend. Big Slaw attempted to cheer everyone up by shoving two fillets down his top to create a cleavage, but no-one was in the mood to find it funny so early in the week.

By the time Little Slaw joined them to help get the last delivery out on time, Gina and Michelle had fallen into silence, both lost in their own thoughts. Michelle was feeling sorry for herself as she contemplated the futility of her quest now that the vodka-induced high, when she'd thought marrying George Clooney was the answer to everything, was over. Gina, on the other hand, was weighing up the pros and cons of suggesting to Michelle that they form their own religion, to which they could recruit celebrities such as . . . George Clooney.

'So where we are?' asked Little Slaw.

'Where we are indeed,' muttered Michelle.

'No, where we are with Josie, with George Clooney?' he pressed.

'Funny you should ask that,' Gina butted in. 'Nowhere, that's where, because she doesn't like any of my ideas.'

Little Slaw didn't say anything, just silently tucked three breasts into their blue bed.

'I wonder if you are too grand, Gina. You must be simple,' he said, brow furrowed.

'Who are you calling simple?'

'You mean her ideas, don't you?' said Michelle, trying not to smirk. 'He wasn't calling you simple, Gina.'

Little Slaw said nothing. More breasts were laid to rest.

'How would you get a man?' he said eventually, looking at Michelle.

Michelle looked back, confused.

'You know, like normal, how would you get a man?'

Gina's turn to smirk.

'Alcohol, of course,' said Gina before Michelle could answer.

'Alcohol?' questioned Little Slaw.

'Er, let me see, just give me a moment,' said Gina,

holding up her fingers and ticking them off with her eyes closed, deep in thought.

'Gary Crabtree?' she fired at Michelle, her eyes flashing open.

'First time I ever drank gin,' Michelle muttered. 'Never touched it since.'

'And what about that Tony you pulled on holiday in Devon?'

'I blame Scrumpy for that one. If I'd been sober I definitely would have noticed his wooden leg.'

'True,' Gina sympathised. 'Well, by my reckoning then, every bloke you've ever pulled has been alcohol induced.'

Gina, Michelle and Little Slaw stared at each other, all slightly horrified by this fact. An empty nest sneaked by, bereft of occupants. Little Slaw spotted it and gave chase, sprinting alongside the conveyor, hurdling over a pallet before being brought down by a rogue cardboard box and sending packing foam flying in all directions.

'What the hell?' roared RB1, otherwise known as Rotten Bastard 1, as opposed to RB2, who was otherwise known as Rotten Bitch 2, the other factory floor supervisor.

'Much apologies,' said Little Slaw as RB1 bore down

on him. 'I was to rescue empty packet but it did not happen.'

'One word,' breathed RB1. 'Retirement.'

'You okay, Little Slaw?' said Michelle, rushing over. 'Had we better get you to first aid? Better get that in the accident book, eh? That's dangerous, someone leaving a box lying there to be tripped over. It could lead to a possible injury claim,' she continued, glaring at RB1.

'I'm fine,' said Little Slaw, getting up and brushing himself down.

'See, he's fine,' said RB1, suddenly jovial. 'Nothing to worry about. Now get back to work and we'll say no more about it.'

Michelle, Gina and Little Slaw resumed their positions at the conveyor and life went on.

'So, alcohol, you say,' said Little Slaw.

'Looks like it,' replied Michelle, now even more depressed as she scanned her memory, desperately trying to come up with a relationship that had not begun in a drunken haze.

'What am I doing?' she said suddenly, slamming five breasts into a blue tray that should only hold three. 'It's stupid. What the hell am I thinking? Let's just forget

George Clooney. It's never going to happen, and even if in some ridiculous universe it did, it probably wouldn't stop Josie sleeping with Sean and shacking up with him anyway, so I should stop wasting any more time thinking about it.'

'No way!' shrieked Gina. 'I love thinking about it. You can't give up already. What will I think about then?'

'It's stupid and pointless, Gina,' Michelle said despondently.

'What, and discussing what flavour crisps we're having for lunch isn't? Oh, that's so much more interesting,' retorted Gina. 'Tell her, Little Slaw – wanting to marry George Clooney is not stupid and pointless.'

'Wanting to marry George Clooney is not stupid and pointless,' repeated Little Slaw.

'You're just saying that,' said Michelle.

'No, I believe it,' he insisted. 'And what has changed since the wedding?'

'I've come to my senses. I will never marry George Clooney, so I shouldn't waste my time trying.'

'So instead you will show Josie how to give up, just like that. How to quit before you start. How to have no belief in yourself.'

'But I will *never* marry George Clooney,' Michelle repeated.

'You cannot answer that,' said Little Slaw, slamming the side of the conveyor belt with his fist. 'You are getting in the way of your dream. Just you. When really the only person who stand in your way is him, George Clooney. So we work out how to ask him. Then you will know. Then you can look your daughter in the eye and tell her you followed your dream no matter what.'

A dozen blue trays trundled by unfilled as Michelle, Gina and Little Slaw stared at each other.

'You are right,' Little Slaw added gently. 'Marrying George Clooney is not likely to stop the shagging or the shacking as you call it. But showing Josie how to get out into big wide world and follow her dreams might. You must get out of your own way, Michelle. You show Josie how to get out of her own way then sky is limit.'

'You see,' said Gina, bouncing up and down. 'It isn't stupid and pointless. And I've just thought of a foolproof idea on how to track him down.' She paused to take a deep breath and to ensure her audience was captive. 'If you become his stalker you'll see him in court,' she declared. 'I don't think George has his own stalker. It's a vacant position. You stalk him, he takes you to court, and you've got him. Ask him to marry you there and then. He's in a courtroom, he can't get away. Rude to the judge and all that.'

Michelle filled several blue trays before she looked back up at an expectant Gina and Little Slaw.

'If we're doing this we are not breaking the law,' she said eventually. 'We will find a way to George in a law-abiding fashion and show that daughter of mine how to follow her dreams.'

'Get in,' hollered Gina, punching the air.

'Before she Sean shags,' added Little Slaw.

'Before she Sean shags,' Michelle nodded.

Chapter Five

Michelle was weighed down by chicken. She could still feel its slimy, sticky texture on her hands despite several minutes of scrubbing with industrial cleaner. And she could still catch a whiff of its meaty tang despite taking several deep breaths of fresh air when she walked out into the dazzling sunlight at the end of her shift. To top it all, two kilos of the damn stuff dangled off each arm as she slogged her way down the hill to deliver her mother's weekly order from the factory shop. The town sprawled out below her looking pretty much identical to when she used to run full pelt down the hill from school as a teenager, excited by the opportunity to roam the streets and parks with Gina for a few hours before dark. She would never run towards the town now. She was held back by chicken and a daily desire to run in the other direction.

She shouldered her mum's back door open and then slapped the dead meat onto the table, weary from the journey and the emotional rollercoaster she'd been through all day, with the whole will-she-or-won't-she marry George Clooney thing. She clicked on the kettle, praying her mother would be too wrapped up in a thrilling final on *Countdown* to come through and rant about something or other.

No such luck.

'Where the hell have you been?' said her mum, bursting into the kitchen and switching the kettle off. 'You're late.'

'Late for what?' Michelle flicked the kettle straight back on again.

'I cannot believe you have forgotten what day it is,' her mother declared.

Michelle glanced over and noticed for the first time that her mum was wearing her best blue dress, which if she was trendy would be classed as vintage but on her was just plain out of date. She was also wearing red lipstick, a colour usually only selected for extra special occasions or if Michael Parkinson was on the telly.

'It's not your birthday until next month, is it?' said Michelle, racking her brains to recall the significance of the day.

'We discussed this, Michelle. Some time ago.' Kathleen was busily wiping down worktops that didn't need wiping. 'Now I know you've been busy with Gina's wedding and all that, but there really is no excuse for forgetting today of all days.'

'What?' screeched Michelle, too weary to play guessing games. 'For crying out loud, what day is it?'

Her mum threw the dishcloth into the sink and turned to address Michelle, hands on hips.

'Your sister would have been forty today. That's what day it is,' she said sternly.

'Oh,' was all Michelle could say before sitting down with a thud. What with George Clooney and everything, she'd forgotten. Actually, she couldn't blame George, since she and her mother had discussed Jane's significant yet non-existent birthday a couple of weeks ago. She had chosen to forget about it, hoping her mother would too.

'Don't you remember? We said we were all going to

visit her grave together. Me and your dad and you and Josie.'

'And do what exactly, sing "Happy Birthday"?'

Her mum stared back at her defiantly.

'Yes, actually.'

'And who's going to blow out the candles?'

'I haven't put any candles on it.'

'You made a cake?'

'Yes. It would have been her fortieth birthday, Michelle. We can eat it on that bench near the lychgate.'

They continued to stare at each other while Michelle hovered over a variety of possible responses she could give.

Eventually she settled for, 'Don't you think we might all look a bit stupid, singing to a lump of rock and then eating cake?'

'She forgot, didn't she?' said Josie, arriving in the kitchen and slamming an empty mug on the side. 'I told you she would, Gran. Tell her to go home and put on the dress she wore for Ben's christening. It's the only one she owns that doesn't expose too much cleavage for a woman of her age. Then tell her we'll meet her at the church gate in twenty.' Josie stalked out of the room without even looking at Michelle. She had refused to speak to her ever since Gina's wedding.

'Oh, and tell her under no circumstances should she wear any eyeliner,' she added, reappearing in the doorway. 'She hasn't a clue how to put it on.'

Michelle staggered up the road to the church, feeling awkward and flustered. Josie had failed to give any instruction on what shoes were acceptable to wear with the teal coloured dress, and, given her daughter's fierce demands regarding every other part of her outfit, Michelle was petrified of getting it wrong.

She had teal shoes that matched with pretty flowers on, but they seemed wrong for this particular party. Black would normally have been safe, but all her black shoes were six-inch spikes which could pass as sexy in the dark, but at six o'clock on a windy September afternoon would make her look like a hooker on her way to work. She also feared sinkage into the soft grass, which could lead to an embarrassing falling over incident she felt she would not be forgiven for. So eventually, with moments to spare, she made a snap decision to wear cowboy boots, as they were the only flat shoes she possessed besides the stinky cut-price trainers that she wore to work.

With a faint jangle of fake spurs, she approached the cheerfully dressed group standing outside the church.

'You really have no idea, do you?' said Josie, addressing her directly for the first time in two weeks.

'No, actually, clearly I don't,' Michelle replied. 'I apologise for having no idea what one must wear for one's dead sister's fortieth birthday.'

'Or at any other time, as it happens,' Josie retorted.

'Easy now,' said Michelle's dad Ray, looking smart in his Sunday best rather than his usual postman casuals. Michelle knew that Kathleen would have laid his suit out for him and Ray would have put it on without complaint, having spent decades negotiating an easy life with his wife. 'This is important to your mother, so let's get on with it, shall we?' He turned to open the gate, ushered the three ladies through and they trooped silently in single file up the path to the soundtrack of tinkling cowboy spurs.

Jane's grave was towards the back of the churchyard, past all the ancient stones which were crumbling from decades of weather and neglect, in the section allocated for the newer crop of deceased. Depressingly, however, she was becoming harder to find, as new stones had sprung up all too frequently during the sixteen years since she'd died. As they rounded the corner of the church to reach the area, Michelle's mum screeched and dropped the cake box, and the party came to an abrupt halt.

'Mum, what is it?' asked Michelle, concerned.

'It can't be, can it?' Kathleen said shakily, her face white.

'What can't be?' Michelle was convinced her mum was about to collapse.

'Looks like she's seen a ghost,' said Josie.

'You can't say that in a churchyard,' Michelle hissed.

'Why not?' said Josie. 'It's the obvious place to say it, surely?'

'Don't be ridiculous,' said Michelle.

'I can't believe it,' Kathleen murmured.

'Kathleen, what is it?' Michelle's dad stepped forward to see what the problem was.

Kathleen stared at her husband, then gave him the biggest smile he'd seen in a very long time.

'Look who it is!' She pointed towards Jane's grave. 'Look who's back! It's a miracle!'

'Kathleen, I think you should sit down for a minute and gather yourself.' Ray had begun to turn a little pale himself.

'No,' she said firmly. 'I'm going to say hello. Especially after all these years.' She marched off in the direction of Jane's grave.

The three who were left behind watched her go.

'This is freaking me out now,' said Josie.

'This is?' said Michelle. 'And you didn't think a cake was freaky?'

'Well I'll be damned!' said Ray suddenly, chuckling. 'Look who it is!' He started to follow his wife.

Michelle and Josie watched Ray walk away in terrified awe and then, for the first time, noticed that Kathleen had her arms around some bloke standing beside Jane's grave.

'Who the fuck is that?' said Josie.

'*Language*,' Michelle admonished, squinting into the sun to try to work out who the mystery figure was. Ray had reached the man now and was pumping his hand up and down in delighted greeting. The stranger, who seemed to have gatecrashed the weirdest fortieth birthday party ever, had his back to them so they couldn't see his face.

The next moment the man turned and waved in their direction. Clearly Michelle's parents had pointed out that there were two further guests waiting to join the party. Michelle squinted again, desperate to work out who it was.

'Never seen him before in my life,' said Josie. 'Perhaps he's a ghost and we're all dreaming.'

Michelle swallowed, feeling an icy chill in her heart. Finally, she had recognised him. She'd not seen him in a very long time and certainly hadn't expected to see him today.

'Fucking hell,' she muttered.

'*Language*,' admonished Josie.

It was the longest walk of Michelle's life, accompanied by the – now very annoying – jangle of cowboy spurs. Eventually they were all crowded around the narrow plot and it all became unavoidable.

'Rob,' she said with a forced smile. 'Fancy meeting you here!'

'Just what I said,' giggled Kathleen. 'Isn't it wonderful? See, I told you it was a good idea to come today, didn't I? If only to see you again,' she added, clutching onto Rob's arm as if he would disappear like a ghost at any moment.

'How are you?' Rob asked Michelle, looking older than his forty years, grey flecks winning the battle with his brown hair and deep frown lines carving a permanently concerned look onto his face. When he smiled at her, however, the old Rob peeked through and she was reminded of his kind eyes and the cute dimples on his cheeks that she used to tease him about mercilessly.

'Oh, I'm fine,' she said.

Silence fell.

Josie stuck her hand out. 'Well, I'm Josie,' she said. 'Since the rest of my family are too rude to introduce us.'

'Josie, love, I'm sorry,' squealed Kathleen, completely overexcited. 'Josie, this is Rob. Jane's boyfriend. Well, ex-boyfriend, I suppose, though you weren't ex at the time, so I guess . . . oh, never mind. And Rob, this is Josie, our Michelle's daughter.'

'Pleased to meet you,' said Rob.

'I can't believe you're here,' said Kathleen in wonder. 'When we stopped getting your Christmas cards I thought you'd forgotten us. Got married or something.'

'I did get married,' said Rob.

'Oh,' said Kathleen, sounding disappointed. 'To a lovely girl, no doubt, though,' she continued.

'She *was* a lovely girl,' said Rob grimly.

'Oh my God!' cried Josie. 'Did she die too?'

The entire gathering gasped and looked nervously at Rob.

'No, of course not,' he said quickly. He looked down at the ground but when no-one collected up the silence he looked back up to be met with the sight of four expectant faces. 'Actually, she had an affair with my boss,' he muttered. 'Our divorce has just come through.'

'Oh, Rob, love,' said Kathleen, putting an arm round his shoulder. 'You poor thing.'

'So, you looking up your exes, then?' asked Josie.

The entire gathering gasped again and turned to stare at Josie.

'Just asking why he's here,' she shrugged.

Everyone turned back to look at Rob expectantly again.

'To be honest, I don't really know,' he said eventually. 'I decided I couldn't work for my boss any more so I got a job back at the Derby brewery, but being here has brought back so many memories. Plus the fact I turn forty next month . . .'

'I remember,' said Kathleen. 'October the fifth.'

'Yes, that's it. Well remembered. Well, what with that and the divorce and being back in the UK after so many years in America, it's just made me wonder where my life went.' He looked down and started gently kicking the edge of the grave. Yet again the Hidderley family left the silence hanging wide open, forcing him to fill it. 'Anyway, I started thinking about Jane and what happened. How things might have turned out if she hadn't died.'

'Oh, you poor thing,' said Kathleen, rubbing his arm so vigorously it must be hurting him.

'So I thought it might help to come here,' he continued, looking up. 'Remind myself that at least I have a life to live and a fortieth birthday to celebrate. Not like poor Jane.' He nodded his head resolutely. 'I actually have a lot to be thankful for and a lot to look forward to.'

'Of course you do,' said Kathleen, wiping a tear away.

'I do, I do,' he said. 'And you know, your life can just change in an instant. That's all it takes. One moment and you're off on an entirely different course. You never know what's round the corner.'

How true, thought Michelle. She certainly hadn't expected to find Rob around this corner. A flock of birds took flight from the silent graveyard, momentarily distracting everyone.

'But look at you,' said Rob, taking the opportunity to remove the focus away from him and extract his hand from Kathleen's. 'You have a grandchild. And Michelle, you're a mother. How amazing.'

'She's a blessing,' said Ray, putting an arm around Josie.

'She really is,' sighed Kathleen. 'I don't know what we would have done after we lost Jane if she hadn't arrived and brought some joy back into our lives.'

'I'm so glad you found someone and settled down,' Rob said to Michelle.

'Michelle has brought Josie up all on her own,' said Ray, moving to put his arm around Michelle. 'And done a fine job, if you ask me.'

Josie spluttered something out the corner of her mouth whilst Michelle wished a grave would open up and swallow her.

'We've helped a lot, of course,' Kathleen added. 'And Josie reminds me so much of Jane. She's so smart, just like our Jane was.'

'Blimey,' said Rob. He looked at Michelle. 'I can't believe all this has happened since the last time I saw you. I had no idea.'

Of course you didn't, she thought. The last time she had seen Rob was just after Jane's funeral. It was lucky that black was so slimming – the perfect colour to hide the slight swelling of her belly from everyone. She'd been thirteen weeks pregnant and barely used to the idea herself, having only really faced up to her missed periods some four weeks earlier. She could still remember watching those blue lines appear on the pregnancy test as she'd sat alone in the toilets of the Rose & Crown at the end of a long shift in the kitchen. She could barely see straight she was so tired, but she knew she had to find out. She couldn't put it off any longer. She'd tried hard not to think about the implications before she took the test – it was too complicated – but as the blue lines had appeared and she'd lurched forward to throw up into the toilet, she'd known that complicated was probably the kindest thing most people would have to say about her circumstances.

For two whole weeks she told no-one, primarily because she wasn't sure who she should tell first. So many people would be shocked by this almighty cock-up that it was impossible to decide where to turn. The list of candidates shuffled round and round in her head until eventually she decided her sister Jane was the right person to tell first. She'd see how she reacted before she faced anyone else.

She'd mentally relived that day so many times that now every moment looked like one of those silent home movies shot on cinefilm. She'd arranged to meet Jane after work in a bar in Derby. She was late, of course. The bus from Malton to Derby seemed to take forever as it carried her closer and closer to her confession. She'd rushed in and been surprised not to find Jane there. Jane was always on time; she was renowned for it. She'd ordered herself an orange juice and found a quiet corner in the back where they could have some privacy.

Half an hour later and she was starting to get worried. Jane often worked late but she would have let Michelle know earlier in the day if she had a problem, she was sure. Jane was good like that. She decided to give it another ten minutes then find a payphone and call her flat.

By six-thirty she was on the bus winding her way back to Malton, having failed to get an answer at Jane's home. She must have forgotten, it was the only explanation. Highly unusual for Jane, but there was always a first time.

She walked through the door of her mum and dad's house and shouted from the hallway.

'Jane hasn't rung, has she?'

Her dad appeared at the door from the lounge. She remembered fleetingly thinking this was strange. Her dad rarely moved from his chair in front of the TV from the minute he got home from work, never mind getting up to greet her in the hallway.

'Come through, love,' he said. 'Something's happened.'

'What?' she asked as he gravely ushered her into the lounge, where Rob sat on the sofa with his arm around a sobbing Kathleen.

Her first thought was that they all knew. They'd guessed the awful mess she was in and this was their reaction. Complete and utter despair. She sat down on her dad's chair with a thud, her legs no longer able to hold her up.

'It's Jane,' her dad said.

Oh my God, thought Michelle. Jane knew and she'd disappeared, that's why she hadn't turned up to meet her. What had she done?

'Now I need you to be very brave,' said her dad, taking both her hands in his and kneeling in front of her. She braced herself for the words she was about to hear, but it wasn't what she expected. She watched her father's mouth make sounds, put words together in a sentence that didn't make any sense. 'There's been an accident,' he said. 'Jane was hit by a car outside work this afternoon and . . . and . . . she's dead, Michelle. Jane's dead.'

The world didn't stop for Michelle at that moment, as

it does for many people when they hear the news of a loved one unexpectedly dying. It carried on in a weird sort of way as her brain grappled with processing what her father had just told her. She couldn't fit it in anywhere – not without falling apart right there and then. At that moment, the only place she could fit this news into was the very large part of her brain that was preoccupied with the fact that she was pregnant.

And so, one moment after her dad's catastrophic words hit her brain, there was a reaction somewhere deep inside her of something akin to relief. Now she would never have to tell Jane the shocking truth about her pregnancy. She would never have to sit in front of her only sister and tell her that the father of the baby growing inside her belly was in fact Rob's – Jane's boyfriend.

Chapter Six

Michelle had never forgotten that nanosecond of relief and had never forgiven herself for it. It haunted her in her dreams and her waking hours. That moment of relief had done even more to shape the rest of her life than Jane's death had, trapping her in a near constant state of guilt. As she lay in her bed that night sobbing into her pillow, the crushing realisation slowly took hold that she would never see her sister again, and she resolved never to tell a soul who the father of her child was. How could she? It would be bad enough admitting she was pregnant, let alone telling everyone she was pregnant by her dead sister's boyfriend. No-one would cope with that.

She waited three weeks to share the news. The first week was hell on earth. Grief and despair consumed every corner of their lives. She stayed off work to sit with her parents as they stared into space or sobbed uncontrollably, while sympathy poured through the door in the form of a steady stream of visitors. As day eight approached, distraction came as they built themselves up for the funeral, busy with decisions on flowers, hymns, readings and cars. 'Just like a wedding,' the bumbling vicar had said, trying to be helpful, but which had probably set her mum back years in her recovery.

After the funeral the remaining members of the Hidderley family were dumped unceremoniously back into what would have to become their new normal. Three and not four. An awkward number if ever there was one. Relationships would have to be adjusted, alliances reviewed, roles re-established.

Michelle waited for nine days after the funeral, managing to keep her swollen belly hidden by billowing, dark, melancholy clothing. Twenty-three days after her moment of relief, hearing the news of her sister's death, the time came to announce that the three of them would actually soon become four. Rob had visited that morning to let them know that he'd decided to take up an offer to go and work in the American head office of the brewing company he worked for in Derby. Michelle's mother had hit the roof, crying and screaming for him to stay, clearly loath to let go of the bit of Jane that remained with Rob. Ray had had to step in, physically removing Kathleen's vice-like grip on Rob's arm, so that he could leave and start his new life away from the family of his dead girlfriend.

Ray and Michelle had stood at the gate and waved him off. Michelle fought the urge to run after him and tell him she was carrying his child so he wouldn't leave her there to cope on her own. But she couldn't get in the way of his opportunity to escape and get over Jane's death. She would have given anything to escape herself at that moment. Sombrely, they'd trooped back in, and before she could be asked to put the kettle on for the millionth time that week, she decided that now was the time. Rob being out of the way was the sign.

'I need to tell you something too,' she said as they filed into the lounge and resumed their sad positions.

'Oh, what now?' wailed Kathleen. 'I can't take any more.'

'No, this is good news, really,' said Michelle, bracing herself.

Ray and Kathleen looked at her, sceptical that any good news could exist in this current state of loss.

'I'm pregnant,' she announced.

Silence filled the room.

'Are you sure?' asked her mother.

'Yes, Mum. I'm sure.'

Tears started to overflow from her mother's eyes.

'Look,' said Michelle, hoisting up her hoody to reveal a clearly swollen belly.

Kathleen lurched towards her.

'It's Jane,' she sobbed as she bent to cup Michelle's belly. 'A new life, thank God!' she cried, smiling and hugging Michelle with real warmth for the first time she could ever remember.

Ray stood back, reeling from the double shock of Michelle's news and the fact that Kathleen was hugging the daughter who had long been classed as the black sheep of the family for not living up to the angelically high standards of her sister.

'But . . .' he started to say.

Don't ruin it now, Dad, Michelle thought. This is going much better than expected.

'But I didn't even know you had a boyfriend,' he continued.

Kathleen gasped an agreement.

Michelle already had her lie worked out.

'Well, the thing is,' she said, trying hard to hold their surprised gaze, 'it all happened when I went on that catering course up in Scotland.' She swallowed. This was going to be the hard bit. 'We had a bit of a party on the last night and there was this guy I liked and, well, one thing led to another . . .' She couldn't look at her father so stared at the floor. 'We haven't seen each other since. I don't even know where he lives or works.'

No-one spoke. Kathleen was still staring at Michelle's bump. She wasn't even sure if her mother was listening to what she was saying. Her father was taking it all in, though, that was for sure.

'But you'll find him, won't you?' he said.

'I don't want to, Dad,' she replied as steadily as she could. 'I want this baby. I know he won't. It will be much simpler if he doesn't know.'

'But Michelle . . .' her father pressed.

'I've made my mind up, Dad,' she said firmly. 'I don't want him coming along and confusing me. He might want me to get rid of it. I'd rather not live with that kind of rejection. For my sake and the baby's.' She reached over and took her mother's hand and placed it on her belly. 'Just be happy for me. Please, just be happy that we have a new life coming into the family.'

'Of course,' said Kathleen, openly weeping. 'It's wonderful news, Michelle. It's a gift, it truly is. And you'll stay here now, won't you? You'll stay here with me and your father so we can help you with the baby. There's no way you can go and work in that restaurant in London now, is there? You won't go, will you, Michelle?'

There was silence as Kathleen's plea hung in the air. The instant Michelle had found out she was pregnant she'd known that the career she had longed for in the upper echelons of the restaurant world would be a fatality. She just couldn't see a way round it. And since Jane was dead and she was carrying her boyfriend's baby, sacrificing her career seemed a suitable start to the life sentence of guilt Michelle must serve. Saying it out loud, however, was a different matter. Saying it out loud meant that was it. No going back. Dream over. She was stuck here.

'I won't be going to London,' she said, tears springing to her eyes. 'Of course I'll be staying here.'

Ray and Kathleen fell on her, tears of joy finally replacing the rivers of sadness they had wept in the last few weeks. Michelle stared ahead, numb.

*

'Bloody dog!' shrieked Josie, suddenly streaking off across the graveyard. 'Get off it, you hound!' she cried, waving her arms around in a demented fashion. She stopped at the corner of the church and they watched as a Jack Russell sped off looking pleased with itself. The next thing they saw was Josie holding up an empty cake tin.

'Sorry, Gran,' she shouted across. 'The dog got Auntie Jane's cake.'

'Cake?' mouthed Rob to Michelle.

'Don't ask,' Michelle mouthed back.

'Look,' said her dad. 'Why don't we all go down the Red Lion and have a drink together? You'll join us, Rob, won't you?'

Kathleen had had the makings of a thunderous face until Ray had cleverly suggested the inclusion of Rob.

'Oh, you must,' she said. 'Let's raise a glass to Jane, eh? She'd want us to all be together – today of all days – the people who loved her most.'

Dear God, muttered Michelle under her breath. Please let him say no.

'I'd love to,' he said.

'That's settled then,' said Ray. 'It's your round,

mind,' he added, slapping Rob on the back and striding off, the imminence of a pint putting a spring in his step.

'You staying for the quiz?' asked Daz, slapping some sheets of paper in the middle of the table. 'Hi, 'Chelle. Good to see you.'

Jesus, thought Michelle. Could this get any worse? The last five minutes had already proved to be probably the most excruciating of her life, as her mother dithered over the seating arrangements around the tiny round table in the corner of the Red Lion. Who was going to sit the other side of Rob was clearly a hugely strategic matter. Of course Kathleen herself would sit one side of him, clucking like some old mother hen, but her selection of who should take pride of place on the other side was causing her problems. When Ray plonked himself down next to Rob he was instantly rejected as a suitable candidate and dispatched to go and order drinks. Michelle couldn't decide who would be least damaging sitting next to Rob: her or Josie. The three women hovered as Rob sat alone until Josie declared she was off to help her granddad and Michelle sat herself in the prize seat, deciding she couldn't bear to see Josie sitting so close to her own father . . . and yet so far.

'Starts at seven,' Daz ploughed on. 'Fiver a team. Crate of Fosters for the winners. I don't believe we've been introduced?' He thrust his hand out to Rob.

'Daz, you remember Rob,' gushed Kathleen. 'Rob was our Jane's boyfriend.'

Daz squinted at Rob, clearly having no recollection of him. Rob stood up and shook his hand as Daz looked him up and down suspiciously.

'You probably don't remember me,' said Rob. 'I've not been around for a long time.'

'Oh yeah,' said Daz. 'Where you been then?'

'Well, I've been living and working in America, actually.'

'America, eh?' said Daz. 'I thought of moving over there once, but the UK is the centre of the music industry, so it really just didn't make sense for me.'

'Right,' nodded Rob. 'So you work in music then? That must be interesting.'

'Well, you know,' Daz said. 'I play my part.'

'We've just been up to visit Jane's grave,' Kathleen interrupted. 'And there Rob was. Isn't it amazing?'

'Yeah, awesome, Mrs H,' replied Daz. 'So, are you all

going to do the quiz then? I had you in mind with some of these questions, Michelle. I think you might be in with a chance.'

'No, we're not stopping long,' Michelle said quickly.

'Another time maybe,' said Rob, sitting down again.

'Nonsense!' cried Kathleen. 'We'll do the quiz,' she said, seizing a pen from the pint pot in Daz's hand. When Rob tried to speak she laid a firm hand on his arm.

'Please,' she said. 'Stay.'

He glanced at Michelle. 'Of course I'll stay.'

'Now where's Ray got to with those drinks?' said Kathleen, looking round. 'He'll be chatting to someone and have forgotten all about us. You used to like nuts, didn't you, Rob? I'll ask him to get you some nuts too. Now don't you move. I'll be back in two ticks.'

'She's not changed,' Michelle commented after Kathleen had bustled off to hurry her husband along.

'She always did like to mother me,' sighed Rob. 'More than my own mother, in fact. So, how about you? Have you inherited her mothering skills?'

'I don't think Josie would say I have any mothering skills.'

'I can't believe that,' said Rob. 'Is she at a tricky age? How old is she?'

Michelle froze.

'Fourteen,' she said quickly, praying the rest of the family weren't on their way back to the table. She had no idea if Rob had any recollection of that fatal night but it was a risk she wasn't prepared to take. Fourteen put Josie well out of the range of possibility of Rob being involved in her conception.

'Wow, she seems pretty grown up for fourteen,' he said.

'Yeah, well, they grow up so much quicker than when we were teenagers.'

'Nuts!' cried Josie, approaching the table and throwing a bag of dry roasted at Rob, who just managed to catch it and stop it flying over his shoulder onto the next table.

'Aren't you seeing Sean tonight?' Michelle asked when Josie had sat down and ripped into a bag of cheese and onion. Josie eyed her mother suspiciously. She never asked if she wanted to see Sean.

'He's gone fishing.'

'*Fishing?*'

'Yeah, what's wrong with that?'

'Well, don't you take up fishing when you're, like, sixty?'

'I do apologise, Mother. You're right. I made a mistake.

He's actually gone down town to get paralytic then pop a few pills before he shags some tart. Happy now?'

'I didn't mean that. I'm just surprised, that's all.' Michelle could see Rob's eyeballs virtually popping out of his head at the mother–daughter exchange.

'Please let me apologise for my mother,' said Josie, addressing Rob. 'It's so long since she had a relationship that she's jealous of anyone else who manages it.'

'One, two, one, two. Can everyone hear me?' came Daz's voice over the microphone, followed by an ear-splitting squeal of feedback, thankfully killing all conversation at the table. 'Have you all got an answer sheet and a pen?' The half-full pub grunted in response. 'Now, following last week's constructive criticism . . .' he began.

'You still limping, Daz?' shouted a hard nut from the next table.

'Luckily the swelling has now reduced, thank you for your concern, Bagsy. As I was saying, in response to certain people being unhappy that the subject of last week's film round was B-movies, this week's film round will be based purely on commercially successful films that I am positive you have all heard of. But please can I beg you all to go home and watch the genius that is *The*

Incredibly Strange Creatures Who Stopped Living and Became Mixed-up Zombies, because it is quite frankly one of the best movies ever made.'

Oh Daz, just get on with it, Michelle willed him.

'So without further ado and if you are all sitting comfortably, we'll begin. Oh, and just so you know, for this round there are two points per question. I'm going to read out a quote from a film and you have to give me the name of the actor or actress who said it and what film it came from. So that's not the name of the character from the film, the real name of the actor or actress.'

'For fuck's sake, ask a bloody question, Daz!' shouted Bagsy. 'Or you'll be doing more than limping.'

'I just need to make sure everybody understands. Let me repeat for one last time . . .'

'Ask a bloody question or I'm going down the Feather's quiz!'

'Right, quote number one. Who said, "I see dead people"?'

Josie stuck her elbow in Michelle's side. 'Mum did, in the graveyard earlier.'

'No, I didn't!' cried Michelle. 'It was you who said there must be a ghost.'

'You saw a ghost, Josie?' exclaimed Kathleen. 'Do you think it was Jane?'

'No, no, forget it, Granny. Mum was just being stupid.'

'It wasn't me,' pleaded Michelle.

'*The Sixth Sense*,' interjected Rob, recognising the need to halt the ghost talk. 'That was the film, but I can't remember the boy's name. Was it Harry something?'

'Haley Joel Osment,' said Michelle.

'Rob said it was Harry,' challenged Kathleen.

'No, she's right,' Rob said. 'That's his name.'

'Look, Rob, if you think it's Harry let's stick with Harry,' urged Kathleen.

'No, seriously, Michelle is bang on.'

'I'm definitely right, Mum,' Michelle said.

'Alright,' sighed Kathleen, slumping back in her chair. 'As long as Rob is sure.'

Terrible feedback from the microphone heralded the arrival of the next question.

'Quote number two,' said Daz. 'In what film, who said "Hasta la vista, baby"?'

'Oooh,' jumped in Rob. 'That'll be Arnie. Arnold Schwarzenegger in *Terminator*.'

'Write it down, Josie,' Kathleen ordered. 'It's such a

good job you're here,' she gushed to Rob. 'We wouldn't have any idea otherwise.'

'Well, I only know because I met him once, actually,' he replied, looking a bit embarrassed. 'The brewery sponsored the Superbowl and he was one of our guests. Every time his team scored he shouted "Hasta la vista, baby!" at the top of his voice. He was really funny. Had us all in stitches.'

'Sounds like you had a good time living in America?' said Michelle.

'Well, there were upsides,' Rob shrugged.

'I'll bet,' Michelle muttered.

'Are you sure it wasn't *Terminator 2*?' Ray interrupted, having been deep in thought. 'I'm sure it was a question on one of them afternoon quizzes on the telly your mother likes. Everyone thinks it's the first one but it was in fact the second one.'

'Oh, you might be right,' said Rob.

'Oh, shut up, Ray,' snapped Kathleen. 'Rob is much more likely to know than you. He's met the man, for goodness' sake.'

'But he might be right, actually,' said Rob.

'Ignore him, Rob,' she said in a conspiratorial whisper whilst looking straight at Ray. 'He hasn't a clue on this sort of stuff. He never gets anything right on them telly quizzes.'

'Quote number three,' Daz announced. 'Now, I think this is quite a hard one but some of you here might remember it. Who said in what film, "What is tiramisu? Some woman is gonna ask me to do it to her, and I'm not gonna know what it is!"?'

'Rob?' said Kathleen immediately.

'No idea on this one,' he replied, shaking his head and taking a big gulp from his pint.

Kathleen looked at Michelle. 'You must know this one. It's food related.'

'For the last time, Mum, I'm not fat!'

'I never said you were, but you love your cooking. Surely you can remember when tiramisu was discussed in a film.'

'Funnily enough, Mum, my ears don't prick up every time dessert gets a mention.'

'So where do you cook these days?' asked Rob. 'I can still remember that amazing pork dish you used to do at the Rose & Crown. Every time I came in I'd have to have it. Just couldn't resist it.'

'I don't cook,' replied Michelle. 'I work in a chicken factory.'

'Oh,' said Rob, clearly taken aback. There was an awkward pause. 'What happened?' he asked eventually.

'Responsibilities.' Michelle shrugged and looked away. This was not the conversation she wanted to be having with Rob, in front of Josie, having not seen him in over sixteen years, in the middle of a stupid pub quiz.

'Quote number four,' Daz ploughed on. 'Listen carefully. This is really hard. "Anybody who ever built an empire, or changed the world, sat where you are now. And it's because they sat there that they were able to do it."'

Silence around the table.

'So no-one knows this one?' asked Kathleen. 'Is it a new film? Would it be something you might have seen, Josie?'

'No way,' Josie said. 'Never heard of it.'

'George Clooney, *Up in the Air*,' muttered Michelle.

'Oh God, not George Clooney,' groaned Josie, putting her head in her hands.

'Isn't it George Clooney?' asked Kathleen. 'Who do you think it is then, Josie?'

'No, Gran, it must be George Clooney if Mum says it is.'

'Why did you say it wasn't, then?'

'I didn't. I was just groaning because it's George Clooney.'

'It's nothing, Mum,' Michelle said quickly. 'Just write it down, Josie. Daz will be asking the next question soon.'

'But it might not be George Clooney,' Kathleen protested. 'Can't you see that Josie isn't happy with that answer?'

'No, Gran, it's the right answer,' said Josie. 'I was just groaning because Mum's making an idiot of herself over him.'

'Over who?'

'George Clooney.'

Rob looked over to Michelle, clearly still confused by the news that she hadn't become the excellent chef she'd been destined to be, and now utterly bewildered as to why George Clooney was causing so much angst around the table.

Fortunately, Daz broke in over the screaming PA system. 'And so here we have number five, the last question in this round.' Finally Daz has his uses, thought Michelle.

'Number five?' shrieked Bagsy. 'But there's always ten questions a round. What you playing at, having just five questions?'

'Two points per question, Bagsy. One for the film and one for the actor. Two times five is ten points, which you may have worked out if you'd ever bothered to go to school.'

'Are you calling me stupid?' said Bagsy, rising from his chair and squaring his shoulders.

'Calm down, lads,' said Rob, getting up to stand between them. 'It's just a quiz, eh?'

'It's alright,' said Daz, looking more upset at Rob's interjection than Bagsy's challenge. 'I can handle myself.'

'I'm sure you can.' Rob sat down again. 'So let's hear this last quote, shall we?' He picked up the pen expectantly.

'Of course,' said Daz. 'That's what I'm here for. So, the final quote for this round is "Way to go, Paula! Way to go!"'

'*An Officer and a Gentleman*,' shrieked Michelle, forgetting her discomfort with how her evening was panning out. 'Oh my God. Best film ever.'

'Never heard of it,' said Josie.

'Oh Josie, you have to watch it,' sighed Michelle. 'Richard Gere is in the navy and he has this thing with Debra Winger, who's Paula, who works in a factory near where he's training. Then he leaves and she thinks he's deserting her, until right at the end when she's in the factory and Richard strides in in his pristine white navy uniform and picks her up and carries her away from the factory, in his arms . . . and great music is playing . . . and she's freeeee.'

Everyone stared at Michelle as she misted over and gazed into the distance.

'Are you sure that's the right answer?' asked Kathleen. 'What do you think, Rob?'

Rob closed his gaping mouth. 'I think Michelle obviously knows what she's talking about,' he said.

'It's definitely *An Officer and a Gentleman*,' Michelle repeated. 'It's one of my favourite films; it has the best happy ending in a film ever. He rescues her from the factory and she escapes to a better life!'

Everyone stared back at her blankly.

'I'm going to go and ring Sean,' said Josie, sliding off her stool and disappearing out the side door of the pub.

'Fancy some pork scratchings, Michelle?' asked her dad. 'They sell the ones you like in here. Go on, I'll treat you.'

'She escapes,' she muttered under her breath, watching Josie leave the room to talk to her waste-of-space boyfriend and Kathleen gaze into Rob's eyes like he was her long-lost son. She got out her phone and sent a text to Gina. It was time to kick it up a gear.

Chapter Seven

'So I got onto it as soon as I got your text,' said Gina. 'Apparently he's currently on set in Japan filming his latest movie.'

'Japan?'

'Yep, Japan,' Gina nodded. 'I know, it couldn't be worse. You can't stand sushi, can you? Raw fish makes you chuck.'

'That is a concern, yes,' said Michelle. 'That and the fact that it's on the other side of the world. What's the film?'

'Couldn't really find any details, but it looks like some kind of war movie. I found a shot of him on one gossip website, on set, in a military uniform.'

'George Clooney in uniform?'

'Looked like it.'

'Can you send me the link?'

'Sure.'

'So I guess the good news is he's making a movie,' said Michelle. 'That means at some point he'll be out promoting it. You know, doing premieres, that sort of thing. That's what might bring him to the UK.'

'You read my mind,' said Gina. 'He's actually due in London in November for a premiere of a film that he's already finished.'

'Really! But Gina, that's perfect! How did you find that out?'

'I called Cousin Jack. He sends his regards, by the way. Asked me to pass on the number of his shrink. Said he thought you might need it.'

'I don't need the number of his shrink.'

'He was quite insistent.'

'Do we have to have this conversation again? He's a depressed, impotent drug addict who is in no position to have an opinion on my mental health.'

Gina was starting to look distressed. 'But he made me promise that I wouldn't tell you about George being in London unless you agreed to see his shrink.'

'Why would he do that?'

'Well, it might have something to do with the fact that I told him about how you're planning to marry George Clooney in order to prevent your daughter shagging her boyfriend. He said he's worried about your delusional and dysfunctional behaviour, and as long as you see a shrink then *he'll* marry you to stop Josie shagging Sean.'

'I repeat, he's a depressed, impotent drug addict, and I am merely desperate.'

'That's what I told him.'

'Good.'

'He said you can call him any time, day or night.'

'Great. Now tell me how on earth he knows George Clooney is coming to London.'

'He has film industry connections.'

'Cousin Jack has?'

'Yeah.'

'How, exactly?'

'His ex-wife works the box office at the multiplex in Derby.'

Michelle raised her eyebrows at Gina as she often did.

'No, wait, listen,' Gina said. 'So he called her to pull

in a favour, as he puts it. Seeing as she left him and all that. He asked if she could find out what film premieres were taking place this year in London, if she knew anyone in the company that might know. She refused to start with, apparently, until Jack threatened to slash the tyres on her boyfriend's Mondeo again. Anyway, somehow she came up with the goods, and bingo. Turns out George's latest film premieres in Leicester Square in November.'

'Well I'll be damned,' said Michelle. 'A big fat thank you to Cousin Jack's ex-wife, I think.'

'And Cousin Jack?'

'Of course,' Michelle nodded. 'This is brilliant, Gina. We know when George is going to be in the country so now all we have to do is get to him.' She stopped swinging, putting her feet down hard on the tarmac. Gina and Michelle always did their best thinking on the swings at the park at the top end of town. They'd gone there straight from work for a pow-wow following Michelle's urgent text to start gathering intelligence on George Clooney's whereabouts. Fortunately, there was a light drizzle which had kept small children at home watching CBeebies.

'However,' Michelle admitted, 'even if he's in London our chances of getting to him are pretty slim.'

'As much as I wish you were wrong,' said Gina, 'I think that actually you're right.'

'So I've been thinking,' said Michelle. 'There's only one thing for it. Whilst he's in the country we just have to get him to come to me.'

'Genius!' cried Gina.

Michelle continued her swinging. No-one spoke until Gina slammed her feet down, bringing her to an abrupt stop.

'How the bloody hell are you going to do that, you idiot? What's going to make a Hollywood megastar just rock up in Malton and pop into yours and ask you out for a swift half?'

Michelle stopped and turned to face her friend.

'I've got one word for you, Gina,' she said. 'Charity.'

Gina looked around, confused. She must be missing something.

'And?' she asked, when nothing appeared to enlighten her further.

'Charity. That might be what brings George to me.' Michelle started to swing again.

'For fuck's sake, stop swinging. I can't concentrate with you looking like a demented hamster.'

Michelle stopped but didn't elaborate.

'So, what?' asked Gina, getting frustrated. 'You're gonna get one of those collection tins and hang around hoping he happens to walk past and put his millions into it?'

'Nope.'

'You're gonna set yourself up as a charity – the "I Will Marry George Clooney" charity – and ask people to give you money until you're so rich you can have, like, a ton of plastic surgery and a hair transplant and pin your ears back a bit until you're irresistible to him?'

'Why would I want to pin my ears back?'

'Because they do stick out a bit.'

'No, they don't.'

'They do.'

'You never told me that before.'

Gina shrugged.

Michelle strutted off to sit on the roundabout. Gina followed.

'So that's it, is it?' Gina pressed. 'You're going to ask for donations in order to get rich enough to marry George Clooney?'

'There are many causes more worthy of donations than me.'

'Well, I didn't like to say,' said Gina.

'Look, you know George,' said Michelle. 'He's clearly

the kindest, most generous, most amazing man on the planet, right?'

'I think you are a touch biased.'

'Well, I reckon he's bound to use his celebrity status to help those in need, isn't he? He's just that kind of guy. He probably works for loads of charities, helping them raise money for people who have nothing.'

'You mean, like when they do those phone-ins,' said Gina, 'and they line the celebrities up on a switchboard and tell you to donate money, because if you do, George Clooney might pick up the phone?'

'That's one thing he may be doing, I guess,' said Michelle.

'Are you going to ring up every charity and hope he picks up the phone at one of them?'

'No, of course not.'

'Phew. Because I was going to have to break it to you that would be a stupid plan.'

'I know it would, Gina.'

'They're fake phones, you know, when you see it all set up on telly. There's no way Gwyneth Paltrow knows how to process a credit card. No way. They're all just acting, pretending to talk to people whilst real people take the proper calls.'

'Glad you've cleared that up, Gina.'

'Didn't want you to be wasting your time, that's all.'

'Thank you,' said Michelle. 'Now, if you'll let me try and explain. I reckon if we can find a charity close enough to George's heart, and then go all out to raise money for it, then he might just come to collect the money. What do you reckon?'

'So, you're actually gonna *do* something for "chariddy"?' said Gina, giving it a bit of jazz hands.

'You got any better ideas? I don't see myself getting within a hundred miles of him otherwise.'

'I think it's a good idea,' Gina conceded. 'People are suffering, Michelle, and your motivation to use that in order to shag a celebrity is truly inspirational.'

'Beautifully put, Gina. But no, I was more thinking that it's a win-win situation. Even if I don't get to marry George Clooney, at least I might have actually done something good, maybe helped someone worse off than me. I kind of like that idea.'

'Cats,' said Gina.

'What?'

'I bet he's a cat lover. You could raise money for homeless cats.'

'I hate cats,' stated Michelle.

'I know, just saying.' Gina shrugged.

They fell silent, spinning around on the roundabout, both wondering what George might care enough about to raise money for.

'Oi, you fat fuckers!' came a loud shout from what was clearly a young person's mouth. 'That roundabout is for us kids, not you freakin' geriatrics.'

A four-foot-high boy came out of nowhere and proceeded to grab hold of the rails on the roundabout and spin it as fast as he could.

'Rio Bentall, you just stop that or I'll tell your mother!' screamed Gina, hanging on for dear life.

'Fuck off,' came the reply. 'You're trespassing, you. I'll tell the police.'

'Trespassing?' yelled Michelle. She paused as she waited to spin round again until she could at least see Rio. 'This is a public park,' she managed as he whizzed past her again.

The spinning was getting faster and faster as the momentum built. There was no option for it, she would have to jump. A James Bond-style roll might just break her fall enough to avoid injuring herself, and then she could spring up and run him off. She poised, waiting for Rio to appear again. Best not to jump on top of him; he was the sort to report her for child abuse. In a flash he appeared and she was flying through the air. Her feet touched the ground and she instantly bent her knees to lessen the impact. Her side came into contact with the spongy, child-friendly surface and she launched herself into an impressive roll – until she stopped, having only achieved a quarter turn, totally forgetting that she had a rucksack on her back. She lay there, legs waving in the air like a distressed tortoise.

It is possible that Rio actually did wet himself as he screamed with laughter at Michelle. She hoped so. Eventually Gina dismounted the roundabout as it came to a standstill and helped Michelle up. They walked away, ignoring Rio's further verbal assault.

'You alright?' asked Gina. 'You could have come a cropper there. You're not as young as you used to be, remember.'

'Of course I'm not as young as I used to bloody be,' said Michelle, humiliated. 'I hate that saying. It's so stupid.'

'You only hate it because it's true.'

'Of course it's true!' screeched Michelle. 'How could I be anything but not as young as I used to be?'

'Alright, keep your hair on,' said Gina. 'You going home now?'

'Yeah. Josie's out, so I can get onto the computer and try and find out about George's favourite charities.'

'Right. I'll call Cousin Jack, shall I, and say his intelligence was of great value to our operation?'

'You been watching *Homeland* again?'

'Yeah.'

'I think Cousin Jack should thank his recruit and keep her under orders.'

'Good thinking. I shall inform agent Jack to abort the mission to slash the Mondeo tyres.'

'Excellent. Let's debrief tomorrow.'

Chapter Eight

'Mum, I need the computer.'

'What for?' asked Michelle, trying to concentrate on what was being said on-screen.

'I said I'd Skype Sean before he went to bed.'

'But you've just been over at his house!'

'I know, but he wants to see my face before he goes to sleep.'

'Well, I'm using it at the moment.'

Michelle felt Josie rear up behind her left shoulder, forcing her to quickly wipe away the tears that were dripping off the end of her nose. She didn't have a tissue, so she was forced to give a loud sniff.

'No, you're not. You're just snivelling over some dodgy George Clooney film,' Josie said scornfully. 'When are you going to grow up?'

'It's not a George Clooney film,' said Michelle, wishing she could get up for a tissue but unwilling to allow Josie to take over the cyberspace and replace George Clooney with Sean's acne.

'Oh really, so who exactly is that, then?' asked Josie, her hands defiantly on her hips.

'It is George Clooney, but not in a movie,' Michelle muttered as she watched his lips move, unable to follow what he was saying over Josie's interruption.

'Whatever,' said Josie. 'There's Clooney porn all over the internet that you can watch whenever you like, but at this very moment I promised Sean I would Skype to say goodnight.'

'Call him on your mobile,' said Michelle.

'You are unreal!' shouted Josie. 'Some dodgy clip on YouTube is more important than me wishing my beloved goodnight!'

'It is, actually,' said Michelle, turning round to face her daughter for the first time, eyes red and cheeks glowing.

'What's up with you? You look weird!' shrieked Josie.

She thrust her thumb towards the screen as if gesturing directly to George to clear off and get out of her Skype time. 'You're thirty-six, Mum, not sixteen, for Christ's sake. You're an embarrassment!'

Michelle got up and rushed to the kitchen to grab a tissue. By the time she'd come back, Josie was already dialling Sean on Skype. He answered immediately, leering topless out of the screen, revealing that his acne problem was not restricted to his face. Michelle thought she might retch as she reached over and grabbed the mouse before clicking the Call Cancel button.

'WTF, Mother?' said Josie. 'You can't do that.'

'I hadn't finished,' said Michelle. 'And you can tell Sean I don't want to see him naked on Skype again.'

'He wasn't naked. He had his PJ bottoms on.'

'How do you know?'

'Because he was in them when I left his house.'

'And what were you in, young lady? Or not, as the case may be.'

'I was in my clothes, Mother. I told you, we're waiting until I'm sixteen before we do anything like that.'

'Oh, how reassuring,' huffed Michelle.

'We are both more than capable of controlling our-selves,' said Josie. 'Unlike some. Exactly why were you all red in the face after watching George Clooney on the internet?'

'Josie!' Michelle exclaimed, mortified. 'It wasn't like that.'

'Look, I know it must have been a long time, Mum, and indeed the internet is well known for allowing some people to relieve their frustration, but really – you? So very disappointing.'

'I was not masturbating whilst watching George Clooney on the internet.' Michelle slammed her fist on the desk table.

'Er, hi,' came a voice out of nowhere.

They both swung round to look at the screen, and there was a smirking Sean, reappearing somehow to participate in this late-night mother–daughter debate.

'I wasn't!' Michelle shouted at Sean in a box.

'It's okay, Mrs H, we've all done it,' said Sean.

Silence fell as Sean grinned inanely out at them. It was the first time Michelle had ever seen his teeth and she was sure it was the longest sentence she'd ever heard him put together.

'But I won't tell anyone if you're embarrassed,' he continued.

Michelle stared back at him for a moment, then

reached down and pulled the computer plug out of the wall.

'Mum!' shrieked Josie. 'You can't do that to a computer! It's really bad for it.' She crouched down to put the plug back in.

'Tell your boyfriend,' said Michelle, pointing at Josie's crouched back, 'that I was not doing what he thinks I was doing.'

'Whatever.' Josie stood up again and sat herself down in front of the computer, concentrating on getting it back up and running. 'No-one cares what you do in your private life anyway.'

Michelle opened her mouth to speak, then closed it again. She was tired and not sure she could face trying to explain the real reason why she was flustered and red in the face after watching a George Clooney clip on the computer. She trudged upstairs and went through her usual night-time rituals: brush teeth, look at dental floss and decide to leave it another night, scrutinise face in the mirror to do a wrinkle check, apply moisturiser, go into bedroom, drag off clothes and dump on floor, pull on passion-killing pyjamas, fall into cold, empty bed.

Except tonight, for once, her head wasn't filled with

the sadness of sleeping yet another night alone. It was buzzing with the images she had watched that evening on the computer. It hadn't taken long for her to discover that George Clooney 'has one of the most charitable hearts in the Hollywood community'. The list of charities he supported appeared to be endless, but it wasn't the quantity of his giving that was most impressive. She'd discovered that in 2008 he was so incensed by some of the terrible things going on in the world that, along with the likes of Matt Damon and Brad Pitt, he'd set up the Not On Our Watch project. This was not about putting their faces in the media and asking people to give money, or pretending to be on a stupid switchboard. This involved actually trying to make a difference, using their celebrity status to increase awareness of the pain and suffering going on in places like Darfur in Africa and Burma in South East Asia. Michelle had wept as she'd watched a woman speak of the ritual rape she was subjected to and seen images of millions of children without homes or food. There were clips of George putting pressure on politicians to change what was happening, to actually do something about the mass atrocities going on around the world. Michelle had watched as George addressed the United Nations, desperately trying to get the voices heard of people suffering at the hands of terrible regimes. He had never looked better.

Chapter Nine

'There you are,' said Michelle, dumping herself down in a slightly damp wicker chair. 'I've been looking for you all over. What are you doing out here?'

'Welcome to my office,' declared Daz, waving his hands around the smokers' hut behind the Empire Social Club in the middle of town. The wind was blowing a gale through the open front and cigarette butts were floating in water-filled ashtrays as a result of an earlier rain shower.

'Are you serious?' asked Michelle. 'It's dark, it's damp, it's dirty, and it stinks of fags.'

'Exactly!' replied Daz. 'I love it. Takes me back to

the good old days when all pubs and clubs were just like this – when you walked in and were hit with that smoky atmosphere and the next morning you could still smell the remnants of a fantastic night out on your clothes. Cigarettes and sweat. Good times, Michelle, good times.'

'You never smoked.'

'I know. I just preferred going home smelling like that rather than of wood polish and Domestos. No atmosphere today, you see. That's why no-one goes to the pub any more. They're so sterile, so cleeeean, so homely, with all their fake old country furniture and pretend vintage tat. Yuck, yuck, yuck,' he concluded, pretending to stuff his fingers down his throat.

'But shouldn't you be inside, manning the decks or something? Aren't you supposed to be working?' she asked.

'Buffet time,' Daz pointed out. 'I'm about to go back in after I've made an important managerial decision. What do you reckon to this?' He turned his iPad around to show Michelle what looked like a logo design.

'Dazzling Daz's Double Dex Disco Machine,' she read out from the riot of colours radiating from the letters on the screen.

'Cool, eh?' Daz said proudly. 'I'm going through some rebranding. See how I've changed the spelling of Decks to Dex. It's to appeal to the youth market. I've spotted a big trend in spelling things wrong.'

'Right,' Michelle nodded. 'And the fact that you don't use decks any more; you use a laptop? Should that not be part of your rebranding?'

'Michelle,' Daz sighed. 'Kids like the retro feel. Most top DJs are using decks again to be authentic. Decks are cool. I can't be arsed, though.'

'I see. So what's this new logo for, then?'

'The new truck, of course. Pat Jones has just sold me his Ford Ranger pick-up. It's the bollocks. Five-seater, beautiful grey trim, CD changer, and my disco kit fits in the back perfectly, now I've got rid of the stink of sheep. I just need to pimp it up a bit, you know. I'll take you for a ride later if you like. Bring back memories of old times, eh?' He winked. 'Me, you and Millie the Metro.'

Michelle recollected awkward pauses in lay-bys on the way back from the pub in Daz's mum's car. Gina and her boyfriend would be virtually swallowing each other in the back whilst Michelle would be chatting ten to the dozen in the front at Daz to avoid any silence which might be filled by Daz moving in for a snog.

'Actually, I've come to see you to pick your brains,' she said quickly.

Daz stared at her before silently raising his finger in a gesture to prevent her proceeding any further.

'I knew this day would come,' he said seriously, glancing down at his watch. 'Hold that thought. I'm due back inside now, so why don't you come and join me and we can continue this conversation behind the decks.'

'Are you sure they won't mind?'

'They won't even notice you're there, believe me.'

They went through a back door into the function room, which allowed them to appear behind Daz's disco kit as if they'd been there all the time. Daz sat down behind his laptop and a bank of speakers and began tapping buttons.

'Just lining up the next track ready for when the eating selection finishes,' he muttered as Michelle peered past the lighting rig to take a look at what kind of crowd was having a party on a Thursday night. Before she could take anything in, however, an elderly gentleman appeared at her side.

'Burt Bacharach,' he shouted in her ear.

'Michelle Hidderley,' she replied. 'I'm just giving Daz a hand. Hope that's okay?'

The man looked at her as though she was out of her mind – so much so she wished she'd told Daz she'd come back when he'd finished.

'Burt Bacharach,' the man bellowed again.

'Pleased to meet you.' Michelle politely offered her hand to shake.

The man shook his head at her then some kind of realisation appeared to dawn on him.

'I'm so sorry,' he apologised. 'It's just you're awfully young to have it.'

'Have what?' she asked, starting to panic at the intense concern that had appeared on his face.

Now it was the man's turn to start panicking. He went bright red and his eyes darted around as he searched for an escape route.

'Of course,' he flustered. 'You won't know if you've got it, will you? I'm such an idiot. I'm so, so sorry. Please forgive me.' She watched him turn and scuttle to the other end of the room.

'Who was that?' asked Daz.

'Burt Bacharach, I think he said his name was.'

'Don't be ridiculous.'

'What do you mean?'

'Burt Bacharach is a very famous American singer-song writer.'

'Riiiight,' said Michelle slowly. 'Oooooh, I bet he was asking for Burt Bacharach, not introducing himself. No wonder.'

'Or he's one of them?'

'One of what?'

'Maybe he has Alzheimer's and thinks he actually is Burt Bacharach.'

'Why would you say that?'

'Doh,' said Daz. 'Because this is an Alzheimer's fundraiser.'

'Riiiiight,' she said once again, her mouth dropping open. 'I think he thought it was *me* who had Alzheimer's.'

'Why?'

'Because I thought *he* was Burt Bacharach.'

'Now I'm confused,' said Daz.

'Me too.'

'Shall we move on?' said Daz briskly. 'You said you needed advice?'

'Yes,' she replied, still staring after the old man.

Daz grabbed her hands, forcing her to look at him. 'I have waited patiently,' he said. 'I didn't want to push my expertise on you, but I can assure you I am totally prepared.'

'Really?' Michelle was beginning to wonder if she might actually have early onset Alzheimer's, given that nothing was making any sense.

'Oh yes,' Daz said. 'I've seen you struggling for some time now, and boy, has it hurt me to hold myself back, but I knew I had to let you come to me, or else you might cast my superior knowledge on this matter aside.'

'What the hell are you talking about, Daz?'

'Music, of course!' he cried. 'I've seen it time and time again. You have a teenager in the house listening to some drivel you don't recognise and you need me to give you a tutorial on the youth music of today so you can communicate with your daughter again. You have no idea how many parents have come to me wanting me to explain the difference between each member of One Direction so they can have an intelligent dialogue with their daughter about the merits of Harry Styles.'

'Josie hates One Direction.'

'What! Is she real?'

'She thinks they're for kids and bored housewives and is mortified I have a bit of a crush on Niall.'

'But it's about the music,' cried Daz, thrusting his hands in the air. 'I keep telling everyone. They do perfect pop music. It's genius. Why does no-one understand?'

Michelle took a step back from the demented arm waving that was accompanying his rant.

'It makes me so mad,' he continued. 'Bands with desperate, overly complicated names who play pretentious bloody crap get all the praise, and they're rubbish. One Direction are brilliant and it's about time they got the critical praise they deserve.' He banged his fist on a speaker.

'Okay, Daz, just calm down. I know you are the number one expert on boy bands, but I need your considerable expertise in another area just now. I want you to tell me all you know about event management.'

Daz paused to look at her then took a deep breath and sat down again in the chair in front of his laptop.

'Well, now you're talking.' He turned his lucky DJ baseball cap around and folded his arms. 'I have witnessed every possible event screw-up known to man.

Did I ever tell you about the hog roast at the bar mitzvah? Epic fallout.'

An elderly lady's head appeared over the top of his screen.

'Frank Sinatra?' she said.

Daz looked over to Michelle and mouthed, 'She is not Frank Sinatra, just so you know.'

'Really,' Michelle mouthed back sarcastically.

'Any particular track?' Daz asked the lady.

'Ooh yes,' she giggled. '"Fly Me to the Moon" is my favourite. It's the first record my husband and I ever danced to. We'd love to dance to it now.'

'How sweet,' grimaced Daz as he tapped at his keyboard. '"Fly Me to the Moon", coming right up.'

'Oh, thank you, dear. I'll go and find Gordon straight away.'

'So,' said Daz, turning his attention back to Michelle. 'Event management, you say? What type of event are you thinking of? Hit me with it.'

'Well,' she said, suddenly feeling nervous. 'I'm thinking of running an event for charity.'

'Charity? Why?'

'Well, to raise money.'

'Who for?'

Michelle took a deep breath.

'For a charity called Not On Our Watch.'

'Never heard of them.'

She took another deep breath.

'They aim to bring global attention to international crises and give a voice to the victims.'

Daz looked at her quizzically.

'And why do you want to help do that stuff you just said?'

She sighed deeply.

'Because I want to meet George Clooney and ask him to marry me.'

'Oh, I see. This is that thing Josie has been telling me about.'

'What!' she exclaimed. 'Josie has talked to you about it? When?'

'Michelle,' he said, clasping her hands again, 'you forget I have the school and village hall disco scene sewn up. I am like a godfather to the teenagers of Malton. They talk to me, they tell me things when I'm sat behind these strobe lights and they're trying to convince me to stop playing Eighties classics, despite the fact that they have to understand that Spandau Ballet are vital to their cultural education.'

'So what did she say?'

'That you are a total embarrassment and that you are trying to marry George Clooney.'

'But *she* said if I married George Clooney she wouldn't sleep with Sean.'

'Right. You are not a freak and it totally makes sense. What the fuck are you talking about? Are you sure you don't have Alzheimer's?'

Michelle put her head in her hands in despair.

'That's the deal. Plus if she sees me trying to follow my dream, perhaps she'll think of a dream beyond shagging Sean and get her act together and do something with her life,' she said into her hands.

'Frank Sinatra?' The elderly lady's head appeared over the top of Daz's laptop again.

'It's on now, love. Can't you hear it?'

'This isn't Frank Sinatra,' the lady said after she'd paused to listen.

'I can assure you it is. "Fly Me to the Moon", just like you asked,' said Daz.

'Don't be ridiculous!' cried the lady. 'I know "Fly Me to the Moon" when I hear it and it certainly isn't this.'

'I am a music professional,' said Daz firmly. 'And this is definitely the song you asked for.'

'Oh dear,' she cried, looking agitated. 'I shall have to fetch Gordon. He won't be pleased.'

Daz turned back to Michelle.

'You really want to marry George Clooney?' he asked, as if it was the most ridiculous thing he had heard that evening.

'Yes,' she replied. 'I want to try.'

'Tell him, Gordon!' The old lady had reappeared with a fraught-looking man in tow. 'Tell him to put Frank Sinatra on and that it's our special song. Tell him how we used to dance to it every Saturday when we were courting, and how wonderful we looked.'

'Look, Barbara,' the man said, putting a gentle hand on her shoulder. 'Why don't you go and get some more of that cheese you like whilst I talk to this gentleman?'

'The red cheese?'

'Yes.'

The old lady turned abruptly and walked off towards the buffet.

'I'm sorry,' the man apologised, turning to Daz and Michelle.

'It's okay, mate,' said Daz. 'Not a problem. I understand.'

'At least she can remember some good times,' said

Michelle, wanting to say something to cheer up the desperate-looking man. 'That must be some comfort.'

'If only,' he sighed. 'She's talking about her ex-husband, Gordon. I'm Ernie,' he explained. 'She can remember dancing to Sinatra with him, not me.'

'Oh, that's terrible,' said Michelle. 'I'm so sorry.'

'Oh, don't you be sorry,' replied Ernie. He let out a long sigh. Michelle could have cried for him.

'Have you been together long?' she asked.

'We were childhood sweethearts,' he said as though it was the saddest announcement ever. 'I was about to ask her to marry me when Gordon quite literally danced her off her feet. And I stood by and let him.' He paused, shaking his head. 'Then she called me out of the blue three years ago. Turned out he was a great dancer but a terrible husband. She'd stuck by him until he'd died the previous year. She said she'd never forgotten about me. We married three months later on her eightieth birthday. It was the happiest day of my life.'

'That's fantastic,' said Daz brightly. The gentleman frowned at him.

'Eight months later she was diagnosed with dementia and now she thinks I'm him – her bastard ex-husband who stole her from me over sixty-three years ago.'

'Wow,' said Daz and Michelle in unison.

'I'm so sorry,' repeated Michelle.

'Yeah, well,' said Ernie, averting his eyes from her concerned and awestruck stare. 'It's my own fault. Should have married her when I had the chance all those years ago. Anyway, if you could just put it on again and I'll dance with her. The good thing about all this is that she can't remember what a rubbish dancer I was.'

'Look after yourself,' Michelle said as he turned away.

They watched as Ernie walked over to Barbara and with a small bow offered his hand to her. She took it and he led her to the dance floor, where they shuffled awkwardly as she smiled proudly at Gordon, who was really Ernie.

'Bloody hell,' murmured Daz. 'That is the saddest story I've ever heard.'

'Too right,' said Michelle in a daze, following their gentle swaying around the hall. 'To think he's probably spent every day of his life regretting not asking her to marry him. It just shows that when it comes to stuff like that you simply have to go for it. You never know what might happen.'

'Exactly,' said Daz, nodding furiously. 'Exactly.'

'So, on that note, marrying George Clooney then?'

she said, snapping her head round to address him. 'I need you to tell me exactly what gets people digging in their pockets for worthy causes.'

He gave her an odd look before he sighed and closed his eyes.

'Let's see,' he said, as if exploring the vast cavern of his mind. 'There is what I call the holy trinity of any decent event.'

'Yes,' she said eagerly.

He opened his eyes and leant forward.

'Food, booze, and of course the all-important . . .'

'Yes?'

'Daz the DJ, of course. Guaranteed for a dazzling event.'

'Right, so that gives me something to work with. Food, booze, entertainment.'

'No, I said food, booze, Daz the DJ.'

'Okay, well, let's break this down,' she said. 'So, food. I did have this idea that maybe I could ask the factory to sponsor it. You know, give us a load of chicken?'

'Oh yeah,' said Daz, his eyes lighting up. 'What about chicken-in-a-basket? Why does no-one do that any more? I can do a great chicken-in-a-basket.'

'No way. I'd do this great dish with fresh chillies and

sun-dried tomatoes and paprika and rock salt. It's the best thing you have ever tasted, seriously.'

Daz stared at her.

'You're doing that Nigella thing again.'

'What Nigella thing?'

'You go all curvy and sexy whenever you talk about food. Makes me fantasise.'

'What about?'

'Nigella, of course!'

'Is that meant to be a compliment?'

'Absolutely. I could have said Gordon Ramsay. Now, stop trying to distract me. I still reckon my chicken-in-a-basket would beat the pants off your fancy pants chicken any day.'

'No way. I trained to be a chef, if you remember.'

'You don't scare me. I watch a lot of *MasterChef*. I know the tricks of the trade. I can make it small and delicate and put the basket on top of a black slate whilst smearing ketchup all over it with a blunt knife thing. My chicken would beat yours in a showdown for sure.'

Michelle stared at Daz, her mind racing over the episodes of *MasterChef* she'd studied, convinced she could do just as well as any of the amateurs. An idea was coming, sparked by her natural desire to be competitive over cooking, given her under-utilised skills.

'You are a genius,' she declared finally, grabbing Daz's jacket. 'That's it! A cooking competition! A chicken cooking competition!'

'Mmmm, okay, could work,' said Daz, contemplating the plan. 'You may have the germ of an idea there, but what about the booze and the DJ? Don't forget the holy trinity of any successful event. Have I taught you nothing?'

'Well . . . well . . .' Michelle stuttered. 'We'll do it in the evening and get everyone drunk and have a party.'

'And call it Chickens For Charity,' declared Daz, suddenly swept along by Michelle's enthusiasm.

She paused, considering his idea.

'Yes, yes, yes!' she said finally, punching the air. 'I love it. I love you!' She flung her arms around Daz in glee.

'Excuse me, dear,' came a voice from behind them. 'I'm so sorry to interrupt, but we'd like to draw the raffle in ten minutes, and then can you play that Sixties montage we talked about?'

'Of course, Clare. Whatever you say,' said Daz, reluctantly letting go of Michelle.

'Right you are, dear.' Clare gave Michelle a questioning look before striding off.

'Sixties montage,' he muttered. 'I told her. I said I'm very good at reading my audience. It's the Alzheimer's Society. They won't remember the Sixties.'

'They haven't all got Alzheimer's, though, have they?'

'I know but let's make the poor sods who have got it feel terrible by bombarding them with the sounds of their golden years which they can't even remember. It's just cruel, Michelle, quite frankly. I told Clare it would be much kinder to do a youthful, upbeat medley that lifts their spirits, including a few great tracks by . . .'

'One Direction?' she interrupted.

'Exactly,' he agreed. 'But would she listen? Well, on her head be it when they're all slitting their wrists at the Sixties dross she's asked me to play. Can't you pretend to be a relative or something and insist your grandpa needs to be uplifted out of his condition by a good dose of "Live While We're Young"?'

'I think I've outstayed my welcome already,' she replied. 'And I need to get home and start thinking about Chickens For Charity. You've been such a help, Daz. Thank you so much. I'll be in touch.'

'Any time, matey. I'll get practising my chicken-in-a-basket, shall I?'

'Let me get my hands on some chicken first, hey?'

'Michelle, I'll do you a chicken-in-a-basket any time, you know that, don't you?'

'I do, Daz, I do.'

Chapter Ten

Michelle spent three whole hours crafting a carefully worded 'suggestion' to go in the factory's suggestion box that stood on a table underneath a large poster listing the 'Employee Values'. The 'Employee Failures', as they had rapidly become known, had come about during a hasty brainstorming session prior to a visit from a high-end food retailer. The bosses had been keen to display what a happy, caring, sharing team everyone was, because happy staff would mean happy chickens, and happy chickens would mean they could charge more. On the day of the factory visit all staff had been ordered to wear clean overalls and converse enthusiastically about the intricacies of giblet removal should they be asked. Hence 'enthusiasm' had been the first key value forced out during the awkward stand-off between bosses and staff, as preparations required opinions to be asked of people who had never been asked for them before.

The opportunity for a few home truths had eventually sparked some 'enthusiasm' from some of the more vocal workers, as they took their chance to tell the bosses who sat in the offices high above the factory floor exactly how they should be doing things. Unable to tell them to pipe down during this period of having to present a 'happy team' face, the boss had eventually found his escape route by offering a suggestion box for all staff to be able to document their 'helpful' ideas for consideration. He had then proudly paraded the suits from retail past the poster of values displayed above the suggestion box before taking them into the refrigeration unit, without offering to take them back to get their coats. This tactic ensured that they would only last in there a few minutes before succumbing to the offer of lunch in a local pub with a roaring fire, allowing the boss to take them off-site, away from the potential hazards that lurked around every corner in the form of a member of staff.

Since that day the suggestion box had remained on its

table, gathering dust and not suggestions, as the workers had realised it held no real opportunity to make any material difference to anything to do with the factory. The only suggestion posted to anyone's knowledge was Little Slaw's request to take the box home and decorate it as a letterbox to give to his grandkids' school to post their Santa letters in. No-one ever got back to him on his suggestion.

'I've posted it in the suggestion box,' Michelle replied when asked by Gina what she had done with her Chickens For Charity idea.

'And you call me stupid!' Gina replied, throwing her blue-gloved hands in the air.

'It's what it's there for,' Michelle protested. 'How else am I going to get to Mr Evans?'

'Just go and see him, why don't you?'

'Are you insane? You go up there and you never come out again. In any case, how do I escape the wrath of RB1 and RB2? They're not just going to let me waltz off to the offices without a good reason.'

'But you have a good reason.'

'What? Excuse me, RB1, but I'm just off to see Mr Evans to discuss how he can help me marry George

Clooney. He'd have me in wash-down for the rest of the day.'

Little Slaw sighed next to them.

'Just him tell the real reason,' he said slowly.

A short pause for translation.

'Genius, Little Slaw,' declared Michelle. 'Hey, RB1, I'm just off to see the boss man so he can help me stop my daughter having sex. Yeah, that would work.'

'No,' he said firmly and a little crossly. He leant over and casually pressed the emergency button, stopping the entire production line. RB2 was at their side in nanoseconds.

'Who stopped the line?' she barked.

'No-one,' replied Little Slaw without a flicker. 'This is third time this week. Out of blue. Kaput,' he continued, his hands raised in amazement. 'Faulty engineer is what we need.'

'Fault Engineer,' hissed Michelle.

'Exactly,' agreed Little Slaw. 'Just what I said. Michelle, go tell upstairs we need Faulty Engineer. She know what she talk about. Off you go, chop-chop. We can't be hanging here all day.'

Michelle stood frozen to the spot, staring open-mouthed at Little Slaw.

'Now,' bellowed RB2. 'We need to reach three thousand units today, and you standing there gawping like a goldfish ain't going to get us there.'

'You go. You go now,' urged Little Slaw, nodding vigorously.

Michelle turned and scurried to the end of the production line before beginning the ascent up the metal open staircase to the gods.

'Way to go, Michelle!' screamed Gina from the factory floor as she disappeared into the upper echelons.

'Hey, Michelle,' said Marianne, Mr Evans's PA. 'What can I do for you?' Marianne was as wide as she was tall, and possibly hired to create a physical barrier between management and staff.

'Well,' Michelle began, 'is Mr Evans free at all?'

'As you can hear, he is currently having a screaming match with a haulage company, but I'm sure he will be exhausting himself any minute.'

Michelle looked through the open doorway to see Mr Evans sitting behind a desk and gesticulating wildly as he talked on the phone.

'What shall I say you want him for once he's come out and screamed at me to release any residual anger?'

Just at that moment Mr Evans slammed the phone down and strode out into Marianne's office.

'If that fat fucker sends me an invoice again for unauthorised fucking transportation, I will not be responsible for my actions. Stupid fucker.'

He swooped around and stalked back into his office, slamming the door behind him without even acknowledging Michelle's presence.

'As I was saying,' Marianne said to a shocked Michelle. 'What shall I tell him you would like to see him about?'

'I'll come back at a better time,' said Michelle quickly.

'Believe me, there is no better time,' said Marianne.

'Erm . . . okay, well, I want to ask him if he would like to be involved in raising some money for charity.'

Marianne said nothing, just raised her eyebrows in a fashion that clearly indicated Michelle would have to do better than that.

'I, I . . . mean the factory,' she stuttered. 'I mean, I need chicken. I really need some chicken for some terrible atrocities that are happening in the world.'

'Chicken going to solve the world's problems, is it?' asked Marianne, her gaze getting more resigned by the second.

'Yes, no . . . I mean, chicken is great, very good for

you, of course, who doesn't love chicken, but you see, chicken could do so much more if it tried, if you see what I mean.'

'No, Michelle, I have absolutely no idea what you are talking about. Why don't you start again and just tell me what you *really* mean?'

Michelle felt herself deflate. It had all been so clear when she'd written it down on paper and shoved it in the black hole of the suggestion box. Now she was up here on the spot she had lost all power of coherent thought.

'Come on, spit it out,' urged Marianne.

'Okay.' Michelle swallowed. 'You see, it's for George Clooney's charity. You like George Clooney, don't you?'

Marianne raised her hand and smoothed down her long, dyed blonde hair.

'I like George Clooney very much, actually,' she said, her voice having dropped an octave.

'Good. That's great,' said Michelle. 'So, he has this charity that does amazing things, and I thought we could raise money for it then we could invite him to come and collect the cheque. But I can only do that if I manage to persuade Mr Evans to give me lots of chicken . . . for free.'

She gulped.

Marianne sat very still, deep in thought. Michelle tried not to stare at the flesh bulging from her bra, peeking out from under her short sleeves.

'Would you invite George Clooney to come here, to this factory?' Marianne fired out suddenly.

'I could . . . of course, yes . . . if you think that would be a good idea.'

'And if he came, hypothetically let's say, you would of course not forget to introduce him to me, the woman who made it all possible?'

'Of course I would, Marianne.'

Marianne contemplated Michelle for a moment more, then she reached for her Post-it notes, selected a fuchsia-pink one and began to scribble some words on it. When she'd finished she heaved her ample frame out of her chair.

'You owe me, George Clooney,' she said before swinging around to enter Mr Evans's office.

'Michelle Hidderley wants a quick word, Mr Evans. She says it's important.'

Michelle watched as Marianne placed the Post-it note in his hand and swooped back out of the room.

'You're on,' she said, flicking her thumb to indicate that Michelle should enter the boss's lair.

Mr Evans was still scrutinising the Post-it note as Michelle entered his office. In stark contrast to the rest of the factory, it was grandly adorned with heavy, dark furniture, central to which was an enormous desk in front of the window looking out onto the rolling hills at the back of the factory. You could almost forget that there was a mass of dead meat right below your feet.

Michelle didn't know whether to wait until she was spoken to or get stuck into what would no doubt be a torturous exchange. Mr Evans cut across her thoughts as she desperately tried to recall her carefully worded proposal.

'So, Marianne,' he said, still reading.

'Michelle,' she corrected. Bollocks, she thought. Strike one. What did she do that for? If he wanted to call her Marianne, who was she to argue?

'Michelle,' he said putting the Post-it note down and looking at her for the first time. 'It says here that you have an idea that will help ease the planning permission through the council for the factory extension.'

What the hell, screamed through Michelle's head. What was he talking about? Was this Marianne's idea of a joke? Was she so outraged at Michelle's ridiculous idea that she thought she'd send her into the boss to get hung, drawn and quartered instead, for wasting his time? She looked round quickly through the open door at Marianne, who was smiling and nodding frantically.

'So,' bellowed Mr Evans. 'Your dad's a councillor, is he? Is that it? You know how I can get on his good side, do you? Oh, I get it. You know exactly how I can get on his good side. He's sent you in, hasn't he, for a bit of a backhander. Give us some dosh and I'll see you right at the hearing. That's it, isn't it?'

'No,' exclaimed Michelle. 'My dad's a postman.'

'Right. Mistress, then. You sleeping with one of them corrupt bastards? If you seriously think I'm going to give you money so I can blackmail a councillor you must be off your rocker.'

Michelle sat speechless.

'You got pictures?' continued Mr Evans. 'Evidence? If you've got that I'll consider it, or else I could have any Tom, Dick or Harry coming up here and telling me they're shagging a councillor.'

'I'm not shagging a councillor!' Michelle protested.

'Right,' said Mr Evans, looking confused. 'Then how the hell do you think you can help me get on the council's good side, then? They hate me. God only knows what I've done to upset them.'

Michelle looked round at Marianne in desperation. What on earth was she playing at? Marianne was now holding up a piece of paper which had one word written on it: CHARITY!

Michelle was still confused, but Marianne was one step ahead. She pulled up another sheet on which was written COUNCILLORS LOVE CHARITY EVENTS, except she hadn't written LOVE, she'd drawn a heart in pink highlighter pen.

Michelle's brain finally started to kick in. She raced to catch up with Marianne's thinking and suddenly clicked where she was going with it – but how would she put it into words?

She turned back to Mr Evans and launched into her pitch.

'Councillors love charity events,' she said with a huge grin and some random jazz hands.

'Don't I bloody know it? Always asking us for bloody donations for this and that, just to make them look good poncing around in a suit and chain, handing a cheque to some mutant. Never does us any bloody good, does it?'

'Exactly!' exclaimed Michelle, her mind running fast to work out exactly what 'Exactly!' meant. 'It's because it's not linked to the factory or chickens or anything,' she blurted. 'No-one knows or cares that we have donated money, least of all the council. So we have to do our own event and make it the biggest and best fundraiser the town has ever seen, so much so that you'll have every councillor there is knocking on your door to be associated with it, and . . . and . . .' She drew breath, struggling to find an and, '. . . and you'll look great and the factory will look great and, like, a great addition to the town and really community minded and all that, so why would the council want to stop it growing and expanding?'

Mr Evans sat back, a little startled by Michelle's sudden rush of confidence and passion.

'You are almost starting to make sense,' he said, his brow furrowed. 'Continue.'

Michelle heard an audible 'yes!' from behind her and the swoosh of a flabby fist pump.

'Well, you see, I had this idea that we could raise money for a good cause and have this big event inviting everyone. We could have it in that big space in the warehouse and have a kind of a *MasterChef* type thing where we invite teams from the town to cook their best chicken dish and serve it up, and then other people can buy tickets and come and test loads of chicken, and they get to vote for the best one, and we have prizes and a beer tent and dancing, and we call it . . . *Chickens For Charity*.'

Mr Evans stared at Michelle. She didn't dare breathe. She looked nervously over her shoulder at Marianne, who was now on the edge of her chair, not bothering to pretend that she wasn't totally listening in on the conversation. She shrugged as if to say she wasn't sure whether Michelle had sold it to him. The silence was endless. Michelle had time to take in the fact that Mr Evans had two grey hairs peeping out of his nose which quivered as he breathed, and that he wore a wedding ring as well as a signet ring. She was just starting to wonder what kind of saint he was married to when he took a deep breath and prepared to speak.

'Chickens For Charity,' he murmured.

Agonisingly, he fell silent again.

'I like it.'

Michelle squeaked. Marianne shrieked a louder 'yes!'.

'Chickens and Charity. That's good, really good,' Mr Evans went on. 'If we get those councillors associating chickens with charity, then how could they possibly turn down our extension allowing us to do even more with Chickens For Charity?'

'Absolutely,' Michelle nodded violently.

'And it's got quite a ring to it. Chickens For Charity,' he repeated, waving his hand in the air as if seeing it in lights on some billboard. 'Tell you what,' he said, getting up and starting to pace the room. 'Head office might go for this. Them poncey southern factories get all the kudos for coming up with ideas. About time I showed them all a good idea when I get one. Chickens For Charity,' he said again, nodding in satisfaction.

'And it's a great charity I've found that we can donate to,' Michelle interjected. 'We can do so much good.'

Mr Evans spun round, his brow furrowed again. Michelle sucked air rapidly through her mouth. She'd screwed it up at the last turn. He was going to want to pick the charity. She knew it, and then all of this would be for nothing, apart, perhaps, from some poxy charity with no-one interesting or even slightly famous running it anyway.

'Just answer me this question,' bellowed Mr Evans.

'Yes,' breathed Michelle. She could hear Marianne flapping behind her in trauma over the possible loss of a very unlikely meeting with George Clooney.

'Will we be saving lives?'

'Helping to, yes, definitely,' Michelle nodded. 'Of course you'll be saving lives, Mr Evans.'

'Excellent!' he roared. 'I just need to be able to tell the council that this chicken factory saves lives. Give the money to who the hell you like. I just want to be able to say THIS CHICKEN FACTORY SAVES LIVES.' He thumped his fist hard on the table. 'I can see the headline now on the front of the *Echo*. CHICKEN FACTORY SAVES LIVES. Can you get me that headline?' he said, bearing down on Michelle.

'I'm sure if we use the charity Michelle is suggesting then I can persuade Richard at the *Echo* to run the story,' said Marianne, bustling in and blocking half the sunlight from the room. 'Now, you have a meeting with HR that started ten minutes ago and I just need to warn you what Patrick's put on the agenda. Michelle can come back next week with a list of what she needs for Chickens For Charity, then I'll get on to the *Echo* and start warming them up.' She was frantically waving her arm behind her back to instruct Michelle to vacate the office as a matter of urgency.

'Yes. Right. Good,' said Mr Evans, already studying the agenda that Marianne had thrust under his nose.

'You may go now,' he said, not looking up. 'Same time next week. Don't fuck this up for me.'

'Thank you, thank you,' said Michelle, bowing out of the room. 'Next week, good, brilliant.'

She was just sprinting her escape across Marianne's office when she heard a bellow.

'What on earth has that fuckwit Patrick put that on the agenda for? Get him in here. I refuse to go to a meeting with "Increasing Holiday Entitlement" on the agenda. Dickbrain.'

Chapter Eleven

Michelle eyed her front door as though it was the tip of Everest. So near and yet so far. Her arms felt like lead weights, clamped down by her sides, weighed down by provisions. Her legs were weak and feeble from a day of trudging miles and miles surrounded by uncompromising, often treacherous territory, and her lips, nose and cheeks could still feel the icy chill from hours of being exposed to below average temperatures. Still, her day at the factory was now over, and if she could just get through the door with what felt like half of Waitrose plus ten pounds of chicken breasts, then relief was somewhere in sight. A cup of tea and a cupcake, guiltily bought from the cake display, which had been screaming at her silently to be given a home in the depths of her belly.

She sighed with relief as she parked her purchases on the doorstep and put the key in the back door. She was secretly hoping to creep in without disturbing Josie, who should be upstairs doing her homework. She was desperate to snaffle the cupcake without any disapproving sneers from her daughter, who was unforgiving of Michelle's reluctance to give up sugar in favour of a figure like Rihanna. Michelle had tried to drill into her that in fact Beyoncé was a much better role model with her awesome curves and excellent booty, but Josie was having none of it. Rihanna dictated the eating rules in their house.

'Hiya, love,' was the first indication Michelle had that her evening was not going to go to plan.

She looked around the kitchen and saw, not only her mum and dad, sitting at the table, cups of tea in hand and open biscuit tin plundered, but also Josie and Sean. Finally, to put a total halt to any hint of relaxation for her that evening, there sat Rob, sipping tea out of a mug with *Best Mum In the World* written on it, which Josie had bought her before she turned into the teenager from hell.

'Josie happened to mention that you were doing that special chicken dish thing tonight – you know, the one your dad really likes, even though he hates chilli. We thought we'd come and help you out with it. You don't want to be just cooking for the two of you, do you? No fun in that. I hate cooking for just me and your dad. It seems so pointless.' Kathleen smiled at her husband.

Michelle dropped her heavy bags to the floor in silence, unsure what to do about the crowd of very unwelcome gatecrashers squatting at her kitchen table.

'Oh, and I rang and invited Rob,' Kathleen continued. 'Thought he needed a bit of family round him. You know, since his divorce and everything. It was such a blessing to see him at the graveyard, and it made me realise that we'd been neglecting him all these years. Rob is as good as family to us and it's about time we treated him that way.' She patted Rob's hand and grinned, smearing special occasion lipstick on her teeth.

Michelle wanted to scream at the mention of Rob and family in the same sentence, and at her mother's hypocrisy. She could remember when Rob had announced he was taking a job in America straight after Jane had died. Kathleen had ranted and raved at his desertion in their hour of need and repeatedly declared that he would never step over their threshold again. And now she had invited him into Michelle's kitchen, when he was the very last person she wanted to see make himself at home.

'Sean's here because he's going late-night fishing and he needs a hot meal inside him before he goes, don't you, Sean?' said Josie.

Sean grunted his agreement whilst smirking at Michelle, reminding her that last time she'd seen him had been in cyberspace, half naked, accusing her of masturbating whilst watching George Clooney porn.

'But I have company coming,' she protested. Of all the nights for her family plus Sean and Rob to decide to descend, this was not a good one.

Kathleen twitched. 'What, who? A man?'

'Yes, but it's only . . .'

'Oh love,' said Ray, getting up and putting his arms around her. 'That's just great. A man here for you. Now we can all meet him.'

'You didn't tell me you had a boyfriend,' Josie leapt in. 'When did that happen? Not someone you met down The Bull, is it? They're all geriatrics in there. He'd better not be older than Granddad or else I'll be beyond mortified. Me and Sean will have to leave. Just disgusting, Mum.'

'No, hang on a minute. It's just Daz coming and we've got something really important to talk about.'

'You're seeing Daz?' Josie exclaimed. 'Dozy DJ Daz is your boyfriend? Are you out of your mind?'

'I always knew she'd end up with him, you know,' Kathleen muttered. 'They were such a lovely couple when they went out together at school.'

'You have got to be kidding me!' Josie stared at her mum as if she'd dated the devil. 'Daz was your boyfriend?'

'When your mother broke up with Daz he was round our house every night for a week, crying and begging for her to take him back,' Kathleen told Josie. 'I told her he was a lovely lad and she could do a lot worse, but she wouldn't have it. Maybe she's come to her senses now.'

'Over my dead body,' said Josie and Michelle simultaneously.

Just at that moment a playful knock came on the back door, which if Michelle wasn't mistaken was the tapping out of the chorus to 'What Makes You Beautiful' by One Direction, and in strode Daz.

'Hiya,' he said as he closed the door behind him, not having clocked the audience awaiting him.

'Fucking spiders,' he said with a jump when he did turn round. 'Wasn't expecting the full family Hidderley contingent.' His gaze landed finally on Rob and he barely disguised a sneer.

'Wine and flowers, eh?' Kathleen nodded, eyeing up the offerings Daz was clutching in his hands.

Michelle swooped in to scoop Daz's gifts away and into hiding.

'You didn't need to bring flowers to a meeting,' she said loudly. She heard her mother muttering behind her about the cost of tulips when they weren't in season.

'They were selling them off at the end of the day on the market,' said Daz. 'Didn't want to see them go to waste.' Kathleen continued her barely suppressed commentary on the cost of tulips.

Then a heavy silence descended on the kitchen, apart from Michelle banging produce around and slamming cupboard doors. Everyone stared at each other awkwardly, until Rob broke the silence by getting up and walking over to the kitchen counter, where ingredients lay strewn in all directions.

'So what can I do to help?' he asked, unbuttoning the cuffs of his checked shirt and starting to roll his sleeves up. 'I'm pretty nifty with a veg peeler.'

'I bet you are,' said Daz, nodding, and failing to hide his disdain at Rob's revelation. 'Well, you ain't seen my culinary skills yet, mister. Mrs Howson said my swiss roll was café quality during our third-year domestic science exam. I'm thinking of applying for the *Bake Off*.'

'Get away, you two.' Kathleen bustled in, grabbing a bag of potatoes and a knife out of the knife block. 'You mix men, knives and vegetables and there'll be nothing left for our tea. I've seen it time and time again with Ray. He starts off with a bag of spuds and ends up with what looks like a muckheap.'

'Sean's brilliant with knives, aren't you, Sean?' said Josie. 'You should see the picture of me he's carved into the desk at the back of the chemistry lab. Do one on a potato to show everyone, Sean. Have you got your knife with you?'

'Fuck off, I'm not doing a potato,' Sean grunted.

'Aw, go on, do it on a potato, Sean,' pleaded Daz. 'Or do me . . . go on, pleeease. I've always wanted to see my face on a potato.' He sat down on the chair vacated by Rob to present his face to Sean.

'Do our Ray, Sean,' Kathleen shouted over her shoulder as she began to attack a potato. 'I bet Ray's face would come out right good on a potato.'

'*COUNTDOWN* IS ABOUT TO START!' yelled Michelle at the top of her voice. Desperate for some headspace to sort out how she was going to deal with the unexpected evening ahead, she'd decided to deploy the TV option, which had always been useful when Josie was small and she'd wanted to 'help' in the kitchen.

'It's never that time already, is it?' said Kathleen, frantically rubbing her hands on a towel. 'Come on, Ray. We need to see if Winston finally gets knocked out today.' She grabbed Ray's arm as she hustled out of the kitchen and within moments the familiar buzz of afternoon telly could be heard.

'Me and Sean are going upstairs. Shout when tea's ready,' Josie stated, shoving a grateful Sean out of the room.

'Why don't you go and put your feet up, Rob, mate?' said Daz, slapping Rob on the shoulder. 'Me and Michelle have got it licked in here, I reckon, haven't we, 'Chelle?'

'Look, both of you go and keep Mum and Dad company next door and I'll cook tea. It'll be easier on my own. Honestly.'

'Course, Michelle, whatever you say. Maybe we could

slide to the pub afterwards, then, and have that chat like we said we would, seeing as it's a bit crowded here,' replied Daz, staring at Rob.

'Do you know what, love?' said Kathleen later as she polished off a plate of Michelle's special Salted Chilli Chicken. 'That was lovely but not as good as the time you did it last New Year's Eve. I think you slightly overdid the chilli tonight, and you know your father doesn't like too much chilli.'

There had been mostly silence in the kitchen as the seven of them crowded round the kitchen table that was meant for four, an array of odd chairs called in from all four corners of the house to accommodate the surprise guests. There was the odd ooh and aah when everyone had first tucked in to the recipe, which Michelle had been honing since her days at culinary school until it was exactly to her liking and was pretty much the best way to eat chicken, even for someone who worked with the damn things day after day.

'That, Michelle,' said Daz, smacking his lips, 'would defo give my chicken-in-a-basket a run for its money. I am going to have to up my game, I can see.'

'That was gorgeous,' said Rob, sliding his knife and

fork together and pushing his empty plate forward. 'You've not lost your touch, have you, Michelle?'

'Nice to have a home-cooked square meal in you, is it, Rob?' clucked Kathleen. 'You know our Michelle loves cooking; I'm sure you'd be welcome round here for food any time, wouldn't he, love?'

Michelle stared at her mother, open-mouthed. The audacity of inviting the oblivious father of her oblivious daughter to eat with them whenever he liked was just too much.

'You trying to fix Mum up with Rob, Granny?' asked Josie.

Michelle dropped her knife and fork down on her plate and looked up to see the colour of her cheeks reflected in Rob's face.

Kathleen laughed heartily, avoiding the need for either party to speak.

'Of course not, Josie,' said Kathleen, still laughing. 'Michelle isn't Rob's type.'

'No, she's not,' Daz agreed rapidly.

'No, Rob likes the quiet, clever type like Jane was, don't you, love?' said Kathleen.

Rob hesitated, then mumbled, 'To be honest, I'm not interested in another relationship just yet. Too soon.'

'I'm not surprised,' said Josie. 'A death and a divorce must've put you off forming any lasting relationship ever again.'

'Something like that,' Rob agreed, before grabbing Daz's wine from the middle of the table and emptying the remaining contents into his glass.

'We'll drink the wine you bought next, shall we?' said Daz, staring pointedly at the empty bottle.

'Sorry,' said Rob. 'I've got beer in my boot from the brewery. I'll go and get some.'

'Beer,' said Ray, rubbing his hands together. 'I knew there was a reason why I missed that boy.'

'Just because he gets free beer doesn't mean you have to drink it,' chided Kathleen.

'But it tastes so much better when it's free,' said Ray. 'Even you agreed with me on that one.'

'That's true,' Kathleen admitted. 'I wonder if he'd be able to get us a few crates for your sixty-fifth birthday party?'

Rob stumbled back in at that point, heaving not one but two crates of beer onto the table.

'Help yourselves,' he declared. 'This lot cost me next to nothing from the brewery shop.'

Daz, Ray and Sean's eyes were wide with awe. All of

them were rendered pretty powerless in the face of a table full of free beer.

'Why don't we stay here and not go to the pub?' said Daz.

'How many am I allowed on a week night?' asked Ray.

'Awesome,' said Sean, reaching up and grabbing a bottle.

'Sean, you are underage for alcohol, and aren't you supposed to be going fishing?' demanded Michelle, snatching the bottle from him. 'Dad, you are nearly sixty-five, you can drink what the hell you like on a week night, and Daz, we're supposed to be having a meeting about you-know-what, aren't we? Not getting pissed on free beer.'

'But it's *free beer*,' said Daz. 'Free beer trumps every card known to man . . . apart from . . . free sex, maybe?' He thought for a moment. 'Not that I ever pay for sex, of course,' he said quickly. 'I was just being hypothetical, you know. Anyway, Michelle, we can have our meeting here – with the free beer.'

This was not going how Michelle had planned. She'd been so looking forward to having another practice at her speciality chicken dish, as well as the opportunity to discuss the details of the Chickens For Charity event with Daz. It was only when she talked to him that it seemed like a remotely feasible plan.

'So what you two meeting about, anyway?' asked Josie. 'Are you planning me a surprise birthday party, Mum? If you're asking Daz to DJ then he *must* agree to my playlist.'

'You know that's not the way I work, Josie, and you know it's for your own good and cultural education,' said Daz. 'But as it happens, me and your mother have much bigger fish to fry than your birthday.'

Michelle prayed silently that Daz wouldn't let the cat out of the bag just yet.

'Your mother and I are planning the charity event to end all charity events. Chickens For Charity will soon be what the whole of Malton is freaking out about, you mark my words.'

'Chickens For Charity?' said Josie. 'Are you kidding me?'

'Oh no, young lady,' Daz continued. 'Your mother may well be a genius. Not only has she come up with a stunningly original idea – with my help, of course – but she's also got the buy-in from the chicken factory.'

'So what exactly will these chickens be doing for

charity?' asked Rob, grabbing a beer and taking a swig. Ray hastily helped himself too now that Rob had started and Kathleen appeared to be distracted by Daz.

'Tell 'em, 'Chelle,' said Daz, leaning forward and helping himself to the stash.

'Well,' she started. She tried not to take a deep breath, as she was sick of doing so every time she attempted to explain her plan. 'For a good cause I have asked the factory if they'll give us a load of chicken and then we're going to get a few teams together to cook the best chicken dish they possibly can and bring it to our event. Then people can buy tickets and come and try the food and then vote for their favourite. And we'll have prizes and a beer tent.'

'And I'll be compering, of course, and providing entertainment,' Daz added.

'So it'll all be for a good cause,' Michelle continued, 'and we can try and get the whole community involved and stuff . . .'

'And I'm going to do my speciality of chicken-in-a-basket,' Daz interrupted again. 'If you think Michelle's dish is good you ain't seen nothing yet.'

'So that's kind of it, really.' Michelle grabbed a beer and downed a massive slug.

The room was silent until Kathleen leant forward to quiz Michelle.

'Are you thinking of doing your Salted Chilli Chicken?'

'Well, yes. Unless I create something else before then.'

'Mmmmmm. You see, if I were you, if I wanted to win, I wouldn't enter a dish with chilli in it. Now I have exotic tastes, but there are other people like your dad who just don't really like chilli.'

'But I like Michelle's Chilli Chicken,' Ray protested.

'I know, love, but that's different,' said Kathleen. 'Take my advice. You're never going to win with a dish with chilli in it. You ask anyone in the Women's Institute, we know about these things.'

'So, now you've told us what not to cook, what would you cook, Mrs H?' asked Daz.

'Well, I don't know offhand,' said Kathleen. 'I'd have to think about it very carefully. Ask Pauline down the WI, she's a dab hand with savoury. Sweets are more my thing.'

'Women's Institute!' Daz exclaimed, slapping his forehead. He turned to face Michelle. 'Women's Institute, that's the answer, don't you see? They're perfect!'

'Not following,' said Michelle.

'Cooking Challenge! Where else do we go to find a

group of over-competitive women who are obsessed with food?'

'That is not all we do in the WI, you know,' Kathleen said tartly.

'The WI are exactly the type of people we should get involved,' Daz exulted. 'You throw 'em some free chicken and the whiff of a rosette and they'll come back with a banquet. Now come on, think of some other groups like that. Competitive people obsessed with food?'

'Let me say again . . .' Kathleen began.

'Shut up, Mum, he's onto something,' said Michelle. 'Right, let me think. People obsessed with food.'

'Dieters,' grinned Ray, polishing off his first bottle and grabbing the next.

'Don't be an idiot,' said Kathleen, slapping him in the gut.

'Brilliant, Dad!' Michelle shrieked. 'A Slimming Club! There's a group meets in the Town Hall every week. Gina still goes post her wedding diet to keep herself skinny for that husband of hers. They could do a low fat option. More ideas, come on, everyone!'

'What about the rugby club?' offered Rob. 'I remember, when I used to play, we'd take it in turns to do a barbecue after a match, and if you so much as burnt a sausage you'd get flung in the showers, fully clothed.'

'And how exactly do you think you're going to get the great unwashed of Malton Rugby Club to give up their free time to cook chicken, eh, clever clogs?' said Daz, sneering at Rob. 'I've done many a rugby club do, and it strikes me they don't do anything out of the goodness of their hearts.'

Rob stared steadily back at Daz, deep in thought, swilling his beer round his mouth.

'You don't know, do you?' Daz challenged. 'A totally useless idea.'

Rob continued to swill beer around his mouth as he placed his bottle on the table.

'I think I know what will make them cook chicken for charity,' he said eventually.

'Oh yeah. Go on, then, hit us with this amazing idea,' said Daz.

'Two words. Free. Beer.'

'Brilliant!' cried Ray. 'The lad's cracked it!'

'There is no way you can get enough free beer to satisfy an entire rugby club,' said Daz, helping himself to his third free beer, courtesy of Rob.

'That would be a lot of beer,' said Michelle, keen to halt the stand-off.

Rob turned to look at her and put his hand on her shoulder. Daz bristled beside her and she prayed Rob would take his hand away as quickly as possible.

'Michelle,' he said gently. She wished he wouldn't say her name like that. The familiarity of it made her want to curl up and sob. 'I'll tell them it's for charity. My wife left me for my boss, who I know for a fact has an employee discount allocation that will more than satisfy the entire rugby team. I reckon he owes me, don't you?'

He took his hand away from Michelle's shoulder and sighed deeply.

'Quite right, son,' said Ray, patting him on the shoulder.

'Oh, you poor thing!' cried Kathleen, leaping up and flinging her arms around him. 'You poor, poor thing!'

'For crying out loud,' muttered Daz under his breath.

Kathleen rounded on him. 'Have some respect! This lad has not only lost the love of his life when poor Jane died, but now he's lost his wife. If you'd ever lost a member of your family you'd know what it feels like. It's like having a limb chopped off, it really is.'

'Come on, love,' said Ray. 'Calm down.'

'My dad buggered off when I was five,' said Daz bleakly. 'I know what it feels like to lose a member of my family. Just 'cause he didn't die doesn't mean I'm not cut up about it every day. You don't see me throwing myself around demanding sympathy, do you? Unlike some.' He folded his arms firmly to his chest and stuck his bottom lip out in a sulk.

'Least you had a dad,' Josie muttered.

'What was that, love?' asked Kathleen, now sniffing into a pink tissue.

'I said at least Daz had a dad,' Josie repeated, staring straight at Michelle. 'At least he knew his dad.'

Michelle froze.

The room fell silent. Everyone looked awkward.

Sean grunted.

Rob began to move. Michelle thought she might throw up. He placed his hand on Josie's shoulder. It was all Michelle could do to stop herself getting up and fleeing the room.

'If it helps, Josie,' Rob said, 'I think no dad's better than a rubbish one. My father never took any interest in me; he was obsessed with building his business. He thinks I'm an absolute failure because I don't want to take it over, and instead I went to work for those "damn Americans". He can hardly bear to speak to me.'

'Really?' she said.

'Really,' Rob nodded sadly. 'I reckon as long as you have people around you that care about you then that's all the family you need, believe me. And it strikes me, looking round this table, that you *do* have all the family you need.'

Michelle was aware her breathing had speeded up, and either she needed to get out right now or she needed to get Rob out, right now.

'Oh, Rob,' sighed Kathleen. 'What a wonderful thing to say.'

'Well said, lad.' Ray slapped Rob on the back and sneaked out his next beer from the crate whilst Kathleen was occupied being tearful.

Josie's eyes were burning into Michelle's, and Michelle wished with all her heart she could come out with the right thing to say to end this nightmare conversation. She watched as Rob squeezed Josie's shoulder.

'You okay?' he asked her.

Josie turned her attention away from Michelle. 'I was just thinking that Auntie Jane clearly had much better taste in men than Mum ever did.'

Chapter Twelve

Was it the seventh or eighth time she'd heard booming baritones from the bar totally destroying 'Wonderwall' by Oasis? They were virtually lifting the roof and Michelle wondered what on earth was kicking off. She hoisted an enormous bag of frozen chips back into the industrial freezer at the back of the kitchen. It had been a busy night for pub meals. She reached for the mop standing in the corner and began sloshing it around the floor.

'You ever going to wipe that smirk off your face?' the

chef enquired as Michelle brushed the edge of his shoes with the grey strands of the mop.

'No.' She looked up at him and allowed the smirk to develop into a massive, full-on grin.

'For the life of me I cannot understand why you would want to leave all this,' he said, sweeping his hand around the tiny, greasy, fume-filled kitchen at the back of the pub. 'Why you want to leave me in the lurch to go and work for some la-di-da restaurant in London is totally beyond me.'

'Not just any old la-di-da restaurant,' Michelle corrected him. 'Only the la-di-da bloody restaurant in the Savoy.'

'I bet you get down there and find they can't teach you how to master a temperamental chip fryer the way I have.' He fished a sausage out from the vat of oil that must have been forgotten at some point in the evening. Michelle shuddered and quietly prayed that she would never again work in the sort of kitchen that cooked frozen sausages in a deep fat fryer.

'I'll just have to content myself with passing my wisdom on to your replacement,' sighed the chef.

'Well, there's no rush,' said Michelle quickly. 'I'll be here until the end of July, until my course finishes. I'll need all the shifts I can get to save up for living in London.' She felt a tremor rush through her body. Every time she talked about living in London it felt so unreal, like it was happening to someone else. She had to keep saying it to make sure it was true.

'That suits me as long as you're not shoving how they do it at the Savoy down my throat every shift.'

'I'll try,' said Michelle, not very convincingly.

'Just you remember, they're lucky to have you. You're good, Michelle. This place is going to really miss you.'

Michelle felt her jaw drop. It was the closest the chef had ever got to paying her a compliment.

'Right,' he said, whipping his apron off. 'I'll buy you a drink.'

'What for?' she asked.

'To celebrate,' he said, smirking. 'Me getting rid of you at last.'

The scene that greeted them as they entered the bar was not for the faint-hearted. The source of the drunken revelry was revealed in more ways than one as they discovered the entire rugby team celebrating a win in the only way they knew how: mass drinking, singing and nakedness. Five of the team were currently standing on chairs at the far end of the bar, where, unfortunately, the haze of cigarette smoke could not hide the fact that they had all just dropped their trousers, as required by the lyrics of the song they were singing.

'Good God!' exclaimed Michelle, covering her eyes. It was not a sight to experience sober.

'Think we need to catch up,' said her boss, nodding at the landlord behind the bar, who magically produced two pints of lager out of nowhere.

'Get that down you,' said the chef. 'Proud of you. Really.'

Michelle grinned. As she gulped down the cool, gold liquid she wondered what she would be drinking on a night out in London with her colleagues after a hard shift in the kitchen. Definitely not lager, she thought.

Suddenly someone boomed into her ear and she was aware of a sweaty arm around her shoulder.

'Brilliant news,' she heard.

She turned to discover who the voice belonged to and found Rob, fortunately fully clothed, standing beside her, grinning his head off.

'Your mum rang this afternoon to tell us,' he said. 'It's amazing. I bet you can't believe it.'

'Actually, I can't,' she said excitedly. 'I really daren't in case it turns out they made a mistake. It wasn't me they wanted, it was someone else.'

'Oh, don't be silly,' said Rob. 'Of course it's you they want. You're a brilliant cook.'

Michelle glowed. She liked Rob. Ever since Jane had started seeing him during sixth form at school and he'd talked to her like an equal and not just some stupid kid sister, she'd known that Jane had found a keeper. They also shared a love of *The Fast Show* and endlessly quoted it at each other, much to Jane's annoyance, who thought it was a bit stupid.

'I'm going to work at the Savoy!' she said, clutching his arm and starting to bounce up and down in excitement. 'In London!'

'I know!' cried Rob. 'Let me buy you a drink.'

She looked round for the chef but he had deserted her for his cronies, who stagnated at the end of the bar every night. She downed the last of her pint and put the empty glass down on the bar.

'Let's do it,' she said, suddenly in the mood to party.

'Give me one good reason why you would want to leave Malton?' Jamie, a rugby pal of Rob's, slurred at Michelle. Having convinced the reluctant landlord to sell them an entire bottle of wine, something he clearly hadn't done before, they'd settled themselves at the bar. Jamie had wandered over to find out what the fit bird was talking to Rob about.

'Well,' Michelle began, 'I've lived here all my life. I just want to get out, see different stuff, do different stuff, have a *life*.'

'But everyone you know is here.' Jamie looked perplexed, swaying slightly and grabbing hold of the back of Rob's stool to steady himself.

'Exactly. I know everyone and everyone knows me,' sighed Michelle. 'In London I can be *me* rather than someone's daughter or sister or cousin or whatever.'

'You'll be back,' declared Jamie. 'Mark my words. Look at Rob here. He came back. Went away to uni then you couldn't wait to get back, could you, fella?'

'Well, it's where Jane wants to be,' Rob shrugged. 'And that's fine by me.'

'Come on,' said Jamie, hoisting his huge, muscly arm around Rob's shoulders and squeezing tight. 'You came back for us, didn't you, mate? Don't be shy. You just couldn't live without us.'

'Yeah, that's right,' Rob nodded. ' I just couldn't live without you, Jamie. You are the love of my life.'

'Come back a right southern wuss, though,' said Jamie, swaying precariously towards Michelle. 'Just can't take his alcohol any more. You watch this.' He winked at Michelle. She giggled. Jamie had been a few years above her in school and had never so much as said a word to her. She wasn't sure if she could take any more good fortune. New job, new city and a gorgeous rugby player actually taking notice of her. She couldn't wait to tell Gina.

Jamie beckoned the landlord over.

'Three tequila shots, please,' he requested. 'Make that two rounds.'

'Not for me,' said Rob. 'Jane's studying for her accountancy exams. I can't roll in drunk and disturb her.'

'Come on, you big wuss,' cried Jamie. 'We're celebrating Michelle's new life in London. Get 'em down yer. Can't let her leave without a proper Malton send-off, can we?'

'To London,' said Michelle, grabbing a shot and raising it in the air. The thrill ran through her again. She was going to live in London. It was real. She chinked glasses with Jamie as he flung his arm around her. Life didn't really get any better than this.

*

'You going to let me walk you home, then?' Jamie asked Michelle, several shots later. He had his arm draped heavily over her shoulder and he was virtually drooling. 'Then when you're a famous chef down London I can tell all me mates that I once escorted you home.'

Michelle giggled. She wasn't drunk, she was sure. She was too high on life to be bothered with anything more artificial. But she could tell a bloke that couldn't really be trusted to walk you home, and as much as she fancied the idea of pulling Jamie, she actually would prefer him at least to be able to remember her name for future reference.

'Come on,' he said, gallantly offering his arm. 'It would be a genuine honour.'

'You're in no fit state to take anyone home,' Rob stepped in. 'Besides, Jane would never forgive me if I let her sister out of my sight when you're on the prowl.'

'On the prowl!' Jamie protested. 'I don't prowl. How dare she!'

'Come on, Michelle,' said Rob. 'I'll take you home. You got your coat?'

It took her some time to work out that her coat was still down in the kitchen where she'd left it at the beginning of her shift. She ran down the long corridor and grabbed it, then did a quick victory run around the steel work counter, breathing in the familiar smell of the greasy kitchen. As she skipped back to the bar, she was mentally trying to work out exactly how many more shifts she had to endure.

She was still skipping as she and Rob made their way through the park on their way home. Totally hyped up, she was in full throttle mode, sharing all her hopes and dreams with Rob. All the things she was going to see and do in London, how hard she was going to work, how desperate she was to learn, how one day she hoped to perhaps have her own restaurant somewhere. She knew it was a pipe dream, but she could dream, couldn't she?

'So what would it be like?' Rob asked her patiently as he watched her swing way too high on a swing in the playground in the middle of the park. She'd insisted they stop for a play. Swinging always made her happy, and today she couldn't get enough of happy.

'Well,' she said, slamming her feet down on the concrete, 'I can tell you exactly what it would be like.' Her eyes were shining in the pitch black.

'Go on, then,' he laughed. 'See if you can excite my taste buds.'

'It would be a pleasure,' she declared, getting up and standing in front of him. 'Now please take a seat whilst I get you the wine menu.' She indicated the toddler-sized toadstool carved out of wood next to a small wooden table.

'Are you serious?' he asked.

'Oh yes,' she grinned. 'Deadly serious.'

Rob sighed, pulling his coat around him and squatting down. The toadstool felt a little damp. He tucked his coat under his bottom and pulled his woolly hat down over his cold ears. Michelle looked so delighted he didn't dare complain at the uncomfortable ambiance in her makeshift restaurant. Taking a scarf from around her neck, giggling, she laid it over Rob's lap to act as a napkin, then from inside her enormous ski jacket she pulled out a bottle of MD 20/20 fortified wine, displaying the bottle for Rob to inspect.

'An excellent vintage if I do say so myself,' she said.

'Where the hell did that come from?' he asked.

'Chef gave it to me as I left,' Michelle grinned. 'One for the road, he said. Would you like to try the wine, sir?' She unscrewed the top and offered it to him.

He took a sip and found he was grateful for the warm sensation that spread through his body.

'It'll do,' he announced, taking a bigger swig before putting it down and blowing on his chilly hands.

'So, for an appetiser I'd like to offer you crayfish in a light sauce served on brioche.' Michelle laid an imaginary dish in front of Rob.

'Crayfish?'

'Crayfish are the new prawn,' she assured him.

'Looks a bit black,' he said, poking around in the dark. 'Are you sure you've not burnt it?'

'Idiot!' laughed Michelle, knocking him playfully on the head. 'Come on, eat up, or your entrée will be burnt.'

'It's quite the best crayfish I have ever eaten,' he declared after smacking his lips a few times.

'Is it the *only* crayfish you've ever eaten, Rob?'

'Yes.'

'Moving on, then. Here in the Mediterranean the abundant sunshine ripens our fresh ingredients to a taste that you've only ever dreamed of.'

'Don't mention sunshine when we're sat here in the dark and cold.' Rob took another swig of the wine to warm his blood. 'You never said your restaurant was going to be abroad.'

'Well, as I say, it's just a dream.'

'You'd live abroad, then, learn a language?'

'God, yes,' said Michelle. 'Live and work in the sunshine. Who wouldn't?'

'The brewery offered me a job in San Francisco,' he told her, almost absent-mindedly.

'Really!' she exclaimed. 'But Rob, that's amazing!'

'We turned it down.' Rob shrugged. 'Jane needs to finish her accountancy exams.' He reached forward and took another slug of his wine before digging his hands deep in his pockets. 'I'd like a hot main course,' he said, looking up. 'I'm bloody cold.'

Michelle was rooted to the spot.

'But . . . but San Francisco?'

Rob shrugged again.

'Maybe I'll be able to convince Jane when she's qualified, if there are still opportunities out there.'

'You must be gutted,' she said.

'I'll live,' he said dismissively. 'When there's two of you, you've got to do what's best for both of you. *You*'ve only got yourself to worry about.'

Michelle was grateful she didn't have a boyfriend who might get in the way of her grand escape to London. 'If you asked me to move to San Francisco I'd be there like a shot.'

Rob hesitated for a moment, holding her gaze.

'Yeah, well, you're not Jane, are you?' he said finally.

'Thank God,' Michelle gasped. 'Mum's got to have at least one daughter in the family she's proud of.'

'What are you talking about?' said Rob. 'Your mum's very proud of you. You should have heard her on the phone this afternoon about this job you've got.'

'Rubbish! If I told her I was giving up cooking to train to be an accountant like Jane it would be the proudest day of my mum's life.'

Rob stared at her as he drained the last of the wine. 'You've got her all wrong, you know. Mind you, if I told her, or your sister, for that matter, that you'd taken to serving imaginary food in the dark, they might both insist you take up a more sensible profession.'

'I think if I told either of them that you sat on a toad-stool whilst I served you your first ever dish of imaginary crayfish, they'd demand we were both certified.'

'Shall we keep this, albeit fantastic, imaginary meal between the two of us?' he suggested.

'It'd probably be best.' She laughed. 'Can you imagine if I told my mum I'd served crayfish? She'd be horrified. No meat? But he's a growing lad!'

Rob started to laugh. His shoulders shuddered and the bobble on his woolly hat bounced up and down.

Michelle creased up, the ludicrousness of the situation along with the adrenaline racing round her blood surging into such an explosion of happiness that she could barely contain herself.

Mesmerised by Rob's stupid hat bobbing about in the moonlight, she made a grab for it and darted away, pulling it over her head.

'Race you home,' she cried as she sprinted off into the darkness.

'Oi, come back here!' shouted Rob. 'My head's cold.'

She pounded across one of the football pitches, breathless from laughter and her desire to outrun Rob. She could hear him gaining on her and she tried to speed up but she was running out of steam. Suddenly she felt herself drop like a stone to the grass. Rob had successfully halted her progress with a rugby tackle. She rolled over, laughing uncontrollably as he tried to grab his hat. She was fighting back, trying to keep his arm at a distance, then the fight between them dissipated and they were somehow left holding each other, then kissing each other, then feeling each other, then . . .

It must have been only a matter of minutes before he was tugging up his trousers and she was pushing her bra back into position. When clothes were back where they should be they lay together, face up on the cold grass, staring up into the darkness in silence, not touching.

'I have no idea how that just happened,' said Rob eventually.

'Me neither,' breathed Michelle.

'Did it really happen?' he asked.

'I'm not sure *what* exactly happened,' she replied, unable to extract any sense out of the last few minutes. She could feel herself start to shake, either from the cold or from shock.

'Let's pretend it didn't happen,' she said, sitting up quickly. 'It didn't happen,' she repeated, shaking her head fiercely and turning round to look at Rob.

Their eyes met. Rob's were wide with the fearful realisation of what they'd done.

'Okay,' he said slowly. 'As long as that's okay with you?' he asked, his brow furrowing in concern.

'Yes,' she said quickly. 'Of course. It's the only answer. It never happened.'

'It never happened,' he agreed, getting up and holding out a hand to help her up. They walked home in silence.

Chapter Thirteen

'So, we're going to play a little game,' said Gina, passing Michelle a Post-it note and a pen. 'I've always wanted to do this, because I reckon I'm right ninety percent of the time.'

Michelle was slouching in her chair at the back of the Town Hall. Gina had advised that they arrive early to get a decent seat and enjoy the complete Slimmers United experience. As if she didn't have enough on her mind, the leader of the meeting, Lizzy, had already assumed that she was a new recruit and thrust a membership form in her hand. Mortified beyond belief that she was clearly such an obvious candidate, she'd had to explain that she was there to talk to the group about her charity event, not to sign up for weight loss.

'Are you sure you wouldn't like to give it a go whilst you're here?' enthused Lizzy. 'It's such a friendly group and we have such fun.'

'No, thank you,' said Michelle, tight-lipped. She didn't agree with Lizzy. No-one looked friendly. Lining up to face the gallows, otherwise known as weighing scales, they all looked terrified at what terrible secrets the little machine on the floor might reveal.

Michelle turned to walk to the back of the hall and sat down next to Gina. She felt sick to the stomach with nerves at the thought of standing up and talking in front of people about the event. Public speaking had put the fear of God in her ever since she'd dared to improvise as the innkeeper in a school nativity play when she was seven. Bravely she'd declared there were no bunk beds at the inn and the restaurant was already closed. Kathleen had shouted at her afterwards for ruining it for everyone whilst Ray had smirked in the background, trying not to laugh. Ever since then Michelle had successfully avoided any similar situations for fear of blurting out something she shouldn't. That was until now.

'Why on earth do you still keep coming to this?' she

asked Gina as she watched a variety of shapes and sizes start to awkwardly shed layers of clothing in preparation for being weighed.

'Everyone gets fat as soon as they get married. A wife should *not* look like a whale,' Gina said firmly. 'Besides, I enjoy it. I love watching the weigh-in and trying to guess if someone's had a good or a bad week. That's what the piece of paper is for. I call it Slimmers Bingo. We both have to write down how much we think each person has lost or gained when they get on the scales.'

'If we must,' sighed Michelle. At least this might provide some mild entertainment that would help get her through the torture of sitting through an entire meeting. It might even stop her thinking about how she was going to prevent herself from running out the door, petrified, as soon as she had to stand up to talk about Chickens For Charity. But it was too much to hope that it could distract her from the whole Rob/Josie nightmare that was currently winning the battle for space in her frazzled head.

'So here we go, first up on the scales,' Gina whispered, as if the poor woman currently removing her shoes on the other side of the room might hear them.

'Now it's crucial to read the signals,' she continued.

'This is a classic move by someone who has had a bad week and probably gained at least three pounds.'

'How can you tell that?' asked Michelle.

'She's taking her socks off.'

'So?'

'Socks off is a sign of sheer desperation for the scales to tip in your favour. She's gorged on chocs all week and probably been drunk every night, but now she's praying that sock removal will make up for it. Definitely marking her as a plus three.'

Michelle wrote plus two on her paper to show that she was willing to take part, before letting her gaze wander half-heartedly to the next victim. A spotty young lad in his twenties, who had clearly been spoilt by his mother in the food department, took off his shoes but left his socks on.

'Definitely a loser,' declared Gina, still in hushed tones.

'Because he kept his socks on?'

'No,' said Gina. 'Jason is the easiest person to guess. Every time he gets off the scales and he's lost weight he smiles and gazes over at Lucy – see her at the front, in the lumpy leggings. Jason is a classic male slimmer in his twenties.'

'In what way?'

'He's here for the sex.'

'What? Here?'

'No,' replied Gina, carefully marking a minus two on her sheet. 'He's bound to be a virgin and reckons if he loses weight he'll get sex from someone, anyone really, he's not bothered, he just wants sex. It'll probably end up being Lucy because she'll be more sympathetic and will have sex with him before he hits his target weight for having sex with a normal person.'

Horrified, Michelle marked a generous minus three on her sheet.

'I often thought you should combine the two,' Gina burbled on. 'A fat virgins' weight loss/dating club. I even thought of a name. Lose the Flab for a Shag.'

'Awesome,' said Michelle absent-mindedly.

'Oh come on, 'Chelle,' said Gina, nudging her hard with her shoulder. 'What's up with you? You'd normally find that hilarious. Did you hear me? Lose the Flab for a Shag. It's genius.'

'Sorry, Gina.' Michelle gave a big sigh.

'Hey, come on. I know that face. I normally only see it when your favourite has been kicked off *Strictly*. What's upsetting you?'

'Honestly, Gina, nothing. I'm fine.'

'Well, maybe this will cheer you up,' said Gina. 'I've been talking to Cousin Jack again.'

'Oh, great,' breathed Michelle.

'No, listen. He's only come up trumps again. Apparently he works with someone who lives next door to someone, whose son works for a film production company in London.'

'So, his colleague's neighbour's son?'

'If you say so,' replied Gina. 'Anyway, he managed to get this guy's email address.'

'How did he do that?'

'You know what he's like. He's very direct. He probably just went round, knocked on the door and threatened arson if they didn't hand it over. Anyway, he emails this guy and it turns out he's just a runner or something. Which apparently means you run around getting everyone tea.'

'So bit of a dead end, then?'

'Well, no, actually. Turns out his girlfriend works for a film publicity company and so she could be useful, couldn't she?'

Michelle thought for a moment.

'She'll know people,' she agreed.

'Exactly,' said Gina.

'She'll know people who might know George,' said Michelle.

'Exactly,' Gina repeated.

'So Cousin Jack is now working on getting in touch with his colleague's neighbour's son's girlfriend?'

'If you say so.'

'That's good,' said Michelle, feeling a little calmer. Maybe something might be going to plan in her life.

'Right, so are you going to tell me why you look like the world's ending now?' Gina pressed.

Michelle felt her shoulders sag again instantly.

'Come on,' said Gina. 'Something's up.'

Michelle knew Gina well enough to realise that she had to throw her some kind of bone or else she would never let it lie.

'Do you remember Rob, Jane's boyfriend when she died?'

'Oh yes. A really nice guy.'

'I suppose so,' shrugged Michelle. 'Well, he's back. From America. Just got divorced.'

'Blimey,' said Gina. 'That guy has no luck with women, does he?'

'Guess not.'

185

'So why is this a problem?'

Michelle hesitated.

'Well, it just drags up bad memories, doesn't it? Brings it all back again.'

'I know,' said Gina, gently laying her hand on Michelle's arm. 'I know it's a long time ago but there are always going to be things that will remind you of Jane. But that's a good thing, surely?'

'Yes,' said Michelle. 'You're right. But . . . well . . . it's just bad timing, that's all.'

'He was bound to come back and visit at some point,' said Gina.

'I know. I should have thought of that.' Michelle realised that she'd ignored the fact that he might re-emerge at any time, which had left her totally unprepared as to what to do if he did. Now she was lying awake every night, churning over the fact that perhaps she had no choice but to reveal the identity of Josie's father. That it was the right thing to do. It was a dilemma she'd managed to ignore whilst Rob was out of sight, but she couldn't any longer. Every time she thought through the process of telling not only Rob and Josie but also her parents, she felt sick at the prospect of their reactions, and terrified that she could end up losing them all.

Gina put an arm around her, causing a tear to escape down her cheek.

'He probably won't hang around for long,' said Gina. 'There's no reason for him to stay here, really, is there?'

Only a daughter, thought Michelle. An absolutely enormous reason. She wondered if the first step was to tell Gina. She felt guilty that she'd never had the guts to tell her in the past, but she was so determined at the beginning not to tell anyone that by the time she thought she was able to take her into her confidence, it felt too late. The world had moved on and everyone had accepted that Michelle neither wanted Josie's father to be part of her life nor wished to share with anyone who he actually was.

She could let it out now. Right here. Confess all. It was fitting, somehow, given the confessional nature of the slimmers who were baring all on the scales. She was also at the point where she thought she might explode if she didn't unburden herself to someone. She turned to face Gina's sympathetic gaze and prepared herself to say out loud the words she'd vowed never to say.

'Bums on seats, ladies and gentlemen, bums on seats,' Lizzy cut in. 'We have a lot to get through today and we have a very special guest here to talk to us at the end about her charity work. Stand up, Michelle. Give us all a wave.'

Michelle stared at the beaming Lizzy then glanced back at a proud-looking Gina, who nudged her to stand up and acknowledge the applause that now filled the room. She thought she might throw up. What was she doing here? How had she put herself in this position of doing something that scared her witless? She stood up and waved meekly before sitting down with a thud.

'Right then,' whispered Gina in her ear. 'Let's see who's nailed this Slimmers Bingo, then, shall we?'

Michelle barely listened to the comings and goings of the meeting. She was vaguely aware of Gina nudging her every time someone's weight loss or gain was announced so they could check who had guessed right. The whole thing was very confusing, however, since everyone clapped and cheered whatever the result, pounds on or pounds off.

'Three-pound gain! Three pounds!' Gina exclaimed in response to a middle-aged, massively overweight gentleman. 'Pathetic.'

'So, John, would you like to share with the group how

you think your week went,' said Lizzy, head cocked at the appropriately sympathetic angle.

'It's my wife's fault,' he mumbled. 'She was away for the week visiting her sister. She left me food to heat up in the freezer.'

'That was good of her,' beamed Lizzy.

'Dozy cow didn't tell me how to use the microwave,' John continued. 'I've had a curry every night.'

The entire room sucked in its breath at the mention of takeaway food.

'Okay, John,' said Lizzy, still grinning away. 'Let's throw it out to the rest of the group, shall we? What could John have done to make a healthier choice?'

'Which curry house do you use?' Gina shouted.

'The Shangri-La,' John replied. 'Bloody lovely.'

'Now there's your mistake, you see,' Gina told him. 'I can lose half a pound in an instant from the after-effects of a dodgy curry. Just like that.' She snapped her fingers for emphasis. 'You are paying way too much for your curry. Downgrade to somewhere like Bombay Nights. A bit of the sub-standard rubbish they serve in there will do your digestive system the world of good.'

'Gina,' said Lizzy, her massive smile slipping. 'As interesting a way of losing weight as that is, I don't think it is one that Slimmers United can endorse. Now, can anyone else offer John some help?'

'She knows I'm right,' Gina muttered. 'Maybe I should be a Slimmers United rep. Wonder how much they get paid?'

'Mushy pea curry,' came a voice from the front row.

'Brilliant!' cried Lizzy. Megawatt smile back in full glow.

'Honestly, John, even you can manage this. It's so easy and it tastes delicious. Tell John what's in it, Sharon.'

'It takes, like, five minutes to cook, seriously. So you fry off some mushrooms and onion and you just add a tin of mushy peas.'

'Yuck,' said Gina, thrusting two fingers down her throat.

'. . . then a tin of chopped tomatoes . . .'

'Yuck . . . yuck,' continued Gina.

' . . . then a tin of baked beans . . .'

'Now I am seriously going to throw up,' said Gina, taking her fingers out of her mouth.

'. . . then add chilli powder and curry powder to taste. Dead simple and it tastes awesome.'

'How can something that mixes tinned tomatoes

with mushy peas ever taste awesome?' Gina enquired.

'I've cooked that loads,' piped up someone to the left of Michelle. 'We have it every week.'

'I cook up a batch at the beginning of the week and eat it every night,' grinned the spotty male virgin.

'That just killed all of his chances of a shag,' muttered Gina.

'Mushy pea curry is on page eight of the Slimmers United Cookbook,' announced Lizzy, 'available from me at the end of the meeting for the bargain price of £4.99. Now we've got through everyone, so it's time to announce the slimmer of the week. So let's give Sue a massive round of applause for her phenomenal loss of five pounds this week.'

Sue almost spat out the potato salad she was tucking into as all eyes turned to congratulate her.

'Five pounds! Are you serious?' exclaimed Gina. 'No wonder she's stuffing her face. She's starved herself all week. You can always tell the ones who've taken it too far. Out comes the Tupperware as soon as they've come off those scales. Bet that's not low fat mayo on that salad either. They might as well draw a kebab van up outside for her, I tell you.'

'Now, next week, people, we shall be discussing

the elephant in the room that is fast approaching,' said Lizzy. 'Can anyone guess what that is?'

'John,' Gina muttered under her breath.

'It is, of course, that fatal time of year that is otherwise known as . . . Christmas!' said Lizzy. 'Now I know it's still a few weeks away, but I always find the more advance planning you do the less likely you are to let Christmas bingeing destroy you. We've all done it, haven't we?'

Low level nodding and muttering filled the room.

'So next week I'll be showing you how to make a fat-free and sugar-free Christmas cake.'

'With the added bonus that it's taste-free too,' Gina whispered into Michelle's ear.

'Now, last but certainly not least, let's give a big, Slimmers United hand for Michelle, who has come to talk to us about her charity and a very exciting opportunity for us.'

Michelle's stomach lurched. She'd not quite recovered from the mention of mushy peas and canned tomatoes in the same recipe and now the moment she had been dreading had arrived. She forced herself to stand up and walk to the front of the room, clenching and unclenching her hands in a bid to control her nerves. She muttered *George Clooney* to herself over and over again as she stepped forward and turned to face her audience, who were eager to escape and devour some of the chocolate they had waiting for them in deep pockets or car glove compartments, safe in the knowledge they had a whole week to repent their sins.

Her opening words were low and stuttering, aimed mainly at the floor. She looked up to see Gina waving her hands to indicate she should speak up. She cleared her throat and grabbed one of the boards she had stayed up making past midnight to show images of what the Not On Our Watch project was all about. The words started to flow as she described their work, doing her best to be snappy and punchy, but she could already tell she was losing her audience as they struggled to relate to what she was telling them and why it was important enough to keep them away from their essential post weigh-in snack.

Using another painstakingly assembled board, she moved on to describe how they could help raise money for this important cause. She described the event and how the factory were providing free chicken, but already a low murmuring of unrelated chatter had begun. She could feel the familiar red rash that always appeared when she was experiencing extreme discomfort starting to emerge from her chest, up her neck and onto her face. This was desperate. She was failing miserably. All she had left was her ace card, which seemed to have worked with the other groups that had been canvassed previously.

'We are also extremely grateful to our other sponsor, Clayton's Brewery, who have agreed to provide free beer from their brewery for all contestants who will be cooking food on the night.'

The room fell silent as all the slimmers looked furtively at each other and then glanced at Lizzy wistfully, hoping for some kind of confirmation that given this was for charity, gorging themselves on free beer would be acceptable and in fact fully endorsed by Slimmers United.

Michelle stood awkwardly wishing the ground would swallow her up as the silence continued. The rugby club players had cheered and done a victory lap around the pitch, such was their excitement over free alcohol, whilst the WI had cross-examined Daz on the types of beer that might be available and had been very specific about what should be brought to satisfy the ladies. In desperation, Michelle looked pleadingly at Lizzy, hoping there was something she could do to rescue her.

'Let's throw it out to the group, then, shall we?'

beamed Lizzy. 'Come on, guys, this is a great way to spread the word about Slimmers United and raise money for this very worthy cause. Every week you tell me some startling creative stories about recipes you have created that are healthy and delicious. So come on. Hit me with it. Who has a great recipe for chicken?'

The room fell silent again. Feet shuffled awkwardly.

'Drumsticks,' came a murmur from the back.

'Good start,' bounced Lizzy. 'Drumsticks without the skin are an option. Anyone else? Come on, don't be shy. We're looking for a healthy chicken recipe we can all get involved in that would delight the taste buds of anyone.'

Michelle had never prayed harder for chicken inspiration.

The girl with the lumpy leggings in the front row raised her hand.

'Yes, Lucy,' urged Michelle.

'Sometimes . . .' Lucy hesitated. 'Sometimes I put chicken in my mushy pea curry.'

'Aw, that's brilliant,' said the fat virgin vigorously, as Lucy smiled back shyly.

'Mushy pea chicken curry,' said Lizzy. 'Brilliant, Lucy. We'll do mushy pea chicken curry, Michelle, how about that?'

'Sounds . . . amazing,' replied Michelle, feeling her stomach churn at the thought. 'Can't wait to try it.'

'Fabulous!' Lizzy began clapping. 'Just fabulous. We'll bring some Slimmers United recipe books with us so that everyone who tries it can go home and make it too. I'd better be sure to bring some membership packs,' she added. 'When people discover they can eat food like that and lose weight, then I'm sure we'll have lots of people interested in joining us.'

'I'm sure,' Michelle nodded.

'Let's have a massive round of applause for Michelle, shall we, everyone? What a truly inspirational person she is,' gushed Lizzy. 'I am always in total awe of anyone who selflessly throws themselves at raising money for charity, and we at Slimmers United are very proud to be associated.'

Michelle nodded and smiled then collapsed in a spare chair on the front row.

'Now, if you need anything from us in the meantime, Michelle, be sure to let us know. I'll send you our corporate logo to be included on all your promotional material and a link to our brand guidelines on our website. All items must be approved by head office, of course, but I'm sure that you're well aware of that, aren't you?'

'Of course.' Michelle nodded, in a daze. She wouldn't know a brand guideline if it smacked her in the face.

'Oh, I've just had a brilliant idea,' announced Lizzy. 'We could offer a free membership as a raffle prize, how about that?'

'That would be great.' Michelle swallowed, thinking they'd better sort a raffle out then.

'You were brilliant,' Gina told Michelle half an hour later, after everyone had left and Lizzy had at last finished talking Michelle through the corporate mission and statement for Slimmers United.

'I was rubbish,' Michelle declared. 'Thank goodness for Lizzy.'

'Well, she is very persuasive,' said Gina.

'She certainly is,' Michelle agreed. 'She just signed me up for a six-week membership.'

'Brilliant!' cried Gina. 'You could do with it.'

'Thanks,' muttered Michelle. 'I really needed to hear that.'

'You're welcome.'

'She blackmailed me, actually. Said she'd only give me a raffle prize if I joined up. She's pretty hardcore.'

'Nah,' said Gina. 'She's not really. She just doesn't mind asking, that's all. A bit like me.'

'Funnily enough, I was thinking about that,' said Michelle. 'How do you fancy setting up the raffle?'

'How do I do that?' asked Gina.

'Well, you could start by asking companies in the area to donate prizes. I wonder if Dominic in Sales at the factory might help as well. Maybe some of his customers might give us something?'

Gina considered the request.

'So I just ring lots of people up and ask for free stuff?'

'Yep, that's about it.'

'I can do that. Leave it with me. Sounds like top fun.'

'Really?'

'Consider it done.'

'Thanks, Gina,' said Michelle. 'I really appreciate your help, you know.'

'Look, Michelle, are you okay?' Gina gently reached out to take her hand. 'Something's up. I can tell with you. You've got that post-Jane-dying, I'm-not-really-on-this-planet look that I've not seen in a while.'

Michelle looked away. The moment had passed. She couldn't face bringing up the subject of Rob again. She looked back at Gina.

'Actually, I think I'm just hungry,' she said.

'Fat Club does that to me, too. Fish and chips?'

'I could murder a fish and chips.'

'Let's get going, then. There'll be a queue by now behind all the other starving slimmers.'

Chapter Fourteen

Michelle stood outside Rob's rented terraced house feeling like Little Red Riding Hood. She was wearing a bright red raincoat and had a basket tucked under her arm with a dish of Salted Chilli Chicken hiding under a red and white checked tablecloth. She hesitated before banging on the knocker. Her heart was beating at a hundred miles an hour and her head was swimming with the rehearsed words she had been contemplating all day, as she built herself up to telling Rob he had a fifteen-year-old daughter.

The night before she'd sat for hours trying to foresee Rob's reaction to make sure she was prepared with answers that might help him adjust to the news. At one point she'd even reached for the photo album that she'd put together of Josie during her first year, thinking that maybe Rob would like to see pictures of his girl as a baby.

She flicked through the obligatory shots of Josie in hospital, all pink and screwed up, followed by her first cuddles with grandparents, first outfit that wasn't a Babygro, first smile, first tooth, first holiday in Whitby, throwing chips at enormous seagulls, and lastly first birthday on Christmas Eve, complete with Santa hat on her grinning head as she stood on her own two feet to blow out a solitary candle.

Michelle felt an overwhelming sadness as it hit her how fast the time had gone and how she would never be able to relive those precious baby moments again. She put the album back on the shelf, knowing that Rob should see them when he was ready, once he had found a way of forgiving her for the time she had deprived him of with Josie.

Pulling down her red hood, she grasped the door knocker and bashed it against the door. When there was no answer she tried again. She could see the flickering of the television behind the curtains in the front room, so she knew he must be in.

No answer.

She stepped across the path to the front window and banged on the glass. Now she was here she wanted to get it over with. Almost immediately the curtain was drawn back and out peered Rob. Well, she thought it was Rob. He looked horrendous. His eyes were red with huge bags drooping underneath them. A dark fuzz cluttered his normally clean-cut face, the result of many days without shaving. He also appeared to be wearing blue towelling. Never a good look at six in the evening. He dropped the curtain and disappeared. Next minute she heard the latch being pulled back and the front door opening.

'It's not really a good time,' he muttered at her.

'What's happened?' asked Michelle, spotting tartan checked pyjama bottoms peeping from underneath the blue towelling.

Rob stared back at her and to her horror he began to cry.

'What's happened?' she asked again.

He sniffed loudly. 'You'd better come in.'

She followed him into the living room, picking her way through a collection of empty pizza boxes and bottles of lager. The room smelt of beer, congealed cheese and miserable man. Rob slumped down on the sofa and reached for the remote control, turning the very loud rugby game on the TV to mute. Moving an empty bottle off the sofa, Michelle sat down next to him and put her basket on the table.

'I bought you some Salted Chilli Chicken,' she said when Rob didn't say anything. He looked up in utter amazement at the mention of food.

'That is so kind,' he gasped. 'So kind.' His face, which had lit up for a moment, crumpled again and he grimaced, clearly trying to hold back some more tears. He was barely recognisable as the smart, calm, confident man that had sat at her kitchen table the week before. She didn't know what to say. Her carefully rehearsed words had been blindsided by the wreck that sat in front of her.

'Amy called,' he said, as if it was painful to let the words pass his lips.

'Is that your wife?' asked Michelle.

'Ex-wife.' He took a tomato-stained handkerchief out of his dressing gown pocket and blew his nose.

'She rang to say that she and Larry have decided to postpone the wedding.'

'Okay,' said Michelle, desperately scrabbling for the

appropriate questions to be asking. 'Did you know they were getting married?'

'Oh yeah. They got engaged eleven days after she walked out.'

'Right,' said Michelle. 'So were you intending to go to the wedding, then?'

'God, no!'

'So why did she call to let you know they're postponing it?'

'Because,' he sniffed. 'Because she's pregnant, that's why, and she doesn't want to be a fat bride.' He leant forward, letting his head drop onto his knees. Michelle didn't know what to do other than lay her hand on his back. Suddenly he reared up.

'How could she?' he gasped. 'She didn't think to ring and tell me she was pregnant. Oh no. She rang to tell me that the wedding is postponed, like that could ever be more important.' He slammed his fist on the table, making Michelle jump. She had never seen Rob angry.

'She kept telling me she wasn't ready for kids,' he said, pushing his screwed-up fists into his eye sockets. 'What bollocks. She just didn't want *my* kids.'

'Well,' said Michelle, panicking now that the

conversation was off the scale in terms of what she had expected. 'Perhaps it wasn't planned, perhaps it was a mistake?'

Rob's eyes appeared from behind his fists, a glimmer of hope glinting somewhere deep inside before he slumped back down again.

'I very much doubt it,' he said. 'She plans everything. She left me on a Friday, you know? Friday is food shop day. She didn't want to waste her time buying food for two.'

'Are you sure that's why it was a Friday?'

'Her last words to me as she walked out the door were that I needed milk and I should start buying single-pint cartons rather than two-pint cartons. When I walked into that supermarket and bought one pint of milk . . . well, I've never felt so alone.' Rob reached for a bottle of beer on the coffee table and took a swig. 'This baby definitely wasn't a mistake. She lied to me, Michelle. Why didn't she just tell me she didn't want to have kids with me?'

'I don't know,' she mumbled. But she did know. She knew only too well how hard it was sometimes to tell the truth. A voice in her head shouted, 'Tell him the truth now!' She took a breath, searching for the right words to begin.

'Why me, Michelle?' he said just as the first sentence was formulating in her brain.

'I'm sorry?' she said.

'Why me?' he repeated, his face creased up in pain. 'Why does this keep happening to me? When Jane died I remember thinking there was no way I could lose someone like that again. It's why I had to go to America. To escape, to start again. Focus on my career, forget about relationships.'

'I know.' She nodded. She knew only too well. How she'd wished she were Rob, wished she could run away from the grief, the sadness, the awful mess she was in.

'Then eventually I met Amy, just as I was starting to forget how terrible it was to lose someone. I thought I could do it. I could try again. I couldn't be unlucky enough to have two women die on me. I never thought I'd lose her this way.' He dropped his head into his hands. 'Why does this keep happening to me?' He gave a deep sigh, then began to weep again.

Michelle had no choice but to put her arms around him and pull him in close, rocking him gently backwards and forwards until his sobs subsided. It was heartbreaking to see him like this. It reminded her too much of when Jane had died and they'd sat together on the front row in church during her funeral and she'd felt every heave of his shoulders as he desperately tried to hold it together. She'd wanted to put her arms around him then but she couldn't. Not in church and not with his baby growing inside her. She felt a tear escape down her cheek as Rob's despair sparked her own. She brushed it away hurriedly with her finger as Rob lifted his head from her shoulder, blowing loudly on his handkerchief.

'I'm sorry,' he said. ' I didn't mean to load all this onto you.'

'It's fine,' she shrugged, praying that he wouldn't notice her watery eyes.

They smiled at each other awkwardly and Michelle knew she couldn't bring herself to tell him now. She would have to bide her time before she piled any more heartache onto his overburdened shoulders. He was in no fit state to handle any further life-changing revelations. She started gathering up empty bottles in an effort to create a diversion and an escape route.

'Look, why don't I tidy this place up a bit whilst you go and have a shower? You'll feel better.'

'You're right,' he nodded, his eyes dragged back to the TV. He went quiet for a moment, watching men silently run in random directions across the screen.

'You're right,' he said again, picking up the remote and turning the screen off. 'Your mother's coming round.'

'My mother's coming round here?'

'Yeah, she called earlier to ask me round for Sunday lunch and I got a bit upset on the phone, so she insisted on bringing a casserole round. She's been so kind to me since I've been back. She really is a great woman, your mum.'

Michelle stared at Rob, incredulous.

'So I guess I should clean myself up a bit, you're right,' he said, getting up. 'Thanks, Michelle. I mean it. What would I do without the Hidderley family?' He gave her a small smile, then turned and left the room.

Michelle stared after him, then looked around at the devastation caused by his misery. She got up and began collecting soggy pizza boxes off the floor, wondering how exactly she had ended up tidying Rob's house to make him look good for her mother.

Chapter Fifteen

Sleep was all she could think about as she counted slowly to ten following a barrage of questions from her mother. It was nine o'clock and the night before Chickens For Charity had finally arrived. It was a Friday and so she'd worked a full shift in the factory before knocking off at five to begin the set-up for the main event the next day. She was currently six feet up a ladder, hanging bunting across the entrance to the warehouse that Mr Evans had agreed to let them use as an event space. She had escaped up there after four very long hours, when she had been asked every ridiculous question known to man by the army of kind helpers who had volunteered, but who in such an alien environment seemed to have lost all power to make any kind of decision. She hoped that her elevated status, balancing precariously on the top rung, would put her out of reach of anyone requiring her attention. Just a few more hours and it would all be over, she told herself, wondering whether she would be able to stay awake long enough to go home and cook an enormous batch of Salted Chilli Chicken. She was exhausted, since every waking hour outside of the factory, as well as some during normal working hours, had been taken up with the avalanche of tasks that required attention in order to make Chickens for Charity happen. She'd thought screwing up the courage to stand in front of people and get them involved in the event was going to be the hard part. She'd had no idea that that was just the start. Her brain had to drag itself out of sleep mode and put itself on permanent high-alert, problem-solving mode, to avoid the whole thing crashing down around her ears. Endless requests from the competitors had kept her busy with such things as finding rotisseries for the rugby club, temporary stoves for the WI, and locations of plug sockets for Daz's disco. On top of that, she'd had to deal with the factory health and safety Gestapo otherwise known as Marianne, who seemed intent on force-feeding Michelle as many legal regulations as she possibly could, which had been a bloody nightmare from start to finish. Michelle felt she had spent the entire week dotting i's and crossing t's until she could no longer see straight, and quite frankly, if anyone else approached her with what looked like a problem she was quite likely to burst into tears. Her escape up a ladder seemed a safe bet to keep her out of harm's way.

However, she hadn't banked on her mother, who was undeterred by talking to Michelle's backside and who was prepared to go to any lengths to make sure the WI had every advantage available to maximise their chances of winning the coveted prize of CHICKENS FOR CHARITY CHAMPION CHEFS.

'Michelle!' she screeched, causing her daughter to overbalance and nearly clatter to the floor in a tangle of recycled jubilee flags. 'Pauline Dimmock has called. You know, the one who's providing her prize marrows for a display in our area. She has two questions. Question one, could someone go down to her house on Arcadia Avenue and fetch the marrows, as her Eric has only just had a knee operation and can't go anywhere? Whoever goes needs a wheelbarrow, because they are exceptionally large marrows. And they need to be strong, because she's worried it might be hard to lift the marrow into the barrow.'

'So let me get this straight, Mum.' Michelle sighed wearily. 'She wants a man and a barrow to fetch a marrow at nine o'clock at night?'

'It's very kind of her to donate them. They're prize-winning marrows.'

'I know, Mum, but I'm not sure anyone will want to go down there now. Can't someone pick them up tomorrow?'

'Apparently not. Marrows don't like to be moved in the daylight. Best to do it at night, apparently.'

'Why on earth . . .?'

'Least disruptive, I assume.'

'Who for?'

'The marrow, of course.'

'That's all very well, Mum, but it's very disruptive for the rest of us. Everyone's kind of busy at the moment.'

'Michelle. Do I need to remind you that this is for charity?'

Michelle counted to ten again before she decided she'd better climb down and tackle the problem from the ground.

'I know it's for charity, Mum, I set it all up, remember?'

'Precisely, which is why you should be grateful for the likes of Pauline, who is willing to hand over her prize marrows for George Clooney's charity. I sincerely hope you'll be mentioning her generosity when you hand over the money.'

'Of course I will, Mum,' sighed Michelle, too tired to argue. She rubbed her temples. 'Is Dad busy? Could he pop down in the car?'

'Good idea. Now question two was to ask if you have on-site security.'

'What for?'

'So nothing happens to her marrows.'

'Nothing's going to happen to her marrows.'

'They're prizewinners.'

Bloody hell, thought Michelle. Who knew that marrying George Clooney would lead to her discussing vegetable security measures?

'Tell Pauline,' she said slowly, 'that there is twenty-four-hour security here three hundred and sixty-five days per year. I will personally tell Brian the security man to keep a special eye on Pauline's marrows, okay? Her marrows couldn't be better protected if they were in prison.'

'Oh, Pauline will be relieved to hear that. Have you got Brian's number and then Pauline can call him with instructions?'

Michelle escaped to find some form of sanity with Gina, who was busy setting up the raffle on a stack of pallets just inside the entrance to the warehouse. She wanted to ensure maximum exposure for the prizes she had harassed local businesses, as well as the factory's customers, into donating. As Michelle approached, however, she was somewhat perturbed to see a tractor and trailer backed into the entrance and a large metal cage being lifted off.

'What on earth is that?' she asked, eyeing up what resembled some kind of torture chamber.

'My God, Michelle, you're such a townie. Surely you know what one of these is?'

'I can assure you I have absolutely no idea.'

'It's a cattle crush, of course.'

'And what would you do with a cattle crush?'

'Crush cattle, stupid!'

'For what purpose?'

'No idea.'

One of the army of lads who were lifting the

contraption off the back of the trailer turned to Michelle to explain.

'It traps the cow inside so you can safely give them injections or check their feet or de-horn them. You can even castrate them.'

Michelle turned to look questioningly at Gina.

'It's our star prize,' she exclaimed gleefully. 'These things are worth a fortune, but it's an old model and the agricultural suppliers needed the room, so they said I could have it if I could get someone to take it away.'

'Who is going to want to buy a raffle ticket to win a cage that helps you castrate animals?' enquired Michelle.

'Well, I thought of that. We're surrounded by farmers, right? So I've had all the agricultural businesses putting up posters for Chickens for Charity and making a big splash about the chance to win a free cattle crush. I reckon we'll have half the farming community here tomorrow. Plus I have a back-up plan for the non-farmers.'

'And what might that be?'

'I got the bookshop in town to donate a load of copies of *that* book. Your very own Red Room of Pain. Ta-da!' she said, parading around the cage like some bikini-clad babe at a fancy car show. 'The guy who donated this thinks it's genius. He's thinking of setting up a bit of a sideline.'

'Gina,' said Michelle, struggling for words. 'Your business acumen really makes me feel that your talents are wasted on the chicken factory floor.'

'Too right,' Gina agreed. 'Every company I rang or visited donated something, Michelle. Every one. And in most cases I got an upgrade.'

'Meaning what, exactly?'

'It was my strategy, not to accept their first offer. You know Dominic, the sales manager here? He suggested it. He said if they offer a bottle of wine, suggest two bottles. The guy who gave us the cattle crush started off with a box of foot rot spray. Dominic says I'm a natural.'

'Gina, you truly amaze me.'

'In a good way?'

'Totally in a good way. Now, have you heard from Cousin Jack's colleague's neighbour's son's girlfriend?'

'Oh my God, yes!' Gina clutched both of Michelle's arms. 'They're with him now.'

'With who?'

'George Clooney, of course,' said Gina, getting her phone out. 'I told you that they were going to the premiere, didn't I? Well, Lisa, that's Cousin Jack's colleague's neighbour's son's girlfriend, sent me this at six o'clock, as they were on the red carpet.' She tapped her phone and a grainy George Clooney appeared in the distance as a jumble of voices shouted out from the phone.

'Look, he's there!' shrieked Gina, pointing excitedly at the screen. 'It's so exciting!'

Michelle peered more closely. Indeed, he was there, behind the other people milling around in DJs and evening dresses. Flashes of light intermittently filled the screen, presumably from paparazzi cameras. Michelle could vaguely hear what must be Lisa's voice in the background, off camera, talking to her boyfriend, the son of Cousin Jack's colleague's neighbour.

'Did they get any closer?' she asked. 'Did they get to speak to him?'

'Lisa said in her text it was mayhem outside the cinema and that was the closest they got. But she has your invite for the event tomorrow night and has promised to give it to the girl she knows in his PR team. She'll text me as soon as she's handed it over.'

'Good, good, that's great. You will tell me, won't you?' Michelle was aware that her voice was getting higher and more desperate. All this effort with Chickens For Charity had to be worth it. All the hassle and the pain and sleepless nights had to come to something. It would be so amazing if somehow George did turn up tomorrow.

'Of course I will,' said Gina, putting her arm around her. 'There's nothing more we can do. If he comes, he comes.'

Michelle sat down on a pile of compost bags that Gina had secured from a garden centre.

'What if he doesn't come?' she said, looking up at Gina. 'What if it's all been for nothing?'

'All this, nothing?' said Little Slaw, appearing out of nowhere like the shopkeeper in *Mr Benn*. Little Slaw's ability to impersonate famous characters from TV and film seemed to be getting better and better. 'You call this nothing?' he repeated, gesturing at Gina's random raffle, Kathleen's elaborate trestle tables and Daz's entertainment centre, which was currently being constructed on the back of a low trailer in the middle of the warehouse.

Kathleen approached with a basket filled with every cleaning liquid known to man tucked firmly under her arm, clearly having decided that, for tonight, her work was done.

'I am very proud,' said Little Slaw just as Kathleen

came into earshot. 'Very proud to know you and count you as a friend. This is not nothing. This is huge achievement already.'

'Well, we'll just have to see about that, won't we?' offered Kathleen as she stripped off her rubber gloves and placed them on the top of her basket. 'I only hope that all this doesn't go to waste when nobody turns up to eat our Supreme of Chicken. Your father isn't going to thank you if he ends up eating chicken every day until Christmas.'

Michelle did what she seemed to be doing a lot lately, when all around her appeared to be falling apart, and her confidence plunged its way back down to the bottom of the barrel. She got up and went to find Daz.

Daz had a bucket full of cable ties and was busy attaching strings of disco lights along the side of the trailer holding up his disco kit. The trailer was parked opposite the entrance and, given his elevated status, it was likely that Daz's Disco would be the first thing people would encounter as they arrived to experience Chickens For Charity.

'It's not going to work, is it?' said Michelle to his back.

'Are you kidding me?' he said, not turning round. 'Do you have no faith in Uncle Dazza? You just stay there, young lady, and I'll show you exactly how it's going to work.' He snipped off the end of the cable tie and hoisted himself up onto the back of the trailer before disappearing behind a bank of speakers. Next minute, Michelle was all but blinded as all the disco lights were switched on and the entire warehouse was lit up in sparkling shades of silver, blue, pink and gold.

'Hello, everybody, and welcome to the one and only, first ever Chickens For Charity event,' Daz boomed out. 'Tonight you will experience chicken as you never have before, as you sample the best in culinary expertise from our fair town – all wanting to entice you with the *ultimate* chicken dish. Take your taste buds on a trip of a lifetime, but don't forget to vote for your favourite, because come nine this evening we will be crowning the Chickens For Charity Champion Chefs. Now, to open proceedings I'd like to invite the awesome, the wonderful, the amazing, the stupendous creator of this event, who's done this all in the name of a fantastic charity whose name escapes me just at this moment. So come on up, Michelle Hidderley, and let's have a few words from you.'

Michelle stood rooted to the spot, the enormity of what could be a massive flop hitting home.

'Come on, mate,' Daz urged her. 'Don't be shy. We need to get you used to this microphone before tomorrow.'

The last thing Michelle wanted to do was practise talking on a microphone in front of what could possibly be a bigger crowd than would be there the following night. Reluctantly, she hauled herself up onto the trailer to go and get Daz to shut up.

'So, Michelle, tell us about the charity we're raising money for here tonight,' said Daz into the microphone before he thrust it under her nose.

'Can you just shut the fuck up, Daz?' she said over the loudspeaker system.

'Interesting choice. Can you tell us why you chose the *Can you just shut the fuck up Daz* charity out of all the worthy causes out there?'

'Here's a tenner,' came a voice out of the darkness somewhere behind the trailer. 'Anything for Daz to put a sock in it once and for all.'

'Charming,' announced Daz before switching off the microphone, having caught sight of Michelle's stricken face.

'It's not going to work,' she repeated. 'No-one's going to come, and certainly not George Clooney. This is all a massive waste of time.'

'What do you mean, no-one's going to come?' asked Daz. 'I have been on Malton Radio three times this week. I swear they're screening my calls now, because I call up for every phone-in, no matter what the subject, and talk about Chickens for Charity. We've been in the *Echo* two weeks running. All the people who are cooking will bring along their friends and family so they can rig the vote. Little Slaw has charmed the entire Polish community of the Midlands into coming. What are you talking about, no-one's coming?'

She stared at him, too tired to think straight.

'Mum says no-one's coming.'

'Mrs H is a bloody nightmare at times. Wait till I see her.'

'I can't pull this off.' Michelle felt all her energy drain from her body. 'I've nearly killed myself trying to make this happen, and what for? I've never made a success of anything, so why on earth should I think this is going to work? Jane was the successful one, not me. I wish she were here. She'd fix it.'

'Bollocks, Michelle. Jane would never have got

anywhere close to something like this. She was a boring frosty knickers without a creative bone in her body.'

Michelle gasped.

'You can't say that.'

'Why not?'

'Because she's dead.'

'Yes, she is, and being dead doesn't transform her from being an accountant and fan of Michael Bolton to someone special like you, who appreciates the merits of One Direction.'

'Well, that just sums it up, doesn't it?' sighed Michelle. 'The best thing you can say about me is that I can appreciate a decent boy band when I see one. How very impressive my life is. Jane was already a success before she died and I'm just a joke who hasn't achieved anything, and after tomorrow I'll be a laughing stock.'

'Not achieved anything!' Daz exclaimed. 'You have single-handedly brought up a daughter.'

'Don't get me started on Josie – the daughter who I've brought up so well she's about to throw her life away over a boy at the age of fifteen. She's a disaster.'

'She's fifteen. We were all disasters at fifteen. It's just a phase. She'll get past Sean, you mark my words. We're all obsessed at that age.'

Michelle thought back to when she was fifteen. Daz was right. She had been obsessed at that age. She'd been lusting over the impossible dream of Charlie, who was eighteen and had left school to go to university, and she'd spent all of her holidays traipsing up and down his road in the hope he was back from college and she might catch a glimpse of him.

'You're right about that.' She sighed. 'Thing is, I'm not sure I ever really got over my obsession.' Occasionally she saw Charlie around town with his wife and young children, and she still couldn't stop her heart racing and a blush forming on her cheeks if he was within a hundred yards of her.

'I know I never got over mine,' said Daz.

Michelle noticed Daz was looking thoughtful, which was unusual. Normally his thoughts didn't linger in his head, just made straight for the open air.

'What happens to us, eh?' she said. 'One minute you're fifteen and full of hope that you're going to have this fantastic life and all your dreams will come true, and the next you're banging on the door of forty and you've let it all slip through your fingers. Why do we do that, Daz? Why do we give up? *When* do we give up?'

'I never gave up on my dream,' he said with a determined shake of his head.

'True,' Michelle nodded. 'Even at school you always wanted to be a DJ. I remember in the sixth-form common room everyone used to get really cross with you because you were forever hogging the stereo, putting your music on.'

'I'm not talking about being a DJ,' he said, staring down at his shoes.

'Oh, right,' said Michelle. 'Sorry, I thought that was exactly what you always wanted. I thought that was your real dream.'

He looked up.

'You must realise what my real dream is?'

'No. You never told me you wanted something else.'

'But you must have guessed?'

'No,' she repeated.

'Well,' he said, blinking rapidly, 'all I ever wanted was you.'

'*What?*'

'All I've ever dreamed of is you.'

Michelle was stunned into silence.

'Me?' she whispered eventually.

'Yes, you.'

Michelle had no response. Nothing. She felt numb, as though all feeling had been zapped out of her.

'But I wasn't your dream ever, was I?' Daz said. His eyes had turned steely and were piercing into her.

Michelle couldn't answer. Eventually she couldn't look at him any longer and dropped her gaze to the floor.

Uncharacteristically, Daz did not fill the silence.

It lasted forever.

She looked up finally and mouthed a tearful no.

Daz blew out through his mouth, as if deflating himself. Then he coughed before stepping forward and placing his hands on her shoulders.

'You, Michelle Hidderley, are the most amazing woman I know and I have loved you since I was fifteen.' He swallowed and coughed again. 'And I believe that you can do anything. Look at this,' he said, waving his arms around. 'All this, and you made it happen.'

Michelle couldn't stop the tears falling, she felt so terrible.

'There's no need to cry,' said Daz, taking her in his arms. 'You know what, you did make a dream come true for me this week,' he said into her hair. 'I never wanted to be a poxy disco DJ. I wanted to be on the radio, and this week that's happened three times. Three times!' He pulled away and held her by the shoulders in front of him. 'You made a dream come true this week and you make my dreams come true every week by being my friend. And by the way, tomorrow is going to be a massive success and George Clooney better bloody turn up, because if he doesn't . . . if he doesn't then he's an idiot to let you slip through his fingers.'

Daz paused to wipe what could have been a tear from the corner of his eye.

'And finally,' he said sniffing, 'do you want to know what I'd want to do right now if I was fifteen again?'

'No,' she muttered.

'Dance with you to this song.' He reached over and tapped a couple of keys on his laptop before closing his eyes to inhale the first few bars of the powerful music coming out of the speakers.

The unmistakable sound of Whitney Houston filled the air as 'I Will Always Love You' boomed its way through the warehouse.

'Please. Dance with me?' breathed Daz. He jumped off the truck and offered his hand up to her.

She allowed him to guide her onto the concrete. They embraced and shuffled in true last-dance style.

'You are my dream friend, you know,' she whispered in his ear.

'I know,' he whispered back. 'I like that.'

They moved together in perfect unison, both lost in their own thoughts, thinking about how to crack the impossible dream of falling in love with the right person, when Gina flung herself on them both.

'She's done it!' she screamed down Michelle's ear. 'She's only gone and done it! Look, look!' She thrust her phone into Michelle's face.

Michelle took the phone out of her hands to read the text that Gina was so excited about.

INVITE NOW IN THE HANDS OF GEORGE'S PA WHO HAS PROMISED TO SHOW HIM. FINGERS CROSSED. XX

Michelle squealed. Daz squealed. Gina squealed the loudest.

Chapter Sixteen

It was ten o'clock and Michelle was up to her arms in chicken in the centre of organised chaos in her kitchen. What on earth had possessed her to dream up something that required her to be knee-deep in chicken, in her own home, on a Friday night, she had no idea. But the fifty portions of thighs would not trim themselves, so she was consoling herself with the company of George as her fingers worked their magic. She'd propped the laptop on the kitchen counter and, after a hasty Google, had found footage of the red carpet procession at the premiere already posted on YouTube.

As chicken fat piled up on the side of her chopping

board, forming a small mountain, she kept glancing up to catch glimpses of the impeccably dressed George Clooney, charming his way through the crowd. He shook hands, touched shoulders, posed for pictures and smiled that famous smile which could reduce the coldest of hearts to a warm mush. Interrupted occasionally by an over-eager TV presenter, he waxed lyrical about the performances of his fellow actors, the stunning special effects team and the debt he owed to quite the best director he'd ever worked with. At one point, possibly bored with the constant flow of predictable questions, he did stop one interviewer in his tracks to inform him that before he asked, yes, the rumours were true. Prince George actually was named after him.

He appeared to be without one of his usually stunning escorts. Michelle allowed her mind to wander, as she boiled up giblets, as to what type of partner for George she would turn out to be on the red carpet. Solid, she decided. Both in structure and in attitude. Compared to all the waifs currently drifting around on the screen, her padded bone structure would appear like an anchor for George, a solid weight keeping his feet on the ground, whilst her East Midlands unpretentious attitude would be like a breath of fresh air, cutting through all the

Hollywood hype. She would have to start having manicures, she decided, as she glanced down at her raw hands, which had been up the backsides of far too many chickens to be fit to shake hands with the red carpet brigade.

She was just allowing her mind to wander to exactly how she would respond to the paparazzi's enquiries as to how she and George had met, when the back door was thrust open by Josie, who then slammed it behind her.

'You'll break the glass doing that,' chided Michelle.

'I don't care,' retorted Josie, before slumping down in a chair and setting her face in a look of anguish and anger, as only a teenager can manage.

'And what's eating you?' asked Michelle.

'Nothing.' Josie kicked the table leg.

'Looks like it,' said Michelle. 'Come here and stir this sauce, will you? Whilst I start deseeding chillies. Hot chocolate?'

'Your special hot chocolate?' asked Josie, looking up for the first time.

'Yes, if you come and stir this for me.'

Josie huffed her way out of her jacket before taking up position at the stove with a wooden spoon.

Michelle silently moved around the kitchen, hoping

the calming effects of stirring and the anticipation of a chocolate rush might coax Josie into spilling the beans on what had sparked this latest strop.

'Can I have a fishing rod for Christmas?' she divulged eventually after the first sip of the soothing liquid.

'What for?'

'So I can learn how to fish and go night fishing with Sean.'

'Do you really want to go out in the cold and the dark and sit by a damp river doing nothing?'

'That's what Sean keeps saying.'

'Finally, the lad talks some sense.'

'I keep asking him if I can go with him and he won't let me. He says I'll get in the way and it's no place for a girl.'

'That's very sexist,' Michelle couldn't help but exclaim.

'I know,' said Josie. 'He says he needs his own interests. That we don't need to do everything together.'

'Well, he's right there, isn't he?'

'I don't see why. We love each other. I want to share everything with him.'

This was the longest conversation Michelle had ever had with Josie about relationships and she didn't want to screw it up by inciting a row.

'But you could get bored of each other if you spend too much time together,' she said tentatively.

'No way,' replied Josie with all the self-assurance of a young girl who has never had her heart broken. 'I could never be bored of Sean and he could never be bored of me.'

Michelle wanted to scream at her, tell her that she was setting herself up for a massive disappointment. Given their age, it was ninety-nine percent certain that at some point one of them would ditch the other. She knew her next sentence was crucial, and sure to shatter the first sensible conversation she'd had with her daughter in weeks. Any advice she could offer was bound to be wrong and Josie would cut her down in flames without hesitation.

'Do you want me to show you the best way to deseed a chilli?'

Josie looked up at her mum as Michelle tried to give her best encouraging eyes.

'Do I get to use your posh chef knives that you never let me touch?' she asked.

'Okay,' nodded Michelle. 'Go and wash your hands and you can slice the rest of these babies.'

*

'Like a pro,' said Michelle to Josie after her fifth attempt. 'Like a pro.'

'These knives are awesome,' said Josie, waving a three-incher around her head. 'No wonder you cook great food with these.'

'There's a bit more to it than a sharp knife, you know.'

'Did you never want to go back to it, Mum?' Josie asked as she got stuck into her next chilli. 'Being a chef?'

'I thought about it,' she replied.

'So why didn't you?'

'I got stuck, I guess, and I didn't have the guts to do anything about it. Then before I knew it I'd let all that time slip through my fingers.'

Josie didn't respond. She picked up the next chilli in silence.

'Josie,' said Michelle, putting her hand on her shoulder. 'I know you think this whole George Clooney thing is ridiculous, but I'm not just doing it because of our bet, you know. I had to do something. Anything.'

Josie calmly slit through the entire length of the chilli.

'I was disappearing,' Michelle continued. 'I needed to do something to get out of this rut I'm in.'

Seeds were carefully deposited in a bowl.

'But most of all I want you to know that if you really

want to do something, you can. You shouldn't get in your own way, like I've always done.' Michelle had no idea if Josie was even listening.

'Josie, don't you see? You're fifteen, you can do *anything*. There is such a big world out there, you just have to reach out and go for it.'

Josie's knife stopped mid-flow and she turned to face her mum.

A grunt accompanied the back door opening.

'Sean!' cried Josie, dropping the knife on the chopping board and flinging herself at him. 'What are you doing here?'

'Fish weren't biting tonight, so I thought I'd call in for a drink on my way home.'

'Oh, brilliant. Mum, will you make Sean some hot chocolate?' she shouted over her shoulder as she disappeared into the lounge with him, virtually jumping with glee.

'Of course,' Michelle called after her. 'I'll make him my extra special hot chocolate,' she said as she spooned a pile of chilli seeds into a mug.

Chapter Seventeen

Michelle leant her forehead against the cold window, watching the raindrops pop up on the pane before they started their haphazard descent. She closed her eyes; the headlamps of the oncoming traffic rushing constantly towards her as they sped down the motorway were making her feel dizzy and disorientated. But when she closed her eyes she could only see one thing. The look of anguish on his face was unbearable as it filled her dark vision. She saw every line around his worn eyes, which were closed as if to block out the sadness. It was not how she had expected the day of her long awaited charity event to end. Not at all.

*

Six o'clock that evening had seen Michelle feeling sick for so many reasons she didn't know where to begin. Firstly she was suffering from obligatory pre-party nerves. She remembered her joint eighteenth birthday bash with Gina, held in the function room of the pub where she worked in the kitchens. They'd slaved all day to make the drab, tired, generally brown interior look like it was a place for celebration, rather than somewhere to contemplate slitting your wrists. Having dashed home for a quick wash and brush-up, which was disappointing in itself, since they had planned to spend at least three hours on getting ready, they'd returned at seven twenty-five, ready to greet guests arriving at seven-thirty. It had been one of the most painful half hours of her life, spent gazing round the vast, empty space, thinking that no-one would come. Michelle and Gina had smiled at each other nervously as they'd watched the hands creep round the clock and offered words of reassurance that neither of them believed. Daz had strode up, two bottles of Diamond White in hand, and they'd taken them off him gratefully, sipping long and hard through straws. In those days Diamond White Magic seemed to transform any evening from potential failure into a night packed with high jinks and adventure. And so it had worked its magic that night. Three quarters of the way down the bottle and at precisely seven fifty-five, the guests had started to stream in and the night was off and running, until Daz had switched off his disco at midnight, much to the anger of the party-hungry, Diamond White Magic doused teenagers.

But it wasn't her eighteenth party she was waiting for now, and she doubted if Diamond White Magic was what was required tonight to make Chickens for Charity a spectacular success. It was people she needed, and lots of them, and she still had a whole hour until the event started to worry about whether anyone would turn up.

'They're here,' Daz announced suddenly, dashing past her out of the enormous doors of the warehouse towards the loading bay at the back.

Michelle turned to see two men get out of a car and get ambushed by Daz. Who on earth was he so excited to see when he should be holding her hand and panicking with her? She watched him shake their hands vigorously before grabbing a bag off one of their shoulders and leading them both towards Michelle.

'This is Jonny Player!' he told her excitedly.

'Very nice to meet you,' she said, extending her hand whilst looking quizzically at Daz, who clearly thought that Michelle should know exactly who Jonny Player was.

'Jonny Player!' he repeated, absolutely beaming.

Michelle looked again at the very ordinary looking middle-aged man in an anorak.

'Jonny Player!' exclaimed Marianne, appearing from nowhere in enough silver lycra to foil-wrap every chicken in the factory.

'I'm your biggest fan!' she cried, engulfing anorak man in a shroud of silver. 'Mr Evans and the Mayor are just over here waiting for you.' She grabbed Jonny's arm in a vice-like grip and started to haul him across the loading bay.

'Oi,' cried Daz, grabbing Jonny's other arm and pulling him in the opposite direction. 'Jonny is here to see me and Michelle, not the sodding Mayor. What the hell has he got to do with it?'

'Jonny,' said Marianne, pasting a dazzling smile on her face. 'Mr Evans is the General Manager of this establishment, and between me and him, we have done everything possible to make sure Chickens For Charity happens, haven't we, Michelle?'

'Well,' Michelle began, still desperate to know exactly what was so special about Jonny.

'There would be no Chickens For Charity without me, now would there, Michelle?' said Marianne.

'No, you're right,' Michelle had to reply.

'Bollocks!' exclaimed Daz. 'Listen to me, Jonny. Michelle and I have put blood, sweat and tears into this. When Michelle first came to me with her idea to raise money for those poor people in . . . in . . . somewhere abroad, I could have cried, I really could. Her passion, her commitment, her drive, her compassion, her brilliance with chicken is what has made this event what it is today. Michelle, tell him. Tell him it's all down to you. *You* deserve this.'

Deserve what? thought Michelle. Who was this man in the anorak with grass stains on the elbows? Just then she was saved by an explanation from the other man wearing an equally boring fleece who had arrived with anorak man.

'Ready when you are, Jonny,' he said, thrusting a Radio Derby branded microphone into his hand. 'We need to get a move on, mate, because you're due back in the studio in thirty minutes.'

'Marvellous,' said Jonny, turning on a smile for the

first time. 'Now let me get this straight. So, Michelle, this was your idea and then you've had help from all these people around you?'

'Yes,' gulped Michelle. Now she knew that boring anorak man was the minor local celebrity presenter on Radio Derby, she suddenly felt very intimidated.

'So we'll start with a few words from you and then I'll get some quality sound bites from your supporters,' Jonny continued. 'Shall we take a step over there away from distractions?'

He led Michelle away from Daz and Marianne, who both looked ready to draw pistols at dawn at each other. They stalked away to opposite corners of the loading bay to review their battle plan and be prepared to pounce as soon as Jonny had finished with Michelle.

Jonny took her back towards his car, where fleece man had the boot open and was twiddling with some equipment.

'We all set, Jim?' Jonny asked him.

'All set,' agreed Jim.

'Okay, Michelle. I'm just going to ask you a few questions about this evening's event. So relax. This isn't live, okay?'

'Okay,' squeaked Michelle, smoothing down her hair for no apparent reason.

'So, we're here in Malton to talk to Michelle about Chickens For Charity,' said Jonny. 'So, Michelle, what a wonderful idea to raise money for all the poor chickens out there. Have you always been a bird lover?'

'Er, well no, actually, Jonny, Chickens For Charity isn't for chickens.'

'Isn't it?'

'No, you see, we're cooking chickens, kindly donated by this factory, in order to raise money for a charity called Not On Our Watch.'

'So what you're saying, Michelle, is that chickens are being needlessly slaughtered in order to raise money for an organisation that does not benefit chickens in the slightest.'

'Not needlessly slaughtered, no. This is a chicken factory. We slaughter hundreds of chickens here every day.'

'Er, what Michelle means to say,' interrupted Mr Evans, appearing from nowhere, 'is that all Pinkerton's Chicken Factories are dedicated to being a part of the local communities they operate in, and therefore, when Michelle approached me to be involved in her fundraising campaign, I came up with the idea of a chicken cooking competition using chicken donated by the factory.'

'Amazing,' agreed Jonny, who was possibly not taking a blind bit of notice of what had just been said. 'And for which charity will you be cooking chicken tonight? Hah hah hah,' he suddenly bellowed with laughter. 'Chicken Tonight? Do you get it? You could have called it Chicken Tonight!'

'It's all for George Clooney, actually,' Marianne interrupted, virtually bowling Michelle over in her desperate attempt to be involved. Michelle's heart sank.

'George Clooney?' exclaimed Jonny. 'He's a charity these days, is he?'

'No,' Michelle chipped in before Marianne could take it any further. 'It's not for him, but we are raising money for his project, Not On Our Watch. They're an organisation committed to stopping mass atrocities and giving a voice to their victims.' Michelle prayed she'd said that right. She didn't want to let George down.

'And what does that actually mean, Michelle?' asked Jonny.

Shit, she thought. What did it actually mean? She

thought back to the hours she'd spent watching George on YouTube standing up for people who were living a nightmare, in terrible situations, and who had no-one else to stand up for them.

'It's about standing up for people who are living a nightmare in the most terrible situations, who have no-one else to stand up for them.'

'Sounds very important work when you put it like that.'

'It is, Jonny, it is.'

'And Pinkerton's Chickens, along with the community of Malton, are doing everything we can to support this very important work, aren't we, Mayor?' added Mr Evans. 'Can I introduce you to the Mayor of Malton, Jonny, who is here along with many of our esteemed councillors to support Pinkerton's Chickens and its Chickens For Charity event?'

The Mayor's chains clanked as he leant forward to shake Jonny's hand and display a well-practised mock royalty face.

'What will this event mean for the town of Malton?' Jonny asked the Mayor.

He smiled through a few seconds of awkward silence before he leant forward to speak.

'We all get to eat some damn fine chicken,' he chortled.

Mr Evans slapped the Mayor on the back and roared with laughter.

'Couldn't have put it better myself,' said Jonny. 'So get yourselves down here to eat some damn fine chicken all in support of . . . tell us again, Michelle?'

'Not On Our Watch,' she repeated. 'Standing up for people who are living a nightmare every day and who have no-one else to stand up for them.'

'How'd it go?' asked Daz, grabbing her as soon as the interview was over. 'Was Jonny like, brilliant?'

'Not really,' she replied. 'He thought we were raising money for chickens. As if we'd do that outside a chicken factory!'

'Really?' exclaimed Daz. 'How do these idiots get brilliant jobs working on the radio? After this I'm going to apply to them again so they can get some real intelligence on the airwaves, rather than the buffoons they seem to have working there.'

'The buffoons are leaving now,' said Jonny, walking up behind Daz.

'Jonny, mate, I didn't mean you,' cried Daz, turning

around, red-faced. 'I meant those idiots down at Malton Radio. Don't know their arse from their elbow most of the time.'

'Well, when you work for the BBC there is a level of professionalism required, of course. Anyway, best of luck with the chickens,' Jonny said, shaking Michelle's hand. 'Loving your work, I really am.'

'Thanks, Jonny,' said Michelle. 'And thanks for coming down. I really appreciate it.'

'Up the chickens,' he said, pumping his fist in the air as he got into the car.

'Fucking clueless,' sighed Daz.

Michelle did one last check around before the gates were due to open at seven o'clock. For once she was massively grateful for her mother's need to interfere in everyone's business. She had single-handedly organised all who were competing in the cook off and Michelle knew she would have left nothing to chance. As she walked over to the line of gazebos, she smiled to herself as she watched Kathleen chastising the rugby team for not having their allocation of paper plates and forks ready at the edge of their table, before getting a comb out of her bag and making one poor guy bend down whilst she tidied his hair.

'It's all in the presentation, you know,' she said as he meekly stood in front of her. 'How on earth will you get people to eat your food with that hideous mess on your head?'

Michelle went over to check with her dad, who was in charge of the Salted Chilli Chicken she'd entered. She'd had a taste and was satisfied that the couple of extra ingredients she'd added had really made the dish special, despite her mum's warnings that she shouldn't do a chilli-based dish.

'It's bloody lovely,' said Ray as he put his arm around his daughter. 'It's all I can do to stop myself eating the whole lot, I can tell you.'

'But your father hates chilli,' said Michelle, mocking her mother's shrill voice.

'One day I will tell her I love chilli,' he sighed. 'It's just her chilli I hate.'

'Didn't I tell her, Ray?' said Kathleen, joining them. 'She'll never win with a chilli dish.'

'I don't want to win, Mum,' sighed Michelle. 'It's my event. It would look terrible if I won.'

'As if you'd ever beat the WI anyway,' Kathleen tutted. 'And as for that ridiculous slop the fat people are serving up – do you realise they are using tins of mushy peas? Tins of mushy peas, I ask you.' She turned to walk away and find fault with some other competitors.

'Have you seen Josie?' asked Michelle, anxious that she should be there to witness what was going on.

'Sean said he might take her fishing,' said Ray, shrugging his shoulders.

Michelle thought she might hit the roof. What was Josie thinking? There was a possibility George Clooney could be arriving any minute and she'd chosen to go fishing with Sean.

'She'll come, love,' said Ray.

'She won't,' she replied, turning around to go before she gave her dad the full force of her frustration, which he didn't deserve. She went to find Little Slaw and his calming influence.

'You all set?' she asked when she found him behind a trestle table setting himself up as chief adjudicator and referee to the proceedings.

'Set, I am indeed,' he said rising from his chair and taking a small bow. 'Although I have to own up to a law-breaking accident.'

'Little Slaw!' exclaimed Michelle, feeling her blood

start to boil again. 'For one night only you are the rule maker here. You can't go breaking the law now.'

'It was only a small law-breaking accident.' He pushed forward a large box. Michelle glanced down and recognised it instantly.

'You stole the suggestion box?'

'I'm afraid so, yes. We needed vote collecting thing,' he grinned.

'Er, where do we buy a ticket?' came a voice from behind them. Michelle turned to see an elderly couple standing behind her.

'Here,' she gasped, pointing wildly at Little Slaw. He did the honours and took their money, explaining where they should go to taste the chicken and how to vote for their favourite. As they wandered through into the warehouse towards the gazebos piled high with chicken, Daz struck up the music and Chickens For Charity was off and running.

For the next two hours Michelle never stopped. First they were running out of forks and she had to find Mr Evans, who was still brown-nosing the Mayor and the councillors, to see if he would let her pilfer the staff canteen for some more. Fortunately she asked him in front of the Mayor, avoiding having her head blown off by the ridiculously inconvenient request. Then she was forced to split up a row that had erupted between the WI and the rugby club. The ladies claimed the boys' tactics, of offering a free kiss to anyone who promised to vote for them, was against the rules. When neither side appeared to want to back down, even when Michelle said that the WI could offer kiss incentives too, she was forced to seek out Rob, who was stoically manning the bar, and ask him if he could have a word with his rugby pals. He returned shortly after, telling her that she needn't worry. The rugby team had agreed to charge for their kisses and donate the money to the charity, which the WI had decided, post a mini committee meeting, was acceptable.

Despite her dashing around putting out fires this way and that, Michelle couldn't help but keep one eye on the gate. She didn't really know who she wanted to see walk in more, Josie or George Clooney. She also wasn't sure which of the two would deem the sight that met them more ridiculous. Josie, who would be incredulous that Michelle would ever think that a higgledy-piggledy group of makeshift gazebos, a disco on the back of a trailer and bowls and bowls of fast congealing, unwanted mushy pea curry would ever lead to her marrying George Clooney. Or George Clooney, who surely would be in shock to meet anyone who could think that mushy pea curry could ever be a force for good. All she could keep thinking was that she had to get rid of the mushy pea curry. George would not be impressed she told herself as she threw bowls and bowls of it into black bin liner bags.

All too soon it was nine o'clock and a small crowd had gathered around her, awaiting her nod to signal they could proceed with the finale of the evening. There was a lively buzz in the air, as Daz's three rules of successful events seemed to have done the trick. Free-flowing beer had put everyone in a jovial mood, Daz's Eighties soundtrack for the evening was going down well with the predominantly forty-something crowd, and the food generally was being well received apart from the mushy pea curry. Michelle was feeling satisfied that abandoned bowls of the gloop had been eradicated but felt her momentary pride fade as Little Slaw, Gina and Daz approached her. She realised the moment had come when they would have to proceed with the event without the two most important guests. Little Slaw coughed expectantly then stepped aside to reveal a bored-looking Josie chewing her fingernails.

'I needed help,' he said. 'I got hold of her and tell her to be here.'

'Oh, thank you, Little Slaw,' gasped Michelle. 'Thank you, Josie. I mean it.'

Josie shrugged.

'Sean's mate rang and said he'd take him fishing up at the reservoir. They cycled, so I couldn't go.'

'Michelle,' said Gina softly, taking her arm. 'Lisa called. George's PA has been in touch. She gave him the invite but George left his hotel at six to go out to dinner in London. Doesn't look like he's coming.'

'Okay,' said Michelle, stunned. She felt like crying. Ridiculous, she knew. It had always been a long shot. 'Six o'clock, you say?' she asked. 'It said on the invite we'd present the cheque at nine o'clock, didn't it?'

Gina nodded.

'Maybe we should wait,' said Michelle, 'just a bit longer, just in case.' She sounded as if she thought it plausible that George would come all the way to Malton for the sake of some chicken. That was because she had to. She'd forced herself to believe he might come because the alternative was too depressing.

There was a pause.

'No,' said Little Slaw finally. 'You finish off now. You do what you said you'd do.'

Michelle couldn't even raise her head.

'No sad face,' said Little Slaw, lifting her chin. 'Time for celebration. Time to enjoy how far you have come.'

Ten minutes later she was standing on the back of the disco trailer along with Little Slaw, in his role as chief adjudicator. Also joining them were Mr Evans, who had been asked to give his opinion on the dishes presented, and the Mayor, who was there to be mute and hand over a trophy to the winners, if he could stand up that long given the amount of free booze Mr Evans had been plying him with. Daz had just played 'The Final Countdown' by Europe at full blast and the rugby team were having a full-on moshing session down the front whilst the rest of the crowd gathered round them. And it was indeed a crowd. Little Slaw reckoned they had counted over 150 voting slips.

'I told you they would come, didn't I?' said Daz, joining her at the front of the stage as they prepared to announce the winners.

'I can't quite believe it,' she replied, feeling a bit

stunned as it slowly started to dawn on her that Chickens For Charity might have been a success. 'I never thought we'd get this many people.'

'Michelle,' said Daz, 'I have lived in Malton all my life. There is nothing that gets this town going more than a dose of healthy competition. But you made this happen, remember that. This is all down to you.'

She surveyed the throng of people gathering eagerly around the makeshift stage as the music died away. She watched as an overexcited rugby player thrust a bowl of cold mushy pea curry in his mate's face. Yep, this had really all gone to plan. She would never, ever touch mushy peas again and she wasn't going to marry George Clooney. Well done, Michelle.

'Ladies and gentlemen, boys and girls, welcome to CHICKENS FOR CHARITY,' bellowed Daz into his microphone, as if he was on stage at Wembley.

'Let me introduce you to Walter Evans, the General Manager of this fine establishment and the chief sponsor of Chickens For Charity. He will give you his summary of tonight's chicken dishes before the Mayor presents the trophy to the Chickens For Charity Champion Chefs.'

'Thank you, everyone,' said Mr Evans, accepting the

microphone. A few boos could be heard from some of the slightly merry workers who had come along to support Michelle.

'When Michelle and I hatched this plan to figure out how this factory could save lives, along with rest of the wonderful community of Malton, we had no idea this would be the kind of fantastic support we'd get. And I'm very happy that the Mayor and the members of the council are here to share the success of this community event with us.'

'Get on with it!' someone heckled from the back amid deafening silence.

'And boy, chicken has never tasted as good as it has here tonight,' he hollered and was rewarded with enormous cheers from the chefs awaiting the results.

'I have personally tasted all the dishes and whilst I have no idea which team has won the vote I would just like to say to the rugby club . . .' Mr Evans's words were drowned out as the rugby club went bonkers. 'The rugby club can certainly handle their breasts better than their balls.' The lads went bonkers again as if they had already been announced the winners. 'And as for the Women's Institute . . .' The ladies smiled smugly at each other. 'The ladies of the Women's Institute have shown me more leg than I ever thought possible.' Their smug smiles slipped slightly.

'Slimmers United . . . A for effort, and I thank you for highlighting the health benefits of eating chicken, though I'm not sure my wife will think there is much benefit to the amount of mushy peas I have consumed this evening.' Classy trumping noises all round from the rugby club.

'And Michelle, see me later for the recipe for your chilli chicken. Just tremendous, truly tremendous. Almost as good as the chicken-in-a-basket. Just could have done with a good dollop of ketchup.'

'He has no class, does he?' muttered Daz to Michelle. 'Does he not know that you have a scrape of sauce these days, not a dollop?'

'So without further ado, I believe someone has the results of the public vote and the Mayor here can award the prize.'

Little Slaw stepped forward to hand an envelope to the Mayor, before dipping a small bow and moving back behind everyone.

There was a painful moment as the Mayor fumbled with the envelope and took out a card before proceeding to squint at it then lean over to Mr Evans to whisper in his ear that he didn't have his glasses.

'For fuck's sake,' muttered Mr Evans, forgetting that he was still holding the microphone and everyone could hear him, 'it says the Women's Institute, you fool.'

'Utter fiasco!' cried Daz, seizing the microphone from Mr Evans as squeals were heard from the older ladies in the crowd, delighted to hear they had won, however the news had arrived.

'Let's hear it for the fantastic ladies of the Women's Institute and their stupendous Supreme of Chicken,' cried Daz, strutting up and down the front of the trailer. 'Come on, ladies, let's get you all up here and present to you the first ever Chickens For Charity Champion Chefs trophy. Come on, boys, let's give them a leg up.'

The rugby lads didn't need asking twice, too drunk by now to care whether they'd won or not. They all grabbed a grannie in a fireman's lift and plonked the poor old dears on the back of the truck.

All Michelle could think was that she was relieved her mum's team had won. Perhaps there was a chance that Kathleen at least would see the night as a successful one.

'Told you, you shouldn't have done chilli,' was all she could say to Michelle, as she brushed past to accept the trophy.

'And to close proceedings for tonight, I'd like to hand over to the founder of Chickens For Charity who would like to thank you personally for all the money you have raised this evening.'

Michelle took one last desperate look at the gate, hoping that somehow George Clooney might emerge out of a cloud of mist. She had no idea how much they had raised, but there, on hand as ever, was Little Slaw holding an enormous cheque that they had had pre-printed just in case George arrived to collect it personally. She couldn't believe her eyes at the number that appeared in the box. Little Slaw had counted up wrong, surely.

'Thank you,' was all she could muster, looking bewildered at Little Slaw. He gestured to the crowd waiting expectantly. 'Thank you so much,' she said, turning to face the onlookers. 'This is amazing. I can't believe what started out really as a stupid idea has actually raised this much money for George Clooney . . . I mean, George Clooney's fantastic charity, Not On Our Watch.' She was having trouble scraping her chin up from the floor. 'I never expected in my wildest dreams that this would happen. It's amazing. You're all amazing. Thank you so much to everyone who has worked so hard to make this event a success. Including you, Marianne.'

Marianne was on stage now, waving enthusiastically at Michelle. 'Oh, and I have to thank Daz and Gina and Little Slaw,' she said. 'Everyone needs friends like them.'

At that moment, she spotted Josie at the back of the crowd with Ray, who was beaming, clearly massively proud of his daughter. Josie was staring around her at the crowd and occasionally glancing up as if to check her mother was still there. Despite instigating this entire thing in a stupid effort to marry George Clooney, Michelle had in fact achieved something that even Josie had to have some grudging respect for. As Michelle gazed over to her, Josie raised her hand slightly in acknowledgement.

'Thank you so much, everyone.' Suddenly Michelle felt exhausted. 'I will make sure that this money gets into the right hands . . . somehow.'

Chapter Eighteen

She was vaguely aware they were pulling off at a junction now. What time must it be? Three, four in the morning? She was tired beyond belief but sleep refused to rescue her. The night's events were still churning around in her brain and the enormous cheque behind her in the back of the truck kept stabbing her in the back of the head, prompting her into thinking about stuff when all she wanted to do was not think. She glanced across at Daz. He was staring straight ahead into the night, a serious look on his face as he concentrated on driving. Somewhere from behind her came Gina's light snoring. Oh, how she wished she were Gina.

*

A few hours previously, Michelle had leapt off the back of the trailer, enormous cheque in hand, totally full of herself. For now the disappointment that George hadn't shown up was drowned out by her euphoria. The event had been a fantastic success. It had been the hardest thing she had ever done but they'd actually raised a shedload of money. It was utterly unbelievable and she was bursting with pride. She couldn't remember the last time she'd felt proud. She liked it. A lot. She needed it, especially when faced with a drunken rugby player who had just thrown up mushy pea curry everywhere.

She buzzed around coordinating the mass clear-up operation as Daz banged out some tunes providing the perfect soundtrack to her uplifted mood. 'We Built this City on Rock and Roll', always the perfect tidy-up song, had her humming as she swept debris across the truck park. Plastic glasses crackled and bounced in front of her broom as she cleared up around the extremely untidy makeshift bar which had been manned by Rob all night. Good to his word, Rob had dragged himself out of his maudlin mood to come and help out. Now he was also bouncing off anything that happened to be in his way as he unsteadily picked up leftover crates of beer and ambled across to put them in the back of his car.

'You okay, Rob?' she asked as he stumbled, the beer landing in the boot more by luck than judgement.

'Marvellous!' he exclaimed, throwing his arms around her and engulfing her in a bear-hug.

'It's been marvellous.' He stood back and held her shoulders, swaying slightly. 'You've been marvellous,' he continued, grinning from ear to ear. Michelle was glad to see the return of the dimples.

'That's great, Rob,' she said. 'Do you think you should sit down?'

'Nooo. Need to finish the job, get cleared up. Can't let you do all this.'

'It's okay, seriously, Rob. Mum and Dad are still here. We'll finish off. You've done enough already. I'm so grateful, I really am.'

He didn't reply, just stared at her, an odd look on his face. He'd stopped swaying. She should have known then. She'd seen that look on his face once before, about sixteen years ago.

'Let me kiss you,' he said suddenly.

She took a step back in shock.

'No!'

'Please,' he pleaded, screwing his face up.

Michelle looked around her, concerned someone might be watching, though a stack of pallets hid them for now.

'It would be wrong,' she said slowly.

'But why?' he asked, suddenly standing up straight as though totally sober.

'Because . . .' she continued, 'you're Jane's.'

He looked as though she'd slapped him in the face. He reeled back then steadied himself. He was Jane's and always would be, despite the fact she was dead. She knew, had he not been Jane's, they could have perhaps stood a chance. He would have just been Rob then. Nice Rob, helpful Rob, actually very lovely Rob – in fact, if she met someone who was exactly like Rob without being Rob, she would have been doing cartwheels now. But he was Jane's Rob. And there was nothing she could do about that.

She watched him crumple in front of her eyes. First his mouth went and then his shoulders, before he drew his hands up to hide his collapsing face. The first sob wrenched Michelle's heart yet again as she watched him fall apart for the second time since he had reappeared in her life.

She moved to put her arm around him, feeling his body thud against hers as he succumbed to his sorrow.

She held him until he regained some control with an almighty sniff, raising his head to take a deep, calming breath.

'I'm sorry,' he said, wiping his nose with his sleeve. 'I'm so, so sorry.'

'You don't have to be sorry.'

'It's just . . . it's just . . .'

Oh God, thought Michelle. A sentence following a hesitant 'it's just' was usually pretty monumental.

'It's just, I cannot tell you how amazing it's been to be back with you and your family. Your mum . . . your mum . . .'

Is a right cantankerous old bag sometimes, crossed Michelle's mind.

'Your mum has looked after me like a son since I got back.'

'That's because she loves you. Jane loved you and so does she. She sees you as the son-in-law she never had.'

'Amy's parents didn't like me,' he said, taking another large sniff.

'I can't believe that.'

'They did. I wasn't Jewish. They wanted her to marry

a nice Jewish boy. I was never good enough for them.' He looked up, staring into the distance. 'Bit like my own parents, really. Not good enough for them either.'

'Well, you won't get any of that with Kathleen. She really does think the sun shines out of your arse.'

Rob managed a small smile.

'Sorry I tried to kiss you.'

'Forget about it.' She looked away quickly, hoping she hadn't reminded him of the last time she'd told him to 'forget about it'.

'And sorry about the other night. I didn't mean to pour all that out to you. It's just . . .'

Here we go again, thought Michelle.

'I know I ran away and everything. Left you all to go back to your old lives without Jane whilst I buggered off and found a new one. Well, I've realised how much I've missed you all, and being part of the Hidderley clan. I never expected it to feel this way, but coming back and being around you and your mum and dad, and even Josie, just makes me feel like I've come home. Back to where I belong . . . to family, even though of course we're not family.'

He looked so sad she couldn't bear it. She should tell him now. He was family; he was the father of her child and therefore tied into the Hidderley clan in a way he had no idea about.

'And it really has been so good to see you again, Michelle,' he continued. 'I've missed you.' He caught his breath, as if surprised by what he'd said. 'Really missed you.'

They stared at each other. Michelle's mind cracked and splintered like one of the plastic glasses discarded on the floor. Her thoughts shot off in all directions as she struggled to gain any kind of control over them. What did he mean by that? So he'd tried to kiss her, but that was alcohol. This was words. Words required the engagement of brain. Why did he have to say that, just at the point she needed to tell him something that was guaranteed to make him hate her? And why was he looking at her like that? And why on earth couldn't she just tell him that he was the father of her daughter?

She only became aware that Rob had reached forward and taken her hand when he dropped it like a stone as Daz and Gina ambushed them.

'Michelle, Michelle!' Gina shouted.

'Brilliant idea, brilliant idea, brilliant idea!' they both chanted, jumping up and down like crazed teenagers.

'What?' she cried. 'Stop jumping, you're making me feel sick.'

'We're going to go and meet George Clooney *now*!' cried Gina, twirling round and round on the spot.

'*What?* How come?'

'I thought of it!' exclaimed Daz, raising his hand.

'Yeah, but my Cousin Jack's colleague's neighbour's son's girlfriend made it possible!' shrieked Gina.

'Yeah, but it's ideas that matter.'

'They don't matter if you have no way of making them happen.'

'You can always find a way,' Daz shouted, right in Gina's face.

'Guys, just tell me what the hell you're talking about,' said Michelle, glancing furtively at Rob, who had taken several steps back from the two crazy people who'd interrupted them.

'So,' Gina began. 'Daz said now we have the cheque we should just take it to George. So I texted Lisa and she found out where he's staying.'

Daz took up the story. 'So I said we should drive down there right now and take him the cheque. If we turn up at the hotel with that baby there is no way he's not getting his arse out of bed to come down and take it off us.'

'We can't get George Clooney out of bed in the middle of the night, you idiot,' said Gina, bopping Daz on the head. 'No, we drive down now, find somewhere to park and have a kip and then make sure we're in reception from the crack of dawn, ready to pounce as soon as he gets up.'

'We're going to meet George Clooney, we're going to meet George Clooney, we're going to meet George Clooney!' Daz and Gina started to chant, jumping up and down again.

'You go,' Rob said quietly. 'I'll finish tidying up and make sure your mum, dad and Josie get home safe. You go and find George Clooney. Go on.'

'Will you be alright?' she asked.

'Of course. I can't compete with George Clooney, can I, eh?' he said, his faint smile not in any way hiding the look of despair in his eyes.

Chapter Nineteen

Michelle, Daz and Gina made an odd sight standing outside the Ballentine Hotel on the edge of Regent's Park, slightly bedraggled, with a five-foot-high cheque propped up against a lamp post next to them. They gazed upward at the grand building slowly emerging from the darkness as the sun rose over London, with only one thought on their minds.

'To think,' breathed Gina. 'He's in there somewhere.'

Michelle's stomach was churning, which could either be caused by the proximity of the man himself or the sausage and egg McMuffin she'd just stuffed down her in the McDonald's in the next street. They'd sat chewing in silence, all still shattered from an uncomfortable few hours of sleep in the van, parked down a back street. Michelle and Gina were also slightly in shock that whilst their back was turned, Daz had taken Chaz (as they'd named the cheque, for ease and familiarity's sake) into the men's toilet with him. The thought of Chaz being handed over to George after recently being in the proximity of a urinal was not a happy one.

'Mint, anyone?' Daz offered.

'Cheers,' they both said, agreeing that they couldn't remember the last time they'd had a Polo.

'Shall we go in then?' asked Daz, after an acceptable length of time had been spent on sucking on their mints. They were all eyeing up the smartly dressed doorman and wondering if he might be a problem.

'Should we split up?' asked Michelle, thinking it might allow the scruffy trio to slip past unnoticed.

'No, just follow me,' Daz said airily. 'The best way to gain access to somewhere you shouldn't be is to pretend it's exactly where you should be. Trust me.'

He grabbed Chaz and ran as quickly as he could past the doorman and into the jaws of the revolving doors where, due to the size of Chaz, they promptly got wedged in and were imprisoned, unable to move backwards or forwards.

'Help!' Daz shouted. 'I'm stuck in here with Chaz.'

'For fuck's sake,' sighed Gina, shaking her head. 'Talk about making a show of us.' She strode forward and tapped the doorman on the shoulder, offering him a huge grin.

'My friend is a fuckwit and appears to have trapped himself in the revolving door along with a charity cheque we are delivering this morning. Please could you get him out?'

'Of course, madam,' said the doorman with a small bow. He turned and gave the door a well-practised shove and Daz was propelled forward into reception, landing on his knees on top of Chaz.

'Mortified,' muttered Gina, sailing through the disabled door to the side of the revolving door as if she were visiting royalty.

The trio regrouped and contemplated the enormous double-height reception area decked out with the most tasteful Christmas decorations they had ever seen. There was no sign of mismatched, multi-coloured baubles, bedraggled tinsel or unevenly placed fairy lights. The festive look was precise, uniform, exclusively white and painfully elegant.

Feeling more out of place than she ever had, Michelle eyed the bank of white suede sofas. 'Dare we sit on one of those and wait until he comes down?' she asked.

'No way,' said Daz. 'We've not come all this way to sit and wait and probably miss him. We are going to reception to announce our existence and explain why we're here on this very important mission.'

'No,' said Michelle firmly. 'They might think we're some weirdo fans or something and chuck us out. Much better if we just sit here, and if anyone asks, say we're waiting for someone, which is absolutely true.' She stepped forward to take Chaz from Daz and get him settled on a sofa.

Daz wasn't going to let go of Chaz that easily.

'But what happens if he leaves by a back entrance or something?' He pulled the cheque out of Michelle's reach. 'They do that, you know, to avoid being seen.'

'Exactly,' said Michelle. 'George wants to avoid being seen. We go shouting from the rooftops that we're here to see George Clooney and we'll be chucked out straight away.' She reached out and grabbed at Chaz, finally managing to secure it.

'Can I help at all?' came a chirpy voice as a young receptionist in a suit and a name badge came up behind them.

They all turned around, dumbstruck, until Daz spoke.

'We're here to see George Clooney,' he said confidently.

'I see. Is he expecting you?'

'Yes,' said Daz.

'No,' muttered Michelle. 'But we've brought money.' She pulled Chaz around to show the girl. 'Look, lots of money for his charity, Not On Our Watch,' she said, wildly pointing at the name on the cheque. 'It's for a very good cause,' she added as the girl looked perplexed.

'But he's not aware of you?'

'No, he's not aware of me,' Michelle admitted.

'But he bloody should be,' cut in Daz. 'This woman has devoted her life to his cause for the last few months. Her life, I tell you.'

'George would want to meet her,' added Gina. 'Really, she's such a lovely person. He'd like her, I know he would.'

'We refuse to hand this money over unless you get George Clooney down here,' Daz declared, stamping his foot.

By now, the girl had taken a step back as Daz and Gina advanced on her. A look of panic had started to emerge on her face as she clearly marked them as crazed stalkers.

Michelle stepped towards her and saw her flinch. 'Last night we raised all this money for George's charity and then we drove through the night to get down here so we could give it to him in person. That's all we want. To be able to hand over some charity money. That's all, *really*.'

The receptionist looked them up and down, assessing the credibility of their case. Michelle was glad she'd scraped the smudged mascara from under her eyes with McDonald's loo paper.

'I'll need to speak to my manager,' the receptionist said, before leaping away in escape.

'See,' said Michelle, turning on Daz. 'There's no way we'll get to see him now. The manager's going to come down here and chuck us out.'

'You don't know that,' said Daz. 'Going to get the manager is a good sign, believe me. Get some seniority on the case.'

They all turned at the sound of staccato tapping heels chasing the determined thud of leather soles across marble as the receptionist struggled to keep up with a swarthy-looking man in his fifties.

We're doomed, thought Michelle.

'Ladies and gentlemen,' said the man in perfect English but with an Eastern European accent. 'I am so sorry, but George Clooney is no longer staying here. He checked out half an hour ago.'

'Liar!' shrieked Daz, throwing Chaz on the floor.

'Please, sir, I promise you,' said the man very coolly. 'He left early to catch a private plane to his home in Italy.'

Michelle slumped on a white sofa. So near and yet so far. It was all over. She'd failed.

Chapter Twenty

'Epic fail,' sighed Gina, chewing on her third bacon and egg McMuffin that morning. They had been back in McDonald's for what felt like hours, eking out food that could be eaten in nanoseconds because they just wanted to be warm and not face the prospect of the journey home and life without George Clooney.

Daz was nowhere to be seen, having disappeared once again into the loos with Chaz. Michelle and Gina didn't care any more.

'How can I ever face Josie?' moaned Michelle. 'Before all this she thought I was a failure and now I'll have to admit to her that I am. And she's going to shag Sean.'

'I can't believe we were so close,' said Gina for the millionth time. She hoovered the dregs of her chocolate milkshake up her straw, part of her third breakfast. Michelle had told her they were really fattening, but Gina had clarified that she didn't follow the Slimmers United regime whilst outside her home county. 'If only we hadn't come here for a McD's we might have actually met George Clooney,' she said.

'Mmmm,' sighed Michelle, barely listening now. All she could think about was the cock-up she'd made of things. She'd chased a ridiculous dream to prove a point and now she looked like a failure.

Eventually Daz emerged from the men's room, Chaz under his arm, staring at his mobile phone. He sat down next to Michelle without raising his eyes and without taking his protective hands off Chaz. They sat in silence until finally Daz stood up again.

'Okey-dokey,' he said. 'If we can't get to meet George then we'll have to go for the next best thing.'

'Brad Pitt?' said Gina excitedly. 'Matt Damon? Is he here?' she asked, looking around wildly as if Matt would be having breakfast at McDonald's just off Baker Street.

'No,' said Daz. 'Don't be ridiculous. Follow me,

ladies. We're going to pay a little visit whilst we're in London.'

Daz and Chaz led the way down a windy Baker Street. Every so often Chaz got swept away in the excitement and flung himself in the air as a gust grabbed hold of him. As they got to the junction with the A40 and crossed the road, Daz's intentions started to dawn on Michelle, although Gina was still none the wiser.

'Oh my God!' squealed Gina. 'I have wanted to go here all my life. My mum would never bring me because she didn't agree with them using real skin.'

'They don't use real skin, Gina,' said Michelle, gazing up at the enormous building housing the iconic Madame Tussauds attraction.

'Oh they do,' said Gina. 'Mum watched a documentary and she said they take a patch from under your foot and then grow skin from it so they can cover the whole body. Mum said it was a disgrace.'

'How old were you when your mum told you this?' asked Michelle.

'Maybe seven.'

'I think your mum just didn't want to bring you.'

'No, it's true, really.'

'Well, let's go in and find out, shall we?' Michelle gave Daz a little smile, grateful he'd thought of a way of cheering them all up a bit.

Half an hour later, after establishing that no real skin was used in the process of creating the frighteningly lifelike wax models, Michelle was lounging on a sofa next to George Clooney with Chaz between them, whilst Daz took photos.

'Tell you what, 'Chelle,' said Gina. 'You've got great taste in men. Up close he's fucking gorgeous.'

Michelle smiled and leant over to touch George's hand. 'It's so lovely to meet you at last,' she said as Daz leapt around in true paparazzi style, catching every moment of the encounter.

'He looks really grateful, actually,' said Daz, pausing to check how his photos were coming out. 'Grateful and bloody photogenic. If he wasn't such a nice guy I could seriously hate him.'

'Bit quiet, though,' said Gina, leaning in close to study his face. 'Look, he's actually got a few freckles,' she said, prodding his cheek gently. 'So cute.'

A party of Japanese tourists arrived and bustled around them as though they were all connected within an elastic band. Camera flashes filled the air along with a flurry of Japanese exclamations, punctuated by the occasional 'George', as they confirmed to each other who was in their presence. Michelle felt embarrassed to be monopolising the seat next to Mr Clooney and got up, to be replaced immediately by three middle-aged women who squirmed and giggled as George looked on stoically.

'We could show this picture to Josie,' said Daz, handing over his camera so Michelle could see the image of her giving the cheque to George Clooney. 'She'd never guess we were in Madame Tussauds.'

Michelle studied the shot. It appeared authentic. George looked as perfect as he always did. Could this help her save face? Could she present this to her daughter as mission accomplished? She looked around the room, designed to make you feel as though you were attending a Hollywood A-lister party. It was full of every famous person you'd ever wish to meet. Well, maybe not Geri Halliwell. But still, everyone was so real it was amazing, and yet it was all totally fake. A fabrication. A complete lie.

'I can't lie to her,' she said, giving the camera back to Daz. 'Not any more.'

*

Michelle sat with Chaz in the back of the disco van on the long drive back from London to Malton. She was vaguely aware of Gina and Daz gabbling away in the front and occasionally bursting into song when a big tune came up on the radio. It crossed her mind at one point that her two best friends were lunatics – both slightly deranged in their own way – and she realised she loved them both massively for it. If there were one good thing to come out of the whole George Clooney business, it was that she and Daz had found a friendship and understanding that she was sure would last a lifetime. Of course, Chaz was also a great thing, she thought as she glanced over to him protectively, looking somewhat battered by his adventure down to the big smoke. Now that her pursuit of George Clooney seemed to be over, she could look back over the mayhem of the last few weeks and realise that those numbers on Chaz the cheque were a pretty amazing result. Yes, maybe her motives had been off when she began. Raising money for charity in order to get close to a celebrity was hardly something to be proud of. But whatever, it had motivated her to achieve something to be proud of. Something she hadn't felt since before she'd realised she was pregnant with her sister's boyfriend's baby.

What was it that Little Slaw had said after Gina's wedding?

'You must get out of your own way.'

Perhaps if she'd faced up to who Josie's father was at the outset, the last fifteen years might have been very different. Now she might be looking at a woman who had made a mistake, faced up to it and moved on. All she'd ever done was back off. All she'd ever shown Josie was how to avoid the difficult stuff until it paralysed you into a corner you couldn't get out of. That's why she'd gone on this ridiculous journey to marry George Clooney. It was a desperate attempt to get out of her corner.

As they passed the Watford Gap service station she realised she couldn't go back to that corner. It was time to show Josie how to deal with the challenges that life threw at you and not let them get in the way of doing what you needed to do.

'Daz,' she said, leaning forward.

'Hang on,' he said, putting his finger to his lips.

The song playing on the radio came to an end, then he spoke again.

'Shed Seven,' he said, shaking his head. 'Seriously one of the best bands of all time and yet woefully undervalued.

"Chasing Rainbows" gets me here every time.' He pounded his heart with his fist.

'Speaking of chasing rainbows,' said Michelle. 'Who fancies a road trip to Italy?'

'Are you serious?' cried Daz.

'Absolutely,' she replied. 'We are finishing this mission off if it kills me.'

'Get in,' said Daz, punching the air.

'Woo-hoo!' screamed Gina.

'Back up north, driver,' Michelle ordered Daz. 'We're collecting Josie, then Italy here we come.'

Chapter Twenty-One

'Beetroot sandwiches.'

'Are you serious?'

'What's wrong with beetroot sandwiches?'

'Everything.'

Kathleen stood defiantly in front of Michelle, Tupperware in hand.

'They may not have beetroot in Italy,' she said, grabbing Michelle's hand and putting the box firmly in it.

'And your point is?'

Kathleen simply tutted.

'Mum, thank you,' said Michelle sincerely. 'Thanks

for reminding me that Italy maybe a beetroot-free zone so I must get my quota of beetroot sandwiches in before we cross the border.'

'You'll be grateful when you're waiting for that ferry, hungry and in need of a beetroot sandwich.'

'Mum, I can assure you I will never be in need of a beetroot sandwich.'

'Did someone say beetroot sandwich?' said Josie, emerging from the house with an enormous suitcase. 'Cheers, Granny, my favourite.' She took the box from Michelle and tucked it under her arm.

'Bloody hell, Josie,' said Daz, appearing from behind the disco van and eying Josie's luggage. 'We're going on a road trip to Italy, not Marbella for a week.'

Personally Michelle had never been so pleased to see a large suitcase in her life. Having decided that she wasn't giving up on George Clooney just yet, she hadn't been sure how to break the news to Josie that she was pursuing him across Europe.

'For crying out loud, Mum, will you stop acting like such a loser!' Josie had said, throwing her arms up in the air in disgust. 'You lost the bet, get over it. You lost, I won.'

'Not yet, you haven't. I told you I was going to ask

George Clooney to marry me and I will. I'm going to finish this.'

Josie stared back at her blankly as if she was speaking some foreign language.

'Now get up those stairs and start packing a bag. You're coming with me. Chop-chop, we're getting the Eurotunnel tonight.'

Josie stared at her mum, open-mouthed.

'Come on,' urged Michelle.

'But . . . but . . . what about school?'

'This is life experience, Josie. I'll sort it with school, and anyway, we won't be gone long. Let me worry about that. You can bring your books with you and study on the road.'

Josie's chin was still on the floor as she desperately tried to process what her mother was saying into something bad that she could have a go at her about.

'Italy?' she mouthed eventually.

'Yes, Italy,' said Michelle. 'We're taking Chaz to meet George Clooney in Italy, come what may.'

The negative side to this trip was clearly eluding Josie, who didn't know how to arrange her face: excited or horrified? Suddenly her eyes lit up.

'Can Sean come?' she asked.

'No!' cried Michelle, causing Josie to fold her arms instantly in a sulky pose. She'd found the chink in the plan.

'You are coming so we can spend some time together, not so you and Sean can spend time together.'

Josie's stance remained firm.

'Okay,' said Michelle. 'You decide. Sean or Italy. It's up to you. But if you want to go to Italy you'd better get up those stairs and start packing now.' Michelle turned and stalked into the kitchen, then paused just inside the door, holding her breath. A few seconds later she heard the soft thud of Josie going upstairs and then the sounds of pacing above her head, punctuated by drawers and cupboards being opened and closed. Italy one, Sean nil, thought Michelle, with a smile on her face.

Finally they were all packed up and ready to go, apart from Daz, who was messing about on his iPad to make sure that they had the perfect soundtrack to accompany their road trip.

'Music, you see,' he was telling Josie, 'is absolutely essential to any successful trip. When you look back on this key journey with me and your mother in ten, maybe even twenty years' time, you'll remember the soundtrack, believe you me, and you'll listen to it and a whole host of memories will come flooding back.'

'You'd better be putting some Rihanna on that,' was her input.

'You listen to Rihanna all the time, right?'

'Yes.'

'Which is exactly why there will be no Rihanna whilst we travel through Europe. As a responsible member of the music profession I am honour bound to broaden your musical horizons. Now, as we're on our way to meet a movie star, I thought it only appropriate that the soundtrack to our trip will be . . . soundtracks. Classic movie soundtracks of our time. Get a load of this one.' 'Danger Zone' by Kenny Loggins boomed out of the disco van, nearly causing Kathleen to fall over.

'Never heard of it,' shrugged Josie.

'*Top Gun*, of course.'

'Never heard of it.'

'Okay, I'll try you with another Kenny Loggins track. You must know this one.'

'Footloose' belted out of the van speakers.

'Acceptable,' Josie conceded. 'The original, not the remake.'

'A woman after my own heart,' replied Daz. 'And finally a personal favourite.'

The theme tune to *Star Wars* woke up the rest of the street, who might have been having a quiet nap after Sunday lunch.

'Turn that racket down, Daz!' shrieked Kathleen. 'What will the neighbours say?'

'Sorry, Mrs H.' Daz flicked to a more appropriate Harry Connick Jr classic from *When Harry Met Sally*.

'Sean!' Josie suddenly cried, leaping off the seat next to Daz and dashing to fling her arms around him.

'I thought you weren't coming,' she said after she'd squeezed the life out of him. 'I won't go, you know, if you don't want me to.'

Michelle, who was just checking the Eurotunnel ticket with Daz, took a sharp intake of breath and moved to interject. Daz caught her arm, shaking his head silently.

'S'alright,' Sean shrugged. 'I'm going to be fishing all the time anyway.'

'Oh, thank you,' she said, flinging her arms around him again. 'I'll miss you so much, and I'll text you all the time.'

'No reception where I fish,' he said with another shrug.

'You'll wait and wave me off, won't you?' she asked.

Yet another shrug followed by a 'S'pose.'

'So, let's go, shall we?' said Michelle, keen to prevent any last-minute changes of heart. 'In you get, Josie.'

'Wait!' came a shout from across the road. 'Hold on a minute. You got to take this.' Gina was crossing the street swinging a box with a handle.

'I've just been on YouTube and George loves wine, apparently. I didn't have any bottles in but I had most of a box left in the fridge.'

Michelle stared at the box of wine now in her hands and wondered whether George Clooney even knew you could get wine in a box, never mind actually drank the stuff.

'Thanks, Gina,' she said, giving her a hug. Michelle wished she was coming with them, but unfortunately Gina had used up all her holidays to go on honeymoon. Michelle had left a lengthy message on Marianne's answerphone at the factory explaining her reasons for taking holiday at such short notice and promising her George's autograph. She hoped that would be enough to convince Marianne to square it with the HR department on her behalf.

'So, do you know where you're going?' Gina asked Daz, who was looking at a road map upside down.

'Well, we know the town and we figured we'd ask when we get there,' said Michelle. 'If we show them Chaz I'm sure someone will tell us how to find his villa.'

'What's going on?' said a voice behind them. Michelle froze. They were never going to get to Italy at this rate.

'Oh, Rob love!' cried Kathleen. 'Ray, look, it's Rob. How lovely to see you. You will stay for a meal, won't you?'

'Thanks, but I don't really have time today.'

'Cup of tea then? You come inside. There's some apple pie left over from lunch. Growing boy like you needs to eat pie.'

'What about me, Mrs H? I'm still a growing lad, you know,' said Daz. 'A bit of your apple pie would go down a treat to send me on my way.'

'You're growing the wrong way, Daz. Out and not up,' said Kathleen, turning her beam back towards Rob.

'Well, actually I just popped by hoping I could have a quick word with Michelle?' he said.

Michelle looked to the sky for strength. This wasn't the plan. Rob right now would only throw confusion all over her mission, she just knew it.

'Actually we're just leaving for Italy,' Daz declared proudly.

'Really?' exclaimed Rob.

'Really,' Daz nodded. 'We narrowly missed George in London but we'll get him in Italy, won't we, Michelle?' He put a protective arm around her shoulders.

'I see,' said Rob. 'It won't take a minute,' he continued pleadingly to Michelle. 'Honestly. It's about the other night.'

She looked at her watch. She was desperate to escape in case Rob threw her some kind of curve ball, but he looked so desperate. 'Well, I've probably got ten minutes,' she said. 'Let's go inside, shall we?' She was sure whatever he had to say wasn't for sharing.

He followed her into the sitting room and sat down on the sofa. They both hesitated for a moment. The last time they had been in that room together had been the day Jane was killed.

'A lot's happened since the last time we sat in this room,' Rob announced

Michelle nodded wordlessly.

'I just wanted to apologise,' he said. 'For the other night.'

Michelle nodded again.

'It was unfair of me,' he said, looking away, unable to hold her gaze. 'I shouldn't have put you in that position.'

Silence hung between them. The sound drifted in from outside of Ray trying to tell Daz what route he should take to get to the Eurotunnel, despite the fact he had never been there himself.

'You're right, of course,' Rob continued. 'Jane will always be between us. Always was between us.' He looked up, quickly searching her face, her eyes.

'Even when we . . . when we . . .'

'Don't!' Michelle cried out.

'But we did once . . .' He trailed off.

Please don't say it, thought Michelle.

'I guess I thought it might have meant something to you. Maybe?'

He was staring at her so intensely that she thought he must be able to see right inside her to the truth. That all she wanted at this very moment was for him to put his arms around her and tell her everything was going to be alright. That he had come back to rescue her and Josie from this lie of a life they were living. She looked away unable to bear the caring look on his face that hadn't yet been tainted by what she had done to him. She must focus. She was going to Italy to tell Josie first who her father was. She owed her that. Then she would face up to Rob.

'I clearly put you in a terrible position,' Rob continued. 'So I just wanted you to know that there's no chance of me doing it again.' He shook his head. 'Whenever I get mixed up in your family it always seems to end in tears, literally. So I'm going to request a transfer. We're just opening a brewery in Singapore. You won't have to see me ever again, I promise.'

Michelle gasped. The Hidderleys had forced him into fleeing for his life for a second time. It was like déjà vu in that ten by eleven foot room, only with different wallpaper and a large framed photo of Josie competing for space with Jane's graduation picture on the mantelpiece.

'You can't go,' she whispered, shaking her head in despair.

'But I thought you'd be pleased,' said Rob. 'I thought it would be what you wanted.'

She got up from her chair to sit next to him. Taking his hands in hers, she looked into his bewildered eyes.

'You can't go because you *are* family,' she said.

'Oh Michelle, I know I came out with all that stuff

the other night, but there's no place for me in your family. Not any more.'

'I need you to listen to me,' she said as calmly as she could, holding his gaze. 'There's something I need to tell you about the time when Jane was killed, and I need you to promise me that after I've told you you'll listen to why I didn't tell you then.'

He looked at her, confused.

'It's going to be really difficult to understand, so I need you to listen really carefully, okay?'

'Okay,' he said slowly.

Michelle's heart was trying to beat its way out of her chest, but she knew the truth had to come out now. She couldn't let him leave without knowing. But she still didn't know how to put it into words, and she was petrified of what life might look like after those words had been spoken.

'What is it?' prompted Rob, a deep furrow across his brow making him look old and slightly intimidating.

Here goes. Michelle took a deep breath.

'So . . . so,' she began. Spit it out, she thought to herself.

'You obviously remember that night when we . . . you know, in the park after the pub when we . . .'

'Yeah,' urged Rob, nodding vigorously.

'Well, the thing is . . .' Oh my God! a voice screamed inside Michelle's head. I'm not sure I can do this.

'Just tell me,' said Rob kindly. 'It can't be that bad, surely.'

Oh yes it can, thought Michelle.

'Well, you see, not long after that I found out I was pregnant.'

Rob's brow furrowed more deeply.

'What are you saying, Michelle?'

'I'm saying I found out I was pregnant, and I was going to tell you, I really was . . . and Jane. The day Jane was killed I was on my way to meet her to tell her, but she didn't turn up, Rob. She didn't turn up because she was dead. I was about to destroy her life but she was already dead. Then I came home and you were here, and I should have told you, I know, but Jane was dead. How could I tell you? Don't you see I couldn't tell you?'

Rob pulled his hands out of Michelle's desperate clutch and leant very slowly back on the sofa. His head flopped back on an antimacassar and he gazed up to the ceiling.

'And I was relieved,' Michelle went on, the words suddenly desperate to get out to try and make him understand. 'Relieved that my sister was dead. Can you imagine? For a split second all I could think was that I was relieved that I didn't have to tell her that I was pregnant with your child.' She stopped abruptly and pushed her fingers into her eye sockets in an attempt to block out Rob's reaction.

She heard him take a sharp intake of breath and the next thing she knew he was pulling her hands away from her eyes so she could see his sheet-white face.

'You were pregnant with *my* child?'

'Yes, I was pregnant with your child.'

His eyes bored into her, roving all over her face as if looking for something. When he didn't find it he pulled away again, raking his hands through his hair.

'I don't get it,' he said, shaking his head.

'What don't you get?'

'Anything,' he said desperately. 'I can't take it in, Michelle. I don't understand.'

She was at a loss for words, the shame of not telling him overwhelming her.

'I'm so sorry,' was all she could muster, and it seemed woefully inadequate. 'When you left to go to America it seemed like such a great opportunity for you to start a new life and get over Jane. To escape everything. You said it yourself. You needed to escape. I knew if I told you, you wouldn't have gone and that . . . I know this sounds ridiculous now, but it seemed selfish. I had to let you go. I'd cope somehow with the baby. I had Mum and Dad, after all.'

Rob quite literally did a double take.

'Josie,' he whispered eventually, a look of absolute amazement and shock spreading over his face.

Michelle nodded.

'But you said Josie was fourteen. She can't be mine. I left nearly sixteen years ago.'

'Oh God, Rob, I'm so sorry,' cried Michelle. 'I panicked. I lied. I didn't know what to say. Josie will be sixteen this Christmas.'

He went even whiter as Michelle watched the realisation dawn on him that he was Josie's father.

'I know I should have told you,' she pleaded, 'but what I'm trying to tell you now is that it just seemed for the best for you to have a new life in America. Away from the fact that we'd both cheated on Jane.'

Rob leant forward, dropping onto the floor on his hands and knees.

'Josie,' he whispered again, staring at the carpet. 'Josie out there?' he said, lifting one hand and waving vaguely towards the front window. His chest was heaving up and down, almost as though he was practising labour breathing in his kneeling position.

'I have a daughter,' he whispered, shaking his head.

Michelle didn't dare move or speak.

Rob raised his head.

'Why the bloody hell didn't you tell me?' he exploded. 'She's *fifteen*!'

'I'm trying to explain, Rob, please.' Michelle felt herself start to shake uncontrollably. 'You've got to remember what it was like when Jane died. How terrible it was. How life was totally upside down. Can you imagine throwing into all that pain the fact that me and you were about to have a baby? I was too ashamed, Rob. And you would have been too.'

She was in tears now, desperate to make him understand.

'It was hell, Rob, absolute hell. I had to live with knowing what we'd done as we buried Jane. I couldn't grieve, I felt so guilty. Imagine that. Everyone staring at you at the funeral, not as the poor grieving boyfriend but as the cheating bastard who's slept with her sister.'

Rob was now staring at her, horrified.

'And I had to think of Josie,' she continued. 'I always

thought that if she found out how she came into the world she'd be ashamed of me. I thought she deserved a clean start, not to be held back by my baggage. Turns out I've probably held her back anyway,' she sniffed bitterly. 'I can't believe what a mess I've made of things.'

Rob slowly stood up in front of her and she watched as the portrait of Josie – in which she looked cheerful for once – caught his eye. He studied it and Michelle wished she could curl up and die.

'You must go now.' Little Slaw bustled in, appearing at the door in his Sunday best maroon leatherette jacket. 'You must go now or you miss George Clooney.'

Michelle glared at him, desperate for his special Yoda telepathy to realise now was not the time to be worrying about George Clooney.

'Come, come,' he continued, clapping his hands. 'Chop-chop. He important man. He wait for no woman.'

'We're not going,' Michelle blurted. She couldn't tell Little Slaw why, but she knew there was no way she could leave with things like this.

Little Slaw stared at Michelle before turning his gaze to Rob, who was now holding Josie's picture in his hands and gazing at it, seeming oblivious to Little Slaw's presence.

'You go to Italy,' said Little Slaw, taking a step further into the room.

'Please, Little Slaw,' Michelle begged. 'I can't go to Italy. I can't explain why, but it's all gone wrong.' She glanced nervously at Rob, who had walked over to the window and was staring out at Josie. 'I can't go to Italy now. I'll go out there and tell Daz and Josie it's all off.'

'You go to Italy,' said Little Slaw, striding over to her and grabbing her by the arm. Forcing her to stand up, he made her follow him to the window to join Rob.

'Look at that,' he said. 'If you don't go to Italy now you up fuck big time, I'm telling you.'

Michelle looked past the small front garden to where everyone was still gathered around Daz's disco van, awaiting their departure. Daz was in the front, showing Ray what a satnav was, even though he didn't really know how to use it since he'd only just borrowed it from a mate. Ray was squinting at the tiny screen and then referring to an enormous European road map to check if the satnav knew what the hell she was talking about. Meanwhile Josie, Gina and Kathleen were carefully wrapping Chaz in cling film before Josie loaded it into the back of the disco van, laughing at something Gina was saying.

'You going to tell Josie you're not going to Italy because you getting in your own way again?'

'You don't understand,' said Michelle. 'It's complicated.'

'No, it's simple. You go to Italy. You deal with Josie. You come back to this.' He nodded over at Rob.

Michelle gave a massive sigh. This was all too much. She didn't know where to turn.

'I look after him,' said Little Slaw. 'I give him time. You give him time.'

Maybe Little Slaw was right. Rob needed to let his new status sink in. Going away for a few days would give him a chance to adjust and maybe even consider forgiveness.

'But you must go now,' said Little Slaw, tapping his watch impatiently.

She put her hand on Rob's shoulder to get his attention. He dragged his eyes away from the window.

'I have to go,' she said. 'But I will tell Josie everything whilst we're away. I'll tell her all about you.'

He blinked rapidly as if he'd just woken up and couldn't understand where he was.

'Come on, Mum,' said Josie, bounding into the room. 'Daz says if we don't go now, George might have pissed off again.' She grabbed her hand and dragged her towards the door.

'See you when we get back, Rob,' Josie shouted over her shoulder. 'We'll bring you a pizza.'

Moments later Michelle was in the back of Daz's van, squashed against Josie's enormous suitcase. Gina, Kathleen, Ray and Sean hovered on the pavement. Past them she could see Little Slaw and Rob still standing in the window. Little Slaw had one hand resting on Rob's shoulder whilst he waved cheerfully with the other. Daz was in the front, beaming at his choice of farewell tune which was blasting out from the speakers.

'It's relevant,' he said. 'Believe me, you'll get it any minute.'

'But it's a football song,' said Gina, throwing her hands in the air. 'What the hell has that got to do with you all going to Italy?'

'Jesus, Gina. Do I have to spell it out?'

'Actually, yes.'

'"World in Motion" by New Order was the greatest football song of all time and it provided the theme tune to an epic performance by England in the World Cup in . . . Italy. We will be in spitting distance of the Stadio delle Alpi in Turin. Can you imagine that?'

Blank looks all round.

'Where Gazza cried?' added Daz.

'Oh right, yeah, I remember that,' said Gina.

'Hallelujah!' cried Daz. 'Arrivederci, it's one on one, we're playing for England, Engerland,' he chanted. 'Arrivederci is Italian for goodbye. Arrivederci, my friends,' he cried with a wave as he turned the ignition.

'Arrivederci,' he said again as he confidently moved the gearstick.

'Arrivederci!' he shouted with a salute as he stalled the truck and Chaz collided with the back of Michelle's head.

Chapter Twenty-Two

Malton to Folkestone: 226 miles, 2 toilet stops, 5 coffees, 4 Red Bulls, 12 Krispy Kreme Doughnuts

'Is this really necessary, Daz?' asked Michelle as she stood outside Toddington services holding onto Chaz whilst pretending to eat a Krispy Kreme doughnut.

'Oh, she speaks,' exclaimed Daz. 'Thought you'd turned into a mute or something.' He snapped a picture of her on his phone.

'Just tired,' she muttered. True, she hadn't uttered a word the entire trip so far. She'd thought she'd got away with it, since Daz had been busy enjoying his playlist of top soundtrack tunes whilst Josie had been doing her best to block it out by plugging herself into her phone and listening to God knows what. Michelle had sat in the back silently reliving the last fifteen years, trying to work out exactly when she should have told Rob about Josie. She couldn't see when might have been a better time, but it must have been there somewhere, because it sure as hell didn't feel like a good time now.

'So, how's that?' said Daz, thrusting his phone under her nose. 'Shall I post it?'

Michelle looked at the picture, which showed her stuffing her face whilst holding a five-foot-high piece of card wrapped in cling film. Underneath Daz had written a post.

Three go to Italy Part 1: Michelle eats doughnut on way to take Chaz to live with George Clooney.

'Now what's really clever is that I have my Facebook and Twitter accounts linked, so the minute I post on Twitter it also appears on Facebook. See? Isn't that amazing?'

Michelle stared at the screen as her doughnut-eating skills, coupled with an inanimate object with a name, on its way to gatecrash a celebrity home, were broadcast to the world.

'There is no way George Clooney could ever see that, is there?' she asked.

'George doesn't do social media,' stated Daz. 'Ben Affleck does, though. He's on Twitter. He might see you and call George and tell him you're on your way.'

'Well, let's hope so,' said Michelle sarcastically. 'Where's Josie got to?'

'She's gone to call Sean on a payphone.'

'Why?'

'She can't get hold of him on her mobile, so she's worried the network might be down or something and she's trying his landline.'

Daz and Michelle looked at each other as a wealth of bad dating experiences passed between them.

'Poor kid,' said Daz.

'She'll learn.'

'It'll be the hard way, though,' said Daz, shaking his head in pity.

'Isn't it always?'

'His mum says he's already gone fishing,' said Josie, climbing into the back of the van, Michelle and Daz having waited another fifteen minutes for her to reappear.

'I guess seeing as I'm not around he must be bored, and he'll have headed off early so now he's got no signal.' Michelle and Daz raised eyebrows silently at each other.

'Bet he'll call me later.'

'Of course he will,' said Michelle, putting the van into gear, ready to take her shift of the driving, whilst Daz manned the decks and took them through some Disney Classics.

Michelle, Daz and Josie stared straight ahead, not daring to move. The music from the opening credits to *Pulp Fiction* was blaring out. Michelle and Daz were eyeing the volume control furtively but neither of them dared move given the delicate situation they were in.

Getting out of the UK had been bad enough. There had been a dispute as to whether Daz's disco van should be classed as a commercial vehicle and thus incur an additional fee. Daz had not helped matters when he'd stated that the intention of their visit was to deliver a large sum of money to a very influential man in Italy. A man who, should he be made aware of the potential delay being caused to the arrival of said money, would be very angry and could no doubt pull some strings and have the annoying little ticket man sacked.

Michelle had been forced to apologise profusely for Daz's outburst whilst throwing extra money at the annoying little ticket man.

But all that was nothing compared to the trauma awaiting them on the other side of the Channel. The minute they drove off the train in Calais they were waved to one side by customs officials.

Dogs circled and sniffed whilst mirrors on poles were waved under the chassis. Bags and cases were prodded and poked as Michelle sat, skin crawling, knowing that her utilitarian black underwear would not impress the Frenchmen.

Josie jumped when they opened the door next to her and pointed at Chaz.

'*Qu'est-ce que c'est?*' a gruff voice asked.

'It's Chaz,' Josie replied.

The official stared at her before shutting the door, walking round the front of the van, throwing open the other back passenger door and dragging Chaz out.

'Don't hurt Chaz,' murmured a distressed Daz.

All three stared, horrified, as Chaz was stripped naked of his cling film. Two officials stared, unsure of what they had just unveiled. They glanced back to the truck. Daz smiled and waved hopefully.

'George Clooney?' one of them queried.

They all nodded.

'You movie makers?'

'We are part of his charity,' said Michelle slowly. 'This money is for his charity. We are taking it to him.'

The two men exchanged a few words in French before one shrugged his shoulders and bundled Chaz back into the back of the van. He slapped the side of the vehicle, indicating they should get out of there.

'What did they say?' Michelle asked Josie as they pulled off, hoping her GCSE French was up to customs translation.

'They said we looked like *we* were in need of charity,' she muttered, busily texting, no doubt to Sean.

'This is the worst omelette I've ever tasted in my entire life,' Josie declared, holding up a greasy piece of yellow rubber studded with flecks of grey. They sat having dinner in the cheap hotel they'd found to bed down in on the outskirts of Calais to prepare for a long day's drive the following day. 'I thought the French knew their *œufs* from their onions,' she said, just a bit too loudly.

'Shhh,' said Michelle. 'Don't be rude, Josie.'

'But it's disgusting,' she said, pushing her plate away.

'Well, I guess a cheap restaurant is a cheap restaurant,' said Michelle. 'Just because it's in France doesn't mean to say it's going to be gourmet standard. You do need to eat something, please.'

'If I eat that, my insides will turn to lard,' Josie declared. 'Look, it's dripping with it.'

'Please, just eat it,' sighed Michelle, too tired to be having her daily battle with her daughter over food.

'Look, I'll have it,' said Daz, grabbing her plate and piling the contents on top of his food. 'Why don't you pick something else out, Josie, and eat that? Your mum's right, you need to eat something. We've got a long day tomorrow.'

He beckoned a waiter over and asked if they could have another look at the menu. After a momentary stand-off, during which the waiter shrugged several times, he eventually walked off and thankfully returned with a menu.

'*Votre fille n'aime pas l'omelette?*' he asked.

Daz shrugged his shoulders, unable to speak due to the amount of omelette in his mouth, whilst Josie succeeded in having a coughing fit and spitting Diet

Coke across the table. Daz slapped her on the back and looked accusingly at the waiter.

'*J'ai demandé simplement si votre fille n'aime pas l'omelette, c'est tout,*' said the waiter.

Josie continued to choke on her Diet Coke whilst shaking her head violently. Daz finally managed to swallow his omelette and stood to square himself up to the waiter.

'I must ask you to apologise,' he demanded. 'For whatever you said in that foreign language you speak.'

The waiter took a step back as Daz puffed out his chest and gave the man his best Paso Doble face, as practised during *Strictly Come Dancing*. Shoulders raised, chest out, elbows back, he could give Brendan Cole a run for his money any day.

The waiter stared back, incredulous, before turning to Josie.

'*Je suis tellement désolé que cet homme à la tête d'omelette est votre père,*' he said before turning on his heel.

'And that, my friend,' said Daz, sitting down and tucking into his omelette once more, 'is how you deal with rude people like that. Paso face, works every time.'

'Oh yeah,' said Josie. 'He was dead scared of you. He

just called you an omelette face and then he really insulted me.'

'Oh yeah?' said Daz, banging his cutlery down on the table. 'What did he say?'

'He said he was sorry that omelette face man was my father,' she replied in horror.

Daz was clearly about to leap out of his chair, track down the waiter and take things a stage further with his Argentinian tango face, but then he checked himself and glanced at Michelle.

She looked back at him, unsure how they should deal with the waiter's statement.

Josie looked between the two of them for some kind of response.

'That's it, isn't it?' she said, getting up and throwing her napkin down on the table. 'Omelette face is my father.'

'No!' cried Michelle. 'Omelette . . . I mean, Daz isn't your father, don't be ridiculous.'

'You went out together. It all makes sense now.'

'No, it doesn't,' said Michelle. 'We went out together when we were teenagers, way before you were born.'

Josie looked over to Daz desperately. 'You tell me. Seeing as she hasn't got the guts to,' she demanded.

'Josie, I wish I could,' said Daz, switching to a softer Viennese waltz face. 'Being your dad would make me the proudest man alive. Now it tears me apart to say this, so I want you to sit down before I do, okay, come on . . . sit down here.'

Josie sat down, clearly upset. Daz grabbed hold of her hands and looked deep into her eyes.

'This is as difficult for me as it is for you,' he said, biting his lip. 'But I know you're not my daughter because I only ever had sex with your mother once, on my eighteenth birthday, and I know that if we had ever repeated that quite outstanding performance there is no way I would have forgotten.'

'Too much information, Daz,' said Michelle, quietly putting her head in her hands.

'At least it's some information,' muttered Josie.

It's time, thought Michelle.

'Look,' she said gently. 'Let's go back to our room and we'll . . .'

But Michelle never got to finish the sentence as at that moment Josie's phone lit up and an obscure sounding ringtone filled the restaurant, much to the consternation of their fellow diners.

'Sean!' cried Josie, seizing it. She pressed the Call

Accept button and walked out of the restaurant at a furious pace.

Daz picked up his knife and fork and wiped the last of the omelette around his plate before popping it into his mouth.

'Thought we handled that well,' he mumbled.

Chapter Twenty-Three

Michelle had waited up for an hour and a half for Josie to come back to their room so she could talk to her, rehearsing over and over in her head what she would say and how she would say it. When she finally heard Josie swipe her keycard she sat up and braced herself.

Josie walked in and on seeing Michelle sitting tensely on the end of her bed, immediately went on the defence.

'I was only on that bench outside the restaurant,' she said. 'I hadn't gone off anywhere, I was perfectly safe.'

'I know,' said Michelle. 'I knew where you were, I just thought you needed some time to yourself to talk to Sean.'

Josie gave her mum a confused look.

'I can remember what it's like, you know,' said Michelle. 'With your first boyfriend. I'm not that old.'

Josie continued to stare at Michelle in confusion. Finally her shoulders drooped, giving Michelle the signal that she must start the conversation leading to who Josie's father was. But Josie got in first.

'How many times do I have to tell you, Mum?' she said, planting her hands on her hips. 'This is not some silly little first romance like you might have had. This is for real. Me and Sean love each other and there is nothing you can do about it. End of.' She dropped her bag and stormed into the badly lit bathroom, slamming the door behind her and locking it.

Christ almighty, thought Michelle. Talking to a teenager was like negotiating a minefield. She lay back down on the bed and stared at the ceiling as she listened to Josie go through her lengthy bedtime ritual, dictated by the beauty industry, who claimed that their products would definitely prevent the blight of all teenagers . . . spots. Now there was a whopping lie.

Somehow, pondering the dishonesty of the advertising industry had caused Michelle to drift off to sleep. She woke with a start as the sun rose and light streamed in through the paper-thin curtains. Looking over to check on Josie immediately, she saw she was still sound asleep, looking angelic, snuggled up to a teddy bear she'd had since she was a baby – her bit of comfort which had seen her through pretty much every trauma in life. Michelle wished that she was as much of a comfort to Josie as that teddy bear. Whatever she did seemed to hurt her. Maybe that was why she'd put off, and was still putting off, telling her about Rob. Whichever way Michelle looked at it, she was convinced that it would hurt Josie, and who would willingly do that to their own child? But she knew that she would have to make the strike soon. Inflict the pain and then pray the wound would heal.

She tiptoed outside to find Daz sitting on a bench, an enormous map spread out in front of him and a steaming mug of coffee and a plate of pastries holding the corners down. He glanced up as she approached and looked her up and down.

'You slept in your clothes, then?' he asked.

'Actually, yes.' She grabbed a croissant off his plate.

'Me too,' he nodded. 'Found a few, shall we say, interesting adult channels on the TV and fell asleep fully clothed, trying to understand what the hell they were saying.'

Michelle paused, confused.

'It was all in French,' Daz confirmed.

'Does it really matter what they're saying?' she had to ask.

'When you're watching porn? Oh God, yeah. Makes all the difference.'

For about the twentieth time that trip she gave thanks silently for the fact that she'd ended their relationship when they were nineteen.

'So, I've got a visual now on where we're going,' said Daz spitting pastry fragments over the map. 'Across the top of France via Strasbourg then Basel, straight down through Switzerland and then out the bottom into Italy before we hit Como. Eight hours' driving should do it, so if we get cracking and do two shifts each we should be there by tonight.'

As he sat there wiping spilt coffee off Austria, it struck Michelle that actually none of this would have been possible without him.

'I'm so grateful, you know that, don't you, Daz? I mean it when I say I couldn't have done all this without you.'

'Michelle,' he said, struggling to swallow a mouthful of brioche. He seemed to have had his mouth full constantly since they'd arrived in France. 'Look at me,' he said. 'I'm in France with two delightful ladies plotting our route across Europe to deliver Chaz to George Clooney. Never in my wildest dreams did I think I would be able to say such a thing. You made all this possible. Not me, *you*.'

'But if you hadn't said I could do all this then I wouldn't have. I know I wouldn't. It's down to you, seriously.'

'No, it's not. I'm just the local man with the disco gear, who rarely gets twenty miles away from the town in which he was born. Now I'm here, in France, because of you. And do you want to know something? I'm not going back to just being that. I'm going to make something happen in my life, just like you have. You just watch me, Michelle.'

'Wow, that's great, Daz,' she said.

'Right,' he said, looking at his watch. 'Speaking of making stuff happen, it's time we were on the road and tracking down that George Clooney bloke.'

'So your dad has been at the doctor's again this morning, you know, with his hip.' Kathleen's voice rang out of the speakerphone as Michelle took her stint of the driving through Switzerland.

'Are you listening to me?' Kathleen almost shouted when she got no response.

'Sorry, Mum,' said Michelle. 'I got distracted by the amazing mountains we're passing.'

'The doctor wants to refer him to the consultant.'

'That's brilliant,' Michelle replied, still gobsmacked by the scenery.

'It's not brilliant at all,' said Kathleen. 'Arthur Winslow got referred to the consultant and six months later he was dead.'

'Didn't he have cancer?'

'That's right.'

'Well, Dad hasn't got cancer, has he?'

'No, love, I'm just saying that being referred to the consultant strikes me as the kiss of death in most situations.'

'Consultants are there to make people better, Mum.'

'You try telling Winnie Winslow that.'

'Oh my God!' squealed Josie, sitting up front with her mum.

'Is that Josie?' asked Kathleen. 'What's the matter with her? Is she alright? Are you looking after her?'

'It's a cow, Granny, a cow with a bell!' shrieked Josie. 'I so want a cow with a bell.'

'Is she eating?' asked Kathleen. 'You never make her eat enough, Michelle. She's skin and bone if you ask me.'

'Granny, the food in France was disgusting. You have never seen anything like it. I couldn't touch it.'

'Never trust a nation who believe snails and frogs are the height of cuisine, Josie love. I hope your mother's got you out of there by now?'

'Mother,' said Michelle. 'We hardly needed to escape France.'

'We're in Switzerland now, Granny, it's amazing.'

'Switzerland!' exclaimed Kathleen. 'Switzerland! Are you out of your minds? Please tell me you still have your beetroot sandwiches with you?'

'Josie ate them somewhere around Northampton,' Michelle informed her.

'My God, what will you do now?' said Kathleen, sounding distressed.

'About what?' asked Michelle, starting to panic.

'Sandwiches, Michelle, sandwiches,' said Kathleen. 'You can't afford to eat in Switzerland. You're going to starve. I knew I should have made you more sandwiches, I just knew it. Ray . . . Ray,' they heard her shout. 'They're only stuck in Switzerland without any sandwiches.'

'We'll find something, Mum, don't panic,' said Michelle, taking deep breaths to calm herself down. 'We will survive without your sandwiches. Oh look, Gina's

trying to call, must go. We'll call you from Italy, bye.'
She pressed the button and switched to Gina for a saner
conversation.

'Hi, guys,' Gina rang out. 'Are you sunburnt yet?'

'It's cold, Gina,' stated Josie. 'It's nearly Christmas.'

'I know,' said Gina. 'But Michelle's texted to say
she saw a sign for Austria yesterday. They have hot
Christmases in Austria, don't they?'

There was utter silence in the van.

'Australia!' Daz roared suddenly. 'She means Australia!'

'Oh, right,' said Michelle and Josie in unison.

'We were near Austria, not Australia,' said Michelle to
the phone. 'Now we're just driving through Switzerland.'

'Oh my God,' said Gina. 'No wonder it's cold. It's
always cold there, right? You seen any cows with bells
yet?'

'Oh Gina,' said Josie. 'They are the cutest things you
have ever seen.'

'Awwww, I want one,' said Gina.

'Me too,' agreed Josie.

'You and Gina are so on the same wavelength,' said
Michelle to her daughter. Josie stared at her mother,
horrified.

'So, guys, your fairy godmother has some good news,'

said Gina. 'I only managed to get you an address for George in Lake Como.'

'Gina!' said Michelle. 'You are a star. How'd you manage that?'

'Well, you know. I made a few calls, pulled a few strings and that.'

'Cousin Jack get it for you?'

'Yep.'

'How?'

'I daren't ask this time. So I've emailed it to you along with a map, okay?'

'You're amazing, you know that, don't you?' said Michelle.

'Well, we're all rooting for you here, honey,' said Gina. 'Mike is sick of pasta already, seeing as I've insisted on Italian week in our house since I couldn't come on the road trip with you. And me and Little Slaw have put a map up in the staffroom so we can track your progress.'

'Did Marianne get my message?' asked Michelle. 'Did she manage to sort out my holiday entitlement with HR?'

'Oh yeah,' said Gina. 'I went to see her and she's super excited to get George's autograph. Quite frankly, you could ask her to do anything at the moment. Anyway, no-one's noticed that you're not here, so don't worry.'

'Oh great! So good to be missed.'

'I'm missing you. Lunchtime is very dull without you and George Clooney. Look, I've got to go. Dead meat beckons. Give George one for me, eh?'

'I will, Gina. See you soon.'

'Bye.'

The van fell silent except for the faint tinkling of cowbells in the distance.

'Mum, you do know you'll never get near him, don't you?'

'Why not?' asked Michelle, feeling full of bravado now they had an address and after hearing Gina's encouraging words.

'There'll be like a ten-foot-high fence all around his house and massive iron gates that you'll need a secret code to get through and dogs, lots of dogs stopping you from getting anywhere near.' Josie tucked her headphones into her ears before Michelle could respond.

'But we have a secret weapon,' she whispered to herself. 'Chaz will get us past the scary dogs.' Chaz could get them past anything, surely.

Chapter Twenty-Four

'This is so embarrassing!' Josie screamed. 'Make it stop!' she yelled, putting her hands over her ears.

They'd been outside George Clooney's villa for half an hour now, and there were dogs, just as Josie had predicted, barking and jumping up at the fence, making the most horrendous racket. But the dogs weren't the reason for Josie's distress. It was Daz, jumping up and down on top of his disco van and shouting at the top of his voice, waving poor Chaz above his head as 'A little Less Conversation' by Elvis Presley blared out of the speakers.

'A little less conversation, a little more action, Mr Clooney!' Daz shouted. 'If you don't come out now then

Chaz gets it. Do you hear me? Chaz will be leaving the building!'

Daz didn't notice the taxi approaching but Michelle did. Could this be George? she thought. She waited for the taxi to swerve around the van and enter the enormous iron gates, but it didn't. It stopped, and she saw a tall, dark, handsome man get out of the back seat. Odd for George to get dropped off at the gate, she thought, her heart starting to beat rapidly.

He looked over to her and she saw his face for the first time. A face she had thought of a thousand times over the last few days. A face that made her stand frozen to the spot, her heart now thumping out of her chest. Not George Clooney. *Him.* What the hell was he doing here, and what the hell was she going to do now?

The day had started so well – though maybe not for Daz. Having hit nightfall they had decided not to press on to Lake Como but to stop a dozen or so kilometres short so they could be up bright and early and head over there in daylight. A suitable roadside hostelry had been found and after a hasty pizza they had all retreated to their beds. Even though she'd been exhausted from the long day's driving, Michelle had stayed awake for an hour listening to her daughter trying desperately to track down Sean. No answer on his mobile and no answer at his home had led to a flurry of calls to his mates, punctuated by increasingly frantic sounding text messages. Eventually Josie's phone had rung, and to Michelle's relief she'd heard Josie gasp, 'Sean, where have you been?' as she darted for the bathroom and locked herself in. Assuming that Josie would be quite some time, she'd decided to try and get some sleep. Tomorrow was going to be a massive day in more ways than one.

At seven-thirty the following morning Michelle was battering on Daz's door having showered, changed and even used dental floss. She was concerned that she hadn't found him already down in the hotel restaurant stuffing his face with pastries, which seemed to be part of his daily continental routine. Having decided that the day you could potentially meet George Clooney was an occasion when carbohydrates should be avoided at all costs, she'd downed a coffee and gone to track Daz down in his room. To her relief, having for a moment pictured him murdered in some Alpine massacre, she heard a click from the other side of the door then Daz appeared, slowly opening the door.

'You look horrendous!' she blurted.

Daz grunted back. His eyes were barely open, his hair was plastered down over a sweaty brow and the clothes he'd been wearing the night before were crumpled and marked with red stains.

'Are you okay? What happened?' she asked urgently.

'Wah,' he uttered, before staggering backwards and making a dash for the bathroom. Next thing she heard him noisily throwing up. She took a step into the room but immediately stepped back out again. It stank of booze and of a man who was existing on a gut-churning diet. Peering through the door, she spotted Gina's gift for George Clooney, the red wine box, upended on the carpet next to a crushed plastic bathroom beaker which had clearly been broken whilst still containing red wine.

'You are a disgrace, Daz!' she shouted as he staggered out of the bathroom, clutching a towel to his face.

'Downstairs in ten,' she ordered, then turned on her heel.

'What on earth were you thinking?' she asked once they were all on the road again, her driving, Daz poised over a sick bag.

'I'm sorry,' Daz groaned. 'All I wanted to do was get a great playlist together for meeting George.' He leant back against his seat and swallowed as if talking was really hard. 'I'd left my iPad in the van so I went to get it and I spotted the box of wine. I thought George wouldn't miss a glass. So I took it back to my room and I lay there doing my *Come Clooney* playlist, and one glass led to another, and another, and I had no idea how much I was drinking. Wine boxes are the stupidest invention ever.'

'It was supposed to be for George.'

'I know. I'll buy him another one,' said Daz miserably.

'I wouldn't bother,' said Michelle. 'I don't think George drinks the type of wine that makes you feel like this.'

'I'm sure you're right,' Daz agreed. 'There's no way he's ever been through this kind of hell. He's never experienced pain like I'm experiencing now. He must only drink wine that never gives you a hangover, like magic wine us mere plebs are not allowed to know about.'

'Yeah, I bet he eats magic sausages as well that don't make you fat.'

'Please don't mention sausages,' said Daz, winding down the window and taking huge gulps of fresh air.

Michelle glanced back at Josie, who was staring out the window but didn't appear to be seeing anything.

'We should see Lake Como any minute, Josie.'

A Sean-style grunt came from the back seat. It was all she'd got out of Josie since her conversation with Sean the night before.

They rounded a bend and suddenly it felt as though the whole world had opened up. From their viewpoint high up in the mountains they caught their first glimpse of a glittering Lake Como, bouncing sunlight into their eyes until they were totally dazzled. The cloudless sky was reflected as a stunning blue in the water, framed by a shoreline decorated by clusters of quaint old houses. Pointed cypress trees stood proudly to attention beside stunning villas rising majestically over their reflections in the clear water. Sparkling white snowcapped mountains completed the picture, protecting this enchanting kingdom.

'Wow!' said Michelle, pulling into a layby so they could take it all in.

'Wow,' she breathed again.

They all sat in silence, staring.

Josie poked her head through the two front seats.

'It looks like . . . it looks like . . .'

'Something out of a fairytale,' finished Michelle.

'Yeah,' breathed Josie.

'Like in *Shrek*,' said Daz. 'You know, like Far Far Away Land. Like the three little pigs are going to come dancing around the corner any minute.'

Josie and Michelle turned to stare at him.

'I love that movie,' he said, shrugging his shoulders.

'I was thinking more Cinderella,' sighed Michelle. 'Like Prince Charming could appear at any minute on a white horse, cantering across the mountains.'

'Oh perleeeease,' said Josie, sitting back again.

'Or George Clooney could be waiting for me with open arms and fall instantly in love with me and invite me to live here in this magical kingdom with him happily ever after,' she added.

'Your fairytale ending,' nodded Daz.

'Oh yeah,' sighed Michelle.

'Excuse me a minute,' said Daz, suddenly flinging himself out of the van and throwing up at the side of the road.

As they weaved their way along narrow roads, past countless picture-perfect views, Michelle could feel herself getting more and more nervous, as if she really was on her way to meet George Clooney. Think positive, she told herself. She was going to meet George Clooney;

she had to believe that. They'd come so far, travelled so many miles. He would come out and meet them. He had to.

After half an hour of getting totally lost trying to follow Gina's instructions, Josie shouted for them to stop as they drove around a quaint market square for the fourth time.

'What's up?' asked Michelle, but Josie had already jumped out of the van and was heading towards a life-size nativity scene in the centre of the square. Carved wooden figures stood motionless under a moss-covered roof, staring into a straw-filled crib. Animals, less enamoured with the arrival of the Messiah, were scattered around, including a goat on its back with its legs in the air.

'What *is* she doing?' said Daz as they watched Josie stride purposefully towards the virgin birth. 'Do you think she's got religion or something?'

'Perhaps I should go after her,' said Michelle.

'I wouldn't. Maybe she connects on some level, you know, with her also being born at Christmas.'

'You think Josie connects with Jesus?' asked Michelle, incredulous.

'Yeah,' Daz said slowly. 'And the virgin birth thing – Jesus didn't really know who his dad was either, did he?'

'Wasn't it God?'

'Oh yeah,' said Daz. 'Course it was. But when he was a kid he must have been confused with the whole Joseph thing. I can imagine Mary struggling to explain that one to a child. Bit like you, really.'

'Josie wasn't a virgin birth.'

'I know that, stupid!' Daz shook himself and sat up. 'Just saying it might as well have been, as far as Josie's concerned.'

Michelle wondered if he was still drunk. She looked towards the nativity again to discover Josie engaged in conversation with a middle-aged woman sitting on a bench. The woman pointed at something and Josie nodded vigorously, then headed back towards them.

'Half a kilometre back down this road then left at the crossroads. The entrance is on the right after about two kilometres,' she said, climbing back into her seat.

'Is that where George Clooney lives?' said Michelle in awe. 'You just asked her?'

'Yeah,' Josie nodded. 'I said we were musicians from Jerusalem that he'd booked for a party and we'd got lost.'

'Jerusalem!' Michelle exclaimed.

'No idea where that came from. It was the first place that leapt into my head.'

'I like it,' said Daz. 'Musicians from Jerusalem on a mission. Drive on, Mary,' he told Michelle.

'That must be it.' Daz pointed at the high gates set in the middle of the very high brick wall they seemed to have been driving along for miles. 'Pull in, let's have a look.'

They parked in the small area in front of the gates. They could see nothing past the heavy railings, since the driveway swerved sharply off to the left, a wall of trees hiding whatever beauty lay beyond. It was dark, gloomy and uninviting, the sunshine's rays obliterated by the surrounding trees.

'So,' said Daz, stabbing at his iPad. 'The soundtrack to this particular part of our journey just has to be *Ocean's Eleven*. I think our strategic thinking in pulling off this particular stunt is actually on a par with robbing a casino.'

'I think robbing a casino might have been easier,' muttered Michelle. She got out of the van and walked up to the intercom to the left of the gates. There were two buttons. Two intercoms. She glanced back at Daz and Josie, who were both leaning out of their windows.

'Which button do you think?' she asked.

'What does it say next to them?' said Daz.

'Nothing.'

'It hasn't even got his name there?'

'No, nothing.'

'Press the top one. No, hang on a minute, there's something we have to do first.' Daz jumped out of the van and lugged Chaz over to Michelle, then made her pose for a selfie with the well-travelled cheque.

'Say, Clooney.'

'Clooney,' grinned Michelle.

'Now I'm going to stand behind you with Chaz so that when they click on the intercom, Chaz is in full view. We don't want him thinking we're just some crazy stalkers, do we? He needs to see Chaz to know we're legit.'

'Okay,' breathed Michelle, worried that Daz was actually making some sense, and when Daz made sense you knew you were in trouble. She waited whilst he got into position and gave it the thumbs up.

'Let's have a countdown, shall we?' said Daz. 'Five, four, three, two, one . . . we have lift-off.'

She pressed the buzzer.

She felt herself breathe in and out several times. Daz maintained a manic grin, holding Chaz aloft. Josie checked her phone for texts.

'Try it again,' urged Daz. 'He might be having his morning constitutional.'

She tried again. Nothing.

'Okay, now try the other one,' said Daz, still grinning.

She tried the other one. Nothing.

'Again,' urged Daz.

She tried again. Nothing.

And so it went on for what seemed like hours but was maybe twenty-five or thirty minutes. Manic grins had relaxed into reassuring smiles, which had evolved into desperate grimaces. Neither of them was willing to give up, because they knew exactly what would happen if they did. Precisely nothing. And that petrified the hell out of both of them.

It didn't petrify Josie, however, and having finished her textathon with Sean, who seemed to be communicating again, she took one look at her mother's desperate face and decided it was time to speak her mind. She got out of the van.

'This is so humiliating,' she said. 'You've got to stop making a fool of yourself now.'

'Don't talk to your mother like that,' said Daz angrily. 'You should be proud of her perseverance.'

'But it's pathetic!' she yelled. 'He's clearly not here. It's over. You tried, but it's over. You were never going to meet George Clooney, never mind ask him to marry you. It was stupid to ever think you were. Now let's forget this stupid pipe dream and go home.'

It was then that the dogs appeared at the gate, barking and hurling themselves at the railings. Daz took one look at them and leapt onto the top of the truck, then shouted at the top of his voice, threatening to do terrible things to Chaz if George didn't show his face.

It was no wonder he didn't notice the taxi pull up. He wasn't aware someone had joined them until he noticed Josie and Michelle standing with their mouths open.

'What's this?' Josie shouted to make herself heard above the din of Daz's music and the dogs barking. 'Some kind of pantomime? We'll have Auntie Jane turning up as a ghost next. Are you stalking us or something, Rob? This is ridiculous!'

Rob was making his way towards Josie with a purpose in his stride.

'Josie!' shouted Michelle, glancing terrified between her and Rob.

Josie turned on her mum. 'You're ridiculous,' she said scornfully. 'What the hell's going on? Take me home, now!'

'Josie,' said Rob, reaching out to her.

'What's he doing here?' Josie was starting to look frightened.

'It's alright,' said Michelle. 'Calm down.'

Rob took a moment to glance at Michelle before taking Josie's hand.

'I am your father,' he shouted above Elvis, who was still giving it some from the van's sound system.

The next thing they knew there was a thud followed by a low moan. Daz had fallen off the top of the van.

Chapter Twenty-Five

'Daz!' shouted Michelle, cradling his head in her arms. 'Daz, wake up! Are you okay?'

'Mmmmmmmnnnnn,' he moaned. He opened his eyes and was confronted with Michelle, Rob and Josie staring down at him.

'You fell off the top of the disco van,' said Michelle.

'Fuck,' he said, sitting up quickly. 'Where's Chaz?'

'He's fine. We've leant him against the railings.'

Daz stared around him, looking lost and confused. He'd only been out of it for a moment but he was as white as a sheet and he looked as if he didn't know where he was.

'We're in Italy!' shouted Michelle as though he had turned deaf. 'Outside George Clooney's house. Do you remember?'

But Daz didn't appear to be listening. He was staring at Rob with his mouth open.

'What are you doing here?' he asked.

Rob glanced quickly at Michelle, in distress, but didn't reply.

Daz scrambled to his feet.

'Go steady, eh?' said Rob, giving him a hand. 'You had us worried there for a minute.'

'Don't move,' said Daz. He bent to pick up his iPad, which had also been a casualty of his dramatic fall. A few strokes across the screen appeared to satisfy him of its health before he furrowed his brow, clearly searching for something. Michelle, Rob and Josie all stood staring at him, as if frozen. The next moment 'The Imperial March' from *Star Wars* blasted out.

'Turn it off, now!' shouted Rob, suddenly looking very angry.

'So it's true,' said Daz, his eyes narrowing, making no move to switch off the music.

'No!' shouted Rob above the clamour. 'I am not

341

Darth Vader, therefore I am not Luke Skywalker's father, if that's what you're asking. I *am* Josie's father. Now switch it off.'

Silence immediately filled the air.

Everyone stood stock-still. Daz's potentially catastrophic fall had diverted them all for a moment from Rob's momentous announcement, but hearing the *Star Wars* music had certainly brought the drama back to the party.

Michelle was the first to move, approaching Josie tentatively. Josie backed off, casting her mother a look of absolute disbelief.

'Hhhhhow?' she finally uttered, sending terrified looks between Rob and Michelle.

'You hadn't told her yet!' Rob exclaimed. 'But . . . oh my God, what have I done?'

Transfixed by the look of horror emerging on Josie's face, Michelle ignored him.

'Let me explain,' she said, trying desperately to get closer to her daughter, as if contact would reduce the pain somehow.

'How?' demanded Josie.

'We didn't mean it to happen,' said Michelle quickly. 'It was only once. It was a mistake.'

342

Josie continued to back away, shrinking from what she was hearing.

'It was nothing, so we agreed to forget about it,' Michelle continued. 'Rob loved Jane. I loved Jane,' she said pleadingly.

Josie bent down with her hands on her thighs, staring at the ground. Michelle edged closer and managed to touch her back gently.

'I found out I was pregnant and I didn't know what to do, Josie. It was such a mess.'

Josie said nothing but didn't push her mother away. 'You slept with Auntie Jane's boyfriend?' she said to the ground. Michelle couldn't tell if it was a question or a statement.

'Yes,' she murmured, looking over to Rob, who was motionless some feet away, clearly at a loss as to his role in this highly emotional mother–daughter exchange.

'How could you do that?' cried Josie, rearing up and glaring at her mother.

'I don't know!' cried Michelle, letting out a sob. 'It just happened. Then I discovered I was pregnant and I was just about to tell Jane and then . . . ' she faltered.

'Really? You were going to tell Jane?' Josie interrupted.

'You were actually going to face up to the truth? That so doesn't sound like you, Mother.'

Michelle felt as though she'd been slapped in the face.

'I was at the pub waiting to tell her when she got hit by the car. I never got to tell her.' She was convulsed by racking sobs. She'd give anything to have been able to tell Jane about the baby. If Jane had known about Josie it would mean she was alive. Not dead. Not gone. Right now she wanted her big sister so badly.

'Oh, how convenient!' shouted Josie, cutting through her grief. 'Auntie Jane dying saves the day yet again.'

'No!' Michelle wailed.

'But that's it, isn't it?' Josie clenched her fists in pure frustration and anger. 'It's your pathetic excuse for everything. Auntie Jane died. So fucking what! You didn't die, did you? But it's the perfect excuse, isn't it? I won't be a chef because Auntie Jane died. I'll work in a shitty chicken factory because Auntie Jane died. I'll barely leave the town I grew up in because Auntie Jane died. I'll deny my daughter a father because fucking Auntie Jane died.'

Michelle recoiled in horror. She deserved every word of Josie's tirade but it didn't make it any less shocking to hear.

'Josie,' said Rob, taking tentative steps towards the pair. 'You're bound to be upset . . .'

'Upset!' exploded Josie. 'Epic understatement or what? My mum shagged her dead sister's boyfriend! No, I'm over the fucking moon.'

Rob visibly crumpled. Michelle stood with her head in her hands.

'Josie,' said Daz, taking his turn, holding his iPad in front of him as though it might deflect any outburst that Josie might choose to throw his way. 'This is, like, super intense right now . . .'

'Don't say a word!' spat Josie. 'Not a word.'

'Okay,' Daz agreed, backing away quickly.

They all fell silent for a moment, the three adults cowering in Josie's presence. Finally Rob stepped forward again.

'I'm so sorry that you found out like this,' he said, talking very quickly as if to avoid Josie getting a word in edgeways. 'I knew your mum was going to tell you on this trip and I just assumed she would have by now. I couldn't wait to see you. I've already lost nearly sixteen years with you. I don't want to lose any more time.' He took another step towards her.

'Go away!' Josie screamed at him. 'I don't know you! Just leave me alone!'

'But Josie . . .'

'Leave!'

'Okay,' he said, backing away. 'It's alright. You must be in shock.'

Josie turned her back on him to complete his dismissal. He cast Michelle a despairing look, then turned and walked dejectedly back to the waiting cab. Michelle watched him get in and speak to the driver, then they were driving away, Rob's face staring miserably out of the window at Josie.

'Wow,' said Daz to no-one in particular when the sound of the cab's engine had died away.

'Take me home, Daz,' Josie demanded suddenly, brushing past him and climbing into the passenger seat of the disco van. 'But no talking to me. I repeat, do not talk to me.' She slammed the door shut and looked down resolutely.

Daz looked over to Michelle ,who had her head in her hands, gently sobbing.

'So I'll take Josie home then, shall I?' asked Daz nervously, as if he were giving her a lift back from a party, not halfway across Europe. Michelle didn't reply, incapable of taking any parental responsibility. Eventually she nodded.

'Thank you,' she whispered. 'I'll get a cab to an airport.'

'Are you sure?'

'Yes. The last thing she needs is to sit in a car with me for hours on end.'

'It's probably for the best,' said Daz. 'Let her cool down for a couple of days, get used to everything.'

'Thanks, Daz.' She managed a weak smile.

'I'll drop you off in the town.'

'No, you just go. She can't stand the sight of me at the moment.' Michelle fought back more tears as she looked over to the van where Josie was still staring at the floor.

'I'll get your bag,' said Daz, moving to the back of the van and hauling a rucksack out. He put it on the ground beside her before wrapping her in his arms.

'It'll be okay,' he said.

Michelle tried to smile through the tears raining down her face.

'Just take care of Josie.'

'Like she's my own,' he said, squeezing her tightly, then he released her and climbed into the driver's seat.

Josie didn't look at her mother as Daz drove her away. Michelle gave a pathetic wave to the back of her head.

Michelle had no idea how long she sat slumped against the wall outside George's house, clutching her rucksack. The dogs had stopped barking and appeared to have sloped off in search of drama elsewhere. Chaz stood resolutely on guard beside her. She must have relived the scene with Rob and Josie a thousand times in her head before she was roused from her daze by a voice nearby.

'Are you alright?'

She looked up quickly. She couldn't see a soul.

'Are you alright?' the man's voice repeated.

Michelle stood up, dropping her rucksack to the ground. She was hearing voices in her head; she must be going mad.

'Behind you,' the man said.

She spun around. There was absolutely no-one in sight.

'Go away, leave me alone!' she cried, clutching at her ears.

'I'm here,' came the voice. 'The intercom!'

Michelle stared at the buzzer.

'Are you okay?' asked the voice again. 'Are you in trouble?'

'Who . . . are you?' she asked.

'Oh, I'm just a guy,' said the voice. 'I can see you on the CCTV.'

'You're . . . you're . . . not George Clooney, are you?'

The voice instantly dissolved into peals of laughter. Could it be . . .?

'No,' the voice said finally. 'Well, I sort of am.'

'Sort of?'

'Tell you what. You tell me what you're doing there, sobbing your heart out, and I'll tell you why I'm sort of George Clooney.'

'Okay,' said Michelle, thinking it was slightly weird but certainly not the weirdest thing she'd been involved in lately. 'Well,' she said, not quite knowing where to begin. 'You see, it all started when I had a bet with my daughter that I could marry George Clooney by Christmas.'

She had no idea how long it took her to explain the epic journey which had landed her on George Clooney's doorstep in floods of tears. She didn't hold back, sharing everything from sleeping with Rob, to the death of her sister, to bringing up Josie on her own, to her wasted years in the chicken factory. By the time she'd finished she was totally drained.

'So that's it,' she concluded. 'I've screwed everything up.'

There was no sound from the intercom.

'Are you still there?' she said. No response. Whoever he was, he'd clearly got bored of her story.

It was then that she heard a squeak, and she turned around sharply to see a man opening the enormous gates. He was looking down at the lock so she couldn't see his face, but she could see his signature salt and pepper hair.

'George?' she uttered.

The man looked up.

'Sorry, no,' he said. Michelle stared at him. He was possibly the ugliest man she had ever seen, with his tiny piggy eyes, enormous nose and thin lips. Perhaps he'd had a terrible accident and been disfigured. She tried hard not to recoil as he moved towards her and thrust out his hand.

'Michael Lambert,' he announced, shaking her hand vigorously. 'I'm George's body double. He's letting me crash at his place a while.'

Michelle stared at him, open-mouthed. She squinted

so his face was out of focus then he obligingly moved so he was side on to her with his face turned away, hiding his features.

'You see?' he said.

She could see. It was as if George was standing in front of her . . . until he turned his head and she was physically repulsed.

'In case you're wondering, I'm also his butt double,' he said. 'My butt is way better than his. Trust me.'

'You've seen George Clooney's butt?' she asked.

'Oh yeah. Saggy, wrinkled. He needs to work out more.'

'Right,' gasped Michelle.

'George isn't around, but will I do?' Michael continued. 'I can make sure your cheque, I mean Chaz, gets to him.'

'Really?' she said. 'Would you?' She found herself wishing he would angle himself away again so she could pretend he was actually George Clooney.

'Sure. I don't think he'd want Chaz to go all the way back to England.'

'Well, thank you,' she said. 'That would be good.' She picked up Chaz and solemnly handed him over to Ugly George. But as he took hold of the cheque she found she didn't want to let go. Chaz was perhaps the only really good thing to come out of this whole sorry mess. All she'd have once Chaz was gone was a lonely trip back home to face up to the devastation of her life. She wrapped her arms around Chaz one last time before finally letting him go, fighting against the tears.

'I think I've lost everything,' she choked out.

Ugly George moved to put his arm around her shoulders.

'Do you want to know what George would say if he was standing here now?'

'Okay.' Michelle sniffed.

Ugly George cleared his throat and creased up his eyes in a George-ish fashion before he started to speak.

'Well, anybody who ever built an empire, or changed the world, sat where you are right now. And it's because they sat there that they were able to do it. And that's the truth.'

'*Up in the Air*,' muttered Michelle.

'Uh huh,' nodded Ugly George. 'He really is a genius.'

'You do know it's not really George saying that, don't you?' said Michelle. 'It's just his character.'

'Sure. But when George says it, you listen. That's what makes him a genius.'

'You're right,' said Michelle. 'When George speaks, the world listens.'

'So what are you waiting for?' asked Ugly George.

Chapter Twenty-Six

A week later Michelle was sitting at home alone, channel-hopping on the TV, desperately trying to avoid seeing anything to do with Christmas. Just when she thought she was safe, an elf or an angel or a fake Santa beard would pop out of nowhere and remind her that she was deep into the festive season and facing the loneliest, most depressing Christmas of her life. She'd not set eyes on Josie since she'd got back from Italy, as Josie had taken refuge in her grandparents' spare room. Ray and Kathleen had been round and collected some of her things, giving Kathleen the chance to launch into interrogation mode.

'Why can't we get a word out of her?' she raged. 'She

just sits in her bedroom or disappears out the door without telling us where she's going. What happened in Italy?' she asked, banging her fist on the table. 'I demand to know.'

Michelle had sat down at the table, shaking, as she opened up and revealed what had driven Josie into this state.

'*Rob?*' said Kathleen, stunned, when Michelle had finally let the cat out of the bag. '*Rob* is Josie's father?'

'Yes,' said Michelle. 'Please forgive me,' she begged, looking down at the twisted, sodden tissue in her hand.

Kathleen looked away and stared at Ray in amazement, searching his face for an inkling of comprehension as to what was going on. When he said nothing, she turned back to Michelle and drew in a very long breath. Michelle braced herself for the full force of Kathleen's anger, but it was Ray who got in first.

'Josie couldn't wish for a better father, could she, Kathleen?' he said, moving quickly to cover Kathleen's hand with his and grasp it tightly. Kathleen looked at him sharply and opened her mouth to speak then closed it again. 'We couldn't be happier to have Rob as part of the family, could we?' he said directly to her. 'It means we'll get to see a lot more of him, doesn't it?' Kathleen continued to stare at him. He nodded his head slowly, staring into her eyes until, as if in a daze, she started to join in.

'You're right,' she muttered. 'We will get to see a lot more of him.'

Ray whisked her out of the house soon after, still visibly stunned at the news. Michelle hugged her father harder than she ever had as he stood on the doorstep.

'Thank you,' she whispered in his ear.

'I always hoped it was him,' he whispered back at her.

'What?' she gasped, pulling away from him so she could see his face.

'I never believed that cock and bull story you told us about the chef in Scotland,' he said, shaking his head. 'And I saw the way Rob looked at you sometimes.'

Then he was gone, hurrying after Kathleen, no doubt preparing himself to guide her reaction to the news in a way that would ensure the future harmony of the family.

As the days ticked by, it wasn't her dad's unexpected words that occupied Michelle's thoughts but the growing dread that Christmas was fast approaching, and it seemed ever more unlikely that she would be playing any part in Josie's sixteenth birthday on Christmas Eve. Not only that, she suspected Josie would most probably be spending it shagging Sean. Her mission to marry George Clooney to prevent that happening had totally backfired. If anything, Josie was even more likely to have sex with Sean, given her knowledge that her mother had slept with her dead auntie's boyfriend. She had hardly presented herself as a model of restraint.

She had just switched off the TV in response to an advert for *Love Actually*, making her want to vomit at the sight of Hugh Grant snogging Martine McCutcheon under the mistletoe, when she heard the back door open. Her immediate thought was that it must be an intruder. Searching around for a suitable weapon to defend herself, she grabbed a roll of Christmas wrapping paper and tiptoed towards the kitchen. The door started to open before she reached it and she lifted the laughing snowmen high in the air, ready to thrash the living daylights out of whoever had dared enter her home. Through the door came a bedraggled figure, coat wet through, hair lankly falling on shoulders, red-rimmed eyes staring wildly out.

'Mum!' cried Josie, rushing forward and flinging herself at her.

'Josie!' Michelle dropped the snowmen and hugged her daughter with all her might.

Josie sobbed in her arms. She'd not done that since

357

she was nine, when she'd fallen out with her best mate Lucy over a pencil case. Michelle rocked her gently backwards and forwards, holding her tightly, occasionally murmuring how sorry she was. Eventually the sobs abated and became sniffs and Michelle dug out a tissue and watched her daughter blow her nose, trying to summon up the words that would show Josie how terrible she felt about making her feel this way.

'It's Sean,' Josie announced, handing the damp tissue back to her mother.

'Oh,' said Michelle, taken aback. 'Right. What's happened?'

'He wasn't there,' Josie sniffed.

'He wasn't where?'

'Fishing.'

'Right.'

'I thought I'd go and surprise him,' Josie continued, flopping on the sofa. 'I couldn't find him but his older brother was there, so I asked where he was, and he just laughed at me and told me to try the fishmonger's.'

'The *fishmonger's*?'

'Yeah. So I did. Thought maybe he was catching fish and selling them or something, you know, to save money for our flat.'

'Right, yeah, I'm with you,' said Michelle. 'I can totally see why you might think that.'

'So I went to the fishmonger's and . . . and . . .'

'Was he there?'

Josie nodded, fresh tears springing to her eyes.

'He was in the back. I could see him. Snogging Ellie Crab.'

'The fishmonger's daughter?' Michelle asked, resisting the urge to smirk at the appropriateness of Mr Crab's profession.

'Yes,' sobbed Josie.

'Oh, Josie,' said Michelle, sitting next to her and taking her in her arms again. 'I'm so sorry.'

'He doesn't even have a fishing rod!' Josie wailed. 'He lied about it all, everything, just so he could be with her.'

'I really am so sorry,' said Michelle.

They sat holding each other whilst the next wave of tears ran its course.

'You were right about him all along,' Josie said when she was next able to speak. 'He's such a loser.'

Michelle said nothing. She wished she'd been wrong. Anything to stop her daughter going through this kind of heartbreak. Right now there were only two words appropriate to the situation.

'Hot chocolate?' she asked.

Josie nodded and they retired to the kitchen.

Michelle and Josie sat facing each other at the table, blowing the steam off two mugs of chocolate heaven. Michelle peered at her daughter over the rim of her mug, knowing she had to raise the subject that was currently a whacking great elephant in the room.

'You were right, you know,' she said eventually. 'I was using Jane dying as an excuse.'

Josie said nothing.

'And it's unforgiveable that I allowed that to get in the way of you getting to know your father.' Michelle felt tears spring to her eyes. 'I can't expect you to ever forgive me.'

Josie still said nothing, just slowly stirred her drink. A tear reached the end of Michelle's nose and dropped into her mug.

'But I wasn't there,' said Josie finally, not looking up. 'I don't know how it feels to lose someone you love.' She looked up. 'Rob said . . . he said it was a terrible time. No-one knew what to do. Everyone was a mess.'

'You've talked to Rob?' Michelle gasped.

Josie nodded.

'He came to see me. He brought me a teddy bear.' There was a tear at the end of Josie's nose now. 'Said he had no idea what fifteen-year-olds were into but he hoped that I would teach him.'

Michelle thought her heart would break.

'What did you say?' she asked.

'I told him I had expensive tastes.'

'You didn't!'

'Of course I didn't,' Josie retorted. 'God, you're so easy to wind up.' She looked up and smiled at her mum. Michelle reached across the table and took her hand. They sat there in silence for a long time, holding hands and sipping hot chocolate.

'I like him,' Josie said eventually.

'So do I,' Michelle nodded.

Chapter Twenty-Seven

11.00 a.m., Christmas Eve

'Guess what?' said Gina from across the conveyor belt.

'What?' said Michelle.

'They're only doing turkey-flavoured Pringles. I got some at the Co-op. How Christmassy can you get? I'm going straight home at lunchtime and having them.'

'Not for me,' said Little Slaw, shaking his head as he expertly dropped blue polystyrene trays onto the belt. 'In Poland, no meat on Christmas Eve, just fish.'

'But they're crisps,' Gina protested.

'But you say turkey flavour?'

'It'll never be real turkey, will it?' Gina declared. 'Just, like, pretend turkey.'

'What do you mean, pretend turkey?'

'They actually just taste like stuffing,' announced Michelle, passing blue polystyrene trays to Gina.

'You've tried them!' exclaimed Gina. 'You never said!'

'Josie loves them,' said Michelle. 'But personally I think they should be called "Stuffing-Flavoured Pringles That Make You Think Of Turkey".'

'So they're actually turkey-free Pringles,' said Gina. 'See, Little Slaw, you'll be able to eat turkey Pringles today because they're actually turkey free.'

'To think this will be the last ever crisp discussion we have,' said Michelle. 'I can't believe it's my last day on this factory floor.'

'Me neither,' said Gina.

'Nor me,' sighed Little Slaw.

They all looked up at each other, feeling a little sad, before they sensed a large presence approaching: Marianne.

'Mr Evans wants to see you, Michelle,' she barked.

'Why?' Michelle exclaimed.

'You'd better get up there and ask him, hadn't you?' Marianne turned round and strutted off towards the metal staircase without any further explanation.

Michelle rushed after her, still unwilling to upset Mr Evans, despite the fact that in less than an hour she would no longer be working for him. When she'd arrived that morning and got her overall out of her locker for the very last time, she'd thought she might cry with relief, although she was still a little in shock that she'd actually handed her notice in. But she'd known when she got back from Italy that she had to. Ugly George had as good as told her she had to. Her own daughter had told her she had no excuse to be working there. So she had tentatively replaced the dream of marrying George Clooney with another one. Her own catering business was possibly a long way off, but starting as an assistant chef for an event company would allow her to learn the ropes and get into the swing of things before she branched out on her own. And she really couldn't wait to swap her time in a chicken factory for time in a professional kitchen.

Mr Evans wasn't in his office, but Marianne instructed her to go in and wait. He was just in the warehouse making sure no-one had sloped off early.

After ten minutes of staring out at the hills behind the factory, trying to work out why she was there, Mr Evans strode in to put her out of her misery.

'What do you want?' he said, sitting down without looking at her.

'Er, you asked to see me?'

'Why?' he demanded.

'Er, I don't know. Is it something to do with it being my last day?'

He raised his eyes to look at her for the first time.

'Ah yes,' he said eventually, taking his glasses off and rubbing his eyes. 'It's about your departing gift.'

'Oh,' said Michelle, shocked. 'Well, I wasn't expecting . . .'

Mr Evans waved his hand to indicate she should pipe down. She did. A leaving present, from the factory? How amazing!

'You see, I thought it would be highly suitable if you were to leave for all of us here at Pinkerton's Chicken Factory the recipe for that chicken dish you concocted for that charity event.'

Michelle's mouth dropped open in astonishment.

'Sort of like a legacy,' Mr Evans continued. 'You know what I mean. So we have something to remember you by.'

He leant back in his chair smiling and looking very pleased with himself.

Michelle still couldn't speak.

'I can see that you're extremely moved by the gesture,' he added.

Michelle found her tongue.

'You want me to give you my recipe . . . for free?' she exclaimed.

'No, no, no,' said Mr Evans, shaking his head. 'As a gift, for all your years of service to the factory.'

She couldn't quite work out if she was going mad or Mr Evans was actually trying to screw her over. Suddenly, Marianne appeared at Mr Evans's side and placed a Post-it note in front of him.

'Sorry to interrupt,' she said, waving a piece of paper behind his head so only Michelle could see it. There were three words written in pink fluorescent pen: CHICKENS FOR CHARITY. Marianne left the room as quickly as she'd appeared.

'Surely,' Mr Evans continued, 'it would give you a huge amount of satisfaction to share your recipe with the factory that has kept you in gainful employment for all these years?'

'Do you know what, it would,' said Michelle, nodding. 'I can see where you're coming from.'

'Great, brilliant!' Mr Evans leapt out of his chair.

'Marianne, come back in here quick and write down this recipe!' he shouted through the open door.

'On one condition,' Michelle added, thinking quickly. 'No, actually, two conditions.'

'Okay,' he said slowly, sitting back down again.

'The first condition is that a percentage of any profits made from my recipe goes to Not On Our Watch.'

Mr Evans swallowed hard. 'And the second?'

'That you'll run Chickens For Charity every year.'

'Oh, what a brilliant idea!' enthused Marianne, coming in with her notebook at the ready. 'Keeps up your positive image in the community, Mr Evans, *and*, you never know, you might discover some more fantastic chicken recipes. Shall we say the last weekend in November every year?'

Mr Evans sat staring at both of them open-mouthed in confusion. Clearly his little plan hadn't worked out quite the way he'd anticipated.

'Marianne actually got him to sign something saying he agreed to donate some of the profits,' said Michelle when she slotted herself back into the conveyor line a few minutes later.

'His conscience you prick,' said Little Slaw. 'You affect him.'

'I'm not sure he has one of those. But if it means we get to carry on raising money, then that's just brilliant. I so wanted to be able to carry on doing something for George, I mean Not On Our Watch.'

'It's down to Gina next,' said Little Slaw. 'When she starts in sales it must be go, go, go to sell Michelle's chicken.'

'Piece of cake,' declared Gina. 'It tastes like heaven and part of the profits go to Not On Our Watch? This is going to fly off the shelves, I tell you.'

'Spoken like a true saleswoman,' Michelle laughed. 'You're going to be brilliant, you know, when you start your new job.'

'Honestly,' beamed Gina, 'I can't wait. Dominic says he's going to start by taking me to meet all his customers, says I need to start forming relationships with them, whatever that means. I asked Clare – you know, the woman who works for the big hotel chain I persuaded to give us a free weekend break for the Chickens For Charity raffle? Well, we're Facebook friends now. She told me to just be me.'

'Dominic, despite appearances,' said Little Slaw seriously, 'is a smart man. That's why he give you the job.'

'Well, he said he's never known anyone get stuff out

of his customers like I did for the raffle,' she said. 'That's the only reason he asked me to apply.'

'Your talents were just waiting to be discovered,' said Little Slaw. 'You stop getting in your own way, both of you.' He glanced at Michelle. 'You come such a long way since you decide to marry George Clooney. Best decision you ever made.'

'It's certainly changed my life,' she agreed.

'And you leave factory to follow your dream, your proper dream that I know will come true,' said Little Slaw. 'You will make it happen now because you know how to get out of your own way. You learn this lesson from marrying George Clooney, yeah?'

'I'm going to miss your pep talks, Little Slaw,' said Michelle.

'Well, I learn lesson from you marrying George Clooney too,' said Little Slaw. 'Life too short to spend on chicken floor. I shall enjoy my retirement spent with grandkids being up to elbows in poo and Play-Doh rather than chicken. Happy days.'

'Happy days,' repeated Michelle.

'Happy days,' agreed Gina.

'Would you come to Josie's birthday party tonight?' Michelle suddenly asked Little Slaw. 'It's just me,

Josie, Mum, Dad, Gina, Mike, Rob, Daz and Greta.'

'Greta?' said Gina and Little Slaw in unison.

'Didn't I tell you?' said Michelle. 'Daz has a girlfriend.'

'Daz does!' exclaimed Gina. 'Like, how?'

'It's all down to Josie, actually,' said Michelle. 'They were driving back through France and Josie said Daz was sending her mad because he just wouldn't stop talking to her. Anyway, she spotted a woman with a backpack trying to hitch a ride, and Josie demanded they pick her up so Daz could talk at her instead. Turns out she and Daz got on like a house on fire. Apparently it was love at first sight. They've been inseparable ever since.'

'So what's she like?' asked Gina. 'Have you met her?

'Daz actually brought her round to meet me,' said Michelle. 'It was so embarrassing. They snogged like teenagers on my sofa. She's twenty-nine and she's a professional vlogger from Hamburg.'

'What in the name of cowbells is a vlogger?' asked Gina.

'They showed me.'

'Really?' said Gina, horrified.

'No, it's nothing dirty. She has a blog that she posts videos on talking about stuff she's experienced on her travels. She has over a million followers. Companies are queuing up to pay her to talk about them, apparently.'

'Weird,' said Gina. 'And what does she see in Daz, exactly?'

'Her favourite member of One Direction is Liam.'

'Right. I'm getting the picture,' said Gina, nodding.

'I've never seen Daz so happy,' continued Michelle. 'She let him do some videos for her blog and now he's talking about going to South America with her.'

'He's leaving Malton!' exclaimed Gina. 'I could not be happier. Tonight I will hug and kiss Greta like she is my own sister.'

'It is good for Daz,' said Little Slaw. 'He go to find George Clooney with you and he find another love.'

'Absolutely,' Michelle agreed. She was very relieved he had found another love.

'But I regret I cannot come to Josie's birthday,' said Little Slaw. 'I must eat fish with family for tradition on Christmas Eve.'

'Of course,' said Michelle. 'I understand. Actually, we're having Salted Chilli Chicken. Josie and Rob asked for it especially.'

'Well, of course, if Rob asked . . .' said Little Slaw.

Michelle couldn't stop the colour rising to her face. She stared down at the chicken legs rushing past her on the conveyor, feeling Little Slaw's all-seeing eyes searching her face.

'Such a decent man,' he prompted.

She turned her face up to look at Little Slaw and held his gaze for what seemed like an age before she dared let any thoughts out.

'I don't deserve him,' she began.

Little Slaw didn't respond.

'He's forgiven me,' she continued. 'I certainly don't deserve that.'

'He lose time with his family. He doesn't want to lose any more.'

It was Michelle's turn not to respond. She couldn't. Suddenly, very loud music was being played over the decrepit loudspeaker system, deafening all of them. Little Slaw threw a dozen plastic trays in the air in surprise, causing Gina and Michelle to dive for the floor to collect them before RB1 or RB2 bore down on them. As Michelle picked up the last carton on her hands and knees, the music still squealing through the ancient speaker system, she thought the tune seemed familiar. Then someone clearly saw sense and turned the volume down, making the song finally sing loud and true and be totally recognisable.

Michelle stood up slowly, looking around. Had Mr Evans decided to throw them all a last-minute Christmas party before they all left at lunchtime? She glanced up towards the offices at the top of the steel staircase and nearly fell over. There was Josie.

'Do you recognise it?' she shouted down at her.

'Of course I bloody do!' she shouted back. 'What the hell is going on?'

Then she heard excited squeals coming from behind her in the packing section and she spun round to see what all the fuss was about.

And there he was. A man in white, striding towards her. It wasn't a hygiene overall he was wearing, but full naval uniform, and as he walked purposefully her way, 'Up Where We Belong', blasted out through the factory.

'Way to go, Michelle!' shouted Gina. 'Way to go!' she screamed, jumping up and down on the spot.

And then he was standing right in front of her. She couldn't stop her stomach from twisting up in knots as Rob, looking breathtakingly handsome, smiled nervously down at her. She gingerly reached up to touch one of the dimples that she'd mercilessly taken the mickey out of all those years ago. She felt him relax slightly then he searched her eyes for a moment before he began to speak.

'I've been thinking a lot about what Josie said,' he began, glancing up briefly to where Josie was watching them. 'And I think we can all be accused of not doing stuff because Jane died. Not facing up to things.' He swallowed. 'It's time we all stopped making excuses. We need to stop thinking about the reasons why we shouldn't be together and start thinking about the reasons why we should.'

He searched her eyes again and she nodded ever so slightly. He nodded back.

'I know I'm not Richard Gere, or George Clooney, for that matter,' he said. 'But I wondered if I gave you the film star treatment . . . if I asked you again, would you kiss me?'

Michelle couldn't believe what she was hearing.

'I don't need a film star,' she said, gazing up at him. 'You'd have to be an idiot to want to marry a film star when there's men like you around.'

His face broke into a smile before he bent and lifted her into his arms then pulled her close for a kiss, whilst Gina could be heard screaming somewhere in the background. They were still kissing as he carried her through the factory, out of the door and into the crisp winter air and the best Christmas Eve ever.

Epilogue

In April 2014 rumours first started to emerge that George Clooney had indeed got engaged and could no longer be classed as marriage material. Michelle couldn't have been happier. She'd have felt bad if he was all alone, especially since she had also just got engaged and was no longer available to him. She sent a congratulations card to his villa in Italy, along with an invite to her and Rob's wedding, planned for Christmas Eve to coincide with Josie's seventeenth birthday. She thought it very unlikely he would make it, especially as it was at Christmas. But you never know, do you? It's got to be worth a try . . . hasn't it?

Acknowledgements

I have no idea where the idea for this book came from. It just kind of appeared amidst many other ideas, and thankfully it was the one both I and my agents Araminta Whitley and Peta Nightingale seized upon as 'the one'. So thank you for your support in pursuing this story. It's been a great journey.

Delivering it into the hands of Jenny Geras of Arrow Books, however, was a nerve-racking experience, and I thank her enormously for her speedy response with the words 'I loved it!' Thank you so much for your continued support.

As always, many other people have grabbed my hand

and helped me along during the writing of this book. My writer friends always keep me on track, with a special mention to Jo, Julie, Mel and Sharon. I must also thank the amazing Milly Johnson, who is so generous in her support and advice that she must be the nicest writer on the planet. Also to all the book bloggers, reviewers and readers out there who use their valuable time to talk about books. Thank you so much. I really appreciate it.

Technical support this time came from my parents, in the form of advice on cattle crushes. Who knew there was so much to them?

I have greatly enjoyed writing this book, because I love the idea of people ignoring the reasons why they can't achieve something and just going for it anyway. That's what I did when I started writing, but I found you really need people alongside you who believe you can do it. So thank you, Bruce, Tom and Sally. You spur me on every single day.

JOIN
Tracy Bloom
ONLINE

www.tracybloom.com

 @TracyBBloom

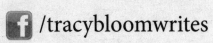 /tracybloomwrites